WAKE THE DAWN

"Snelling (*One Perfect Day*) continues to draw fans with her stellar storytelling skills. This time she offers a look at small-town medical care in a tale that blends healing, love, and a town's recovery.... Snelling's description of events at the small clinic during the storm is not to be missed."

—Publishers Weekly

"Snelling's fast-paced novel has characters who seek help in the wrong places. It takes a raging storm for them to see that the help they needed was right in front of them the whole time. This is a strong, believable story."

—RT Book Reviews

"Lauraine Snelling's newest novel will keep you turning pages and not wanting to put the book down.... *Wake the Dawn* is a guaranteed good read for any fiction lover."

—Cristel Phelps, *Retailers and Resources* magazine

REUNION

"Inspired by events in Snelling's own life, *Reunion* is a beautiful story about characters discovering themselves as the foundation of their family comes apart at the seams. Readers may recognize themselves or someone they know within the pages of this book, which belongs on everyone's keeper shelf."

—RT Book Reviews

"*Reunion* is a captivating tale that will hook you from the very start.... Fans of Christian fiction will love this touching story."
—FreshFiction.com

"Snelling's previous novels (*One Perfect Day*) have been popular with readers, and this one, loosely based on her own life, will be no exception."
—*Publishers Weekly*

ON HUMMINGBIRD WINGS

"Snelling can certainly charm."
—*Publishers Weekly*

ONE PERFECT DAY

"Snelling writes about the foibles of human nature with keen insight and sweet honesty."
—National Church Library Association

"Snelling's captivating tale will immediately draw readers in. The grief process is accurately portrayed, and readers will be enthralled by the raw emotion of Jenna's and Nora's accounts."
—*RT Book Reviews*

"A spiritually challenging and emotionally taut story. Fans of Christian women's fiction will enjoy this winning novel."
—*Publishers Weekly*

Half Finished

Half Finished

A Novel

Lauraine Snelling

New York Nashville

FaithWords
Hachette Book Group
1290 Avenue of the Americas, New York, NY 10104
faithwords.com
twitter.com/faithwords

First Edition: March 2019

FaithWords is a division of Hachette Book Group, Inc. The FaithWords name and logo are trademarks of Hachette Book Group, Inc.

The publisher is not responsible for websites (or their content) that are not owned by the publisher.

The Hachette Speakers Bureau provides a wide range of authors for speaking events. To find out more, go to www.hachettespeakersbureau.com or call (866) 376-6591.

Library of Congress Cataloging-in-Publication Data

Names: Snelling, Lauraine, author.
Title: Half finished : a novel / Lauraine Snelling.
Description: First edition. | New York : Faith Words, 2019.
Identifiers: LCCN 2018039319| ISBN 978-1-4789-2007-6 (trade paperback) | ISBN 978-1-4789-2008-3 (ebook)
Subjects: | GSAFD: Christian fiction.
Classification: LCC PS3569.N39 H35 2019 | DDC 813/.54--dc23
LC record available at https://lccn.loc.gov/2018039319

ISBNs: 978-1-4789-2007-6 (Trade paperback); 978-1-4789-2008-3 (ebook)

Printed in the United States of America

LSC-C

10 9 8 7 6 5 4 3 2 1

Half Finished is dedicated to all of us who love to start new things, try new adventures, and then get sidetracked. Give us the will and encouragement to finish what we've started and the joy of finding homes for them, always cheering each other on.

Half Finished

Chapter One

"This is it. I can't stand this any longer."

Phone to her ear, Mari Jean, better known as MJ, stared at her craft room and rubbed her head where the plastic tub from the top shelf had slid off and smacked her on the way down. "I just can't." The contents of said bin were scattered all over the floor, skeins of yarn and the extra knitting needles. So that was where they had been. No wonder she'd not found them on the last go-through.

"Come on, you've got all that lovely space and storage galore, just start another bin and put it on the shelf." Her best friend, Roxie, chuckled in her ear. "I mean, one more project, perhaps you'll get this one done. After all, you have a deadline this time."

"Since when has a deadline made any difference? I can manufacture more excuses than Walgreens has pills."

"Not surprising. We are highly creative women."

MJ scraped the fingers of her right hand through her newly shorn hair. She always had it cut shorter in the spring just because she hated wasting time messing with her hair during the gardening season. After all, Fond du Lac, Wisconsin, definitely had four seasons, and one especially dripped with humidity, therefore wash-and-wear hair. And no time to complete the abundance of started things. How often had she promised herself she would not start anything new until she had completed at least one of those on the shelves Daryl had built for her? This room, more than any other in their house, showed off his skills as not only a carpenter but a master finish carpenter/cabinet/furniture maker. She brought herself back to the phone conversation.

"What did you say?"

"I said, I heard about what they call a UFO group."

"UFO? Sorry, I'm not into the unknown ga-ga stuff. I didn't know you were either."

"No-o, loony. Unfinished objects. You know, like all the started but not done projects of all kinds. I'm afraid to add up all I have, and you? Why, you would be the winner in any contest."

"Thanks." MJ stared at the upper shelf running around the room about eighteen inches below the ceiling. The shelf that was crammed with plastic bins and containers of all sizes, from shoebox to twenty-quart. Some holding one project, others filled with who knew how many. Knitting, crocheting, attempts at Hardanger, tatting, hand weaving, cards, cross-stitch, fabric painting, quilting, rug making, embroidery, ribbon embroidery, and probably others she couldn't remember. Some of the bins had been through three moves over the years. And now one of them was scattered around her feet.

"Well?"

"A UFO group?" MJ frowned to herself.

"Yes. We'd invite all those we know are in this situation, get together once a month to work on whichever project we choose, potluck lunch if we want, or however..." Roxie paused. "But the clincher is—we agree to not start any new things until we finish all we have."

MJ shook her head. "Sorry, can't agree to that last line. I've got presents to make and—"

"And none of those things in all those bins could be used as gifts?"

Ignoring that last bit of advice, MJ pondered the idea. "You think anyone else would be interested?"

"Who knows? We could talk it up and see what happens. Think about it. We could take turns where we meet or whatever the group decides." Roxie had the gift of getting excited about something and then getting others excited.

"How about we talk about it tomorrow when walking? Looper did not get his morning walk, and he's giving me the mean mother look." She looked down at the sighing basset at her feet. Daryl had said that when he retired, he would walk Looper every evening if she walked him in the morning. Yesterday they both forgot, or put it off due to laziness.

"We could still walk today," Roxie suggested. "I desperately need a latte fix."

"I was going to tie up the daffodil greens today."

"You need a latte fix too—you know you do. Five minutes."

"Ten."

Looper's long red ears perked up, and the white tip of his tail thumped on the hardwood floor.

MJ had just finished adjusting Looper's harness when

she heard Roxie's call from the sidewalk. "Come on, boy, just remember, no jerking me to a stop today so you can read the mail. I need to walk fast to get the old heart rate up. Remember, Anne has treats." At that magic word, Looper picked up his feet and, tail wagging, greeted his walking buddy, Sir Charles, on the sidewalk. Sir Charles, also a rescue but multimix, greeted Looper in the usual doggy way before the four could start down the sidewalk in their usual route, which included Annie's Fountain City Cafe for drinks, lattes for the ladies, and a big bowl holding fresh water for the four-footed customers plus homemade doggy treats.

As she joined Roxie, MJ pointed at the woman's feet. "You're wearing your opera pink shoes. Celebrating?" Roxie changed shoe color according to her moods.

"Just needed a pick-me-up." She rocked one foot back on the heel to study the walking shoe. "Someday I am going to wear one pink and one chartreuse, just to confuse people."

MJ snickered. "It would. You with your shoes and Amalia with her hats. People are going to start calling us the bat-crazy old ladies. And that your hair matches Sir Charles might cause comments."

Roxie leaned over and fluffed the sort-of-maybe-a-spaniel's ears. "They can call us both redheads." She huffed out a breath when she stood up. "At least I don't have to pay to have his colored."

"True." MJ lifted a strand of silvering blond. "I refuse to color mine and Daryl agrees. The kids keep saying, 'Mom, color your hair so you don't look so old. You're retired now, but you don't have to look like it.'"

Roxie snickered. "My Loren knows better than to

make comments like that. She might end up out on her ear." Roxie's daughter, Loren, still lived at home with her mother, but always dreamed of meeting her mate and living happily ever after. Somehow working at the library did not offer many dating opportunities. "So how is retirement going anyway?"

"I don't know. At first it was wonderful. Pure freedom. Now, not so much. Roxie, I supervised fifty-seven people. Now I supervise a basset that is a master at selective listening."

"I can think of a dozen volunteer organizations that need strong leadership. Take your pick."

"I could, but Daryl says, and I kind of agree, that I'm pretty forceful to be doing a volunteer gig. I tend to order people around, not cooperate with them. You had to do that to get stuff moving in the warehouse. Looper, for the love of Pete's sake, find another bush to stick your nose into. That one is sufficiently sniffed." She gave a tug to coax the lackadaisical basset into moving.

"So, did you think more about my idea?" Roxie asked as they picked up the pace.

"The UFO thing? You got to admit, I've not had much time for that." Visions of the yarn still on the floor made her shake her head. "How do you propose getting out info about this rather strange idea of yours?"

"Well, I thought of flyers at the senior center, the Knitting Room, possibly churches, maybe the library on the community board, Mona's Quilting, you know, all the regular places."

"If it gets too big, we won't be able to meet in homes."

"True. I'm dreaming of maybe eight to ten regulars and perhaps some that come and go."

MJ jerked to a stop and looked behind. Sure enough, Looper had found something he could not ignore, unlike the slight jerks on his leash. Sir Charles sniffed around and sat down on the sidewalk. He had learned how to wait for his walking buddy. "Looper, drop it." She twitched the leash. "Drop it." Looper glanced at her and opened his mouth to drop a child's lime green shoe.

Roxie picked it up. "Oh my. A small child's Croc."

MJ wagged her head. "I'll bet some little girl in a car seat is learning how to throw things out of a moving car."

"Or else her mother put it on the roof of the car to unlock it and forgot." Roxie carefully set it on the curb in an open spot, where it was easily seen.

MJ snickered. "You and your shoes; that must really stab your heart."

"At least it's not a dead mouse. That's happened."

"True."

They continued, Looper leading the way.

✿   ✿   ✿

They paused at one yard where the daffodils were nearly done but the tulips were about to bloom. "Their yard is always so lovely." Roxie heaved a sigh. "You never see a mole or gopher."

"Or a weed." The two sighed together. A perfect yard like that would be nice but their husbands were not into gardening like Barb's husband, who could teach Yard and Garden 101. As could Barb. On top of that, she never had UFOs. Everything that was started got finished within a reasonable time frame.

"You two want to come in for tea?" Barb called from the front porch.

"Thanks for the invite," Roxie called back, "but our four-footers need their walk. If we stop now, we'll never get it done."

"Maybe tomorrow?"

"Let's plan on it." With Looper tugging on his leash and Sir Charles pulling in the other direction with his nose to the ground, the two ordered their buddies onward.

"Thank you," MJ muttered. Going in Barb's immaculate house always made her little gremlins of jealousy peek out.

"Welcome."

"How come I got left behind the door when God was handing out doses of perfectionism? I don't want it to the degree of Barb there, but a ticket to pull up when I need it would sure be helpful." MJ deliberately dropped her shoulders from her earlobes. Somehow talking with Mrs. Perfection always did that to her. They picked up the pace after the next cross street in spite of their four-footed companions, who tried to insist on sniffing every smell that came their way

"Come on, you two, I'm thirsty." Roxie tugged on Sir Charles's leash, and for that block, they made good time. "You seen Amalia lately?"

"Saw her ride by this morning in a new blue-and-white boater hat, so yes, but talked with her, no."

"Maybe she'll be at Annie's."

"My mouth is watering for a ginger cookie. Gary makes the best. You know I tried to talk him out of the recipe but no such luck." MJ paused as Looper found yet another enticing aroma.

"I'm counting on lemon bars." They crossed at the stoplight and turned right on the other side. We're not going all around our route today?"

"I not only need a latte, I need the restroom." They looped the leashes over hooks in the low windowsill of Annie's Cafe. She not only provided a lovely place for the dogs to wait, but also kept fresh water in a steel bowl. The maple tree on the corner of the shop gave them shade. Maybe that was a major reason MJ so en- joyed this town. Everyone here seemed to have a heart for pets.

They pushed open the door, to be greeted by the per- fume of something yummy just coming from the oven.

"Good morning, ladies," Anne called from behind the counter. "Your usual?"

"Yes, but what smells so good?" Roxie asked.

"Fresh sticky buns."

MJ made her stop at the ladies' room and joined Roxie. They looked at the Plexiglas display of baked goods on the counter. "No ginger cookies?"

"Sorry, the baker took the night off."

MJ snorted. "The nerve. Then I guess I will have to sacrifice and have one of the sticky buns. I swear you must have an exhaust fan that blows your yummy smells out to the street. When you bake bread..." She wagged her head, eyes closed. "Mmmm-hmmmm."

"I know, compliments of my dad." Annie set the two lattes on the counter. "You said two of each of these?" Her grin made the two women shake their heads.

"Yes, two, one for each of us. Not two each."

"Oh, sorry." Anne's grin came from teasing her good friends.

"Yeah, right." They carried their cups and plates to one of the round wrought iron tables next to the wall decorated with a big painting, done by a local artist. After Anne had waited on another customer, Roxie waved her over. "Got an idea we need to discuss with you."

Anne brought her coffee and pulled out another chair. "What's up?"

"You have any idea how many UFOs you have at your house?"

"UFOs?" Anne moved her head to give them a sideways, you-gotta-be-kidding look. "UFOs are out in New Mexico."

"Not that kind. UFOs—unfinished objects. As in projects, stored at home."

"You expect me to keep count?"

"Nope," Roxie explained, "that's the point. We propose a group that meets once a month to work on UFOs. That way we'll get more done. Working together is always more fun than alone."

"Hmmm." Anne stared from one friend to the other, then gestured around at the café. "This is rather a major one, wouldn't you say?"

"Well, we weren't talking about something like this."

"Where are you going to have it?"

Roxie shrugged. "Haven't gotten that far. But the article I read said that in their group, everyone had to agree to not start any new projects until they finish all their UFOs."

"All?" Anne wore the same horrified look MJ had.

MJ added, "Yeah, I'm with you. I'd never get to start something new in this lifetime. I must admit I'm warming up to the idea, though."

Roxie went on, "But this would be our group and we can set our own guidelines, so that's negotiable."

"You could meet here in the back room." Anne nodded over her shoulder to the comfortable meeting/game/general-purpose room in the back. "You thinking daytime, or evening?"

MJ wagged her head. "Daryl doesn't like me being gone in the evening."

"Why not invite him to come too? He's got plenty of UFOs out in that workshop of his."

"Open the group to men too?" MJ stared at her.

"Well, why not?"

"Hard to move a boat into the back room here."

"He's got smaller projects, I'm sure."

MJ thought about that. Daryl had started building a stitch-and-glue open kayak earlier in the winter. His dream of having it in the water this summer was in dire difficulty, even if he worked all day every day and part of the nights. And yes, he had a shop full of ideas that he had started. They could both come in the evening. "I think I'll offer a contest—whoever gets the closest guess to the number of projects in my sewing/craft room gets one to finish." MJ shook her head at their chuckles. "It's hopeless, I tell you."

"How many tables can you set up back there?" Roxie asked.

"Possibly two eight-footers," Anne replied. "I'm warming up to this idea too. You put together a poster and we can tack it up on the bulletin board. Start with an organizational meeting?" Anne pushed her chair back when the bell tinkled over the door. "I'd say the sooner the better."

"Hold the first meeting here? See how many we get?"

"Sure. We can seat more without the tables." Anne hustled off.

While Anne greeted the new customer and took her order, MJ dug her calendar out of her always-present belt bag. "I'll bet Maureen would love for us to meet at the yarn shop too. She has a lot more space."

"All depends on how many people show up," Roxie replied. "I'll go home and do a mockup on the laptop. I'd say get started meeting in May, on a Monday night at seven." She pointed to Wednesday, April twenty-sixth. "At this organizational meeting we can vote on day and time, but locking in one day each month is easier to remember. That gives us two weeks."

"Okay, April twenty-sixth, seven p.m., here at Annie's. You might add, bring a friend. I'll try to bring Daryl."

"Headline needs to be, YOU GOT ANY UFOs AT YOUR HOUSE? in a big font. JOIN US... and the time, place, etc. You want your phone number or mine?"

"Or both?"

"Sounds good. I'll find a graphic or two."

They paid their checks, thanked Anne for the dog treats she'd baked in-house, waved at another table of women, and headed for the door, only to veer around as if joined at the hips and stop to talk to the other two.

"What are you cooking up now?" Paula asked.

"What makes you ask that?"

"I know you two. You have that look about you." Paula nudged the other woman. "You know, Gail?"

The greetings taken care of, Roxie jumped in. "We have the best idea."

"See, I told you."

As Roxie described their idea, MJ was getting more and more pumped herself. "And so we are making a flyer to put around as an invite."

"UFO party." Paula looked dubious.

"Well, not a party but a group. You know how much more fun doing things together is."

Paula shrugged. "I do my knitting or crocheting in front of the TV when George is watching sports, so that technically, I am with him."

"Me too. Knitting bag is right by my chair, but..." Roxie shook her head, making one curl flop over her forehead. "So put April twenty-sixth on your calendar. We're meeting right here." She pointed to the social room. "You can bring something to work on if you want, but this is for organizational purposes."

Both women nodded. "I will be there. If I got my storage spaces cleared, I would near to faint."

Gail grinned. "Your hubby might too."

"I know, Mr. Organized."

MJ and Roxie waved good-bye and headed for the door again. Their furry-faced friends sat up immediately, tails wagging.

"Yes, we're going home." Both dogs got to their feet, whimpering and dancing, to head out. They nosed for their doggy treats, well versed in the drill, and crunched away, tails wagging all the while.

While on the way there, they'd checked out every smell, so now they pulled against their leads, heading for home.

"I'll call Amalia as soon as I get in. Looper, slower." MJ yanked.

"You could have used your cell."

"I know, but it and I are on a sabbatical. I left it home for that very reason."

"But what if Daryl tried to call?" Roxie snorted.

"Then he might have heard it ringing if he was in the kitchen. I hate being tied to that thing."

"My friend," Roxie said with exaggerated patience, "you've got to come into this century. Tech is here to stay and will only grow." They waited for the light, then strode across.

"We should have gone the other way to get our mile and a half in."

"Yeah, well, we didn't, so sue me. Make sure your computer is turned on, because as soon as I get a rough draft, I'll fire it over to you. You can edit it on the screen or print it out."

MJ rolled her eyes. Roxie was determined to make her use the computer. She knew how but she and it had a love-hate relationship. When it worked right, it was great. When it didn't, she threatened it with a baseball bat. One never knew what kind of mood the thing was in.

Roxie dragged on Sir Charles's leash. "We can each take a handful later this afternoon and post them in the places we discussed. Make sure you have pushpins along."

"You'll have it done by then?"

"MJ, this isn't a book we're writing, but a one-sheet poster. I think I'll make it eleven by fourteen. Bigger will attract more attention. I'll make it plenty bright."

"I need another latte."

Chapter Two

"Looks pretty good." Amalia nodded, setting the blue ribbon on her straw hat to bobbing. Leave it to Roxie and MJ to come up with an idea like this. UFO group. Not that she had so many UFOs since she'd sold her home and moved into the senior apartments in what used to be the Tilden School. The school her children had attended. Seemed strange at times for it to be housing seniors now. But she was plenty comfortable there. Besides, quite a few of her friends lived there now too.

She turned to a woman she knew from church who had also stopped to read the poster on the library's bulletin board. "You have any unfinished projects?"

"Do birds eat seeds? I do have a quilter friend, however, who has none. A big zero. She doesn't even have a stash. Uses her fabrics up and then buys new for the next quilt. You'd think that would be illegal, you know."

"Or she's lying."

"Now, Amalia..."

"You going?"

"I think so, got to check my calendar. You?"

Amalia nodded again. "Oh, yeah, MJ and Roxie'd have my head if I didn't show up. Besides, maybe Gary will have his ginger cookies there. Tried to talk him out of the recipe but he wouldn't budge. Says he has a secret ingredient."

"Well, I better get my books and head on home. My husband gave me a list to pick up for him too. See you there."

Amalia watched her friend as she disappeared in the stacks. She sure wasn't walking as well since that minor stroke she had. Pity. Just the thought caused a thank-you to raise heavenward that she could still ride her bike and walk as far as she needed to. A hip replacement had freed her from the worst pain anyway. She went on over to the desk to pick up the two books she had put on order, checked them out, waved to another friend sitting over by the window reading, and headed out to where she had parked her blue three-wheeled bike with both front and rear baskets. This was her main mode of transportation, other than public, since she'd moved smack-dab in the middle of Fond du Lac. Much easier than when she'd lived a couple of miles out in the country.

Digging her cell phone out of her rear jeans pocket, she punched Roxie's number. "Looks good," she said after the usual greetings. "Where all did you post them?" She nodded as Roxie caught her up. "You got any more? I'll put one up at the apartments. No, on my way home right now. I'll swing by and pick it up."

"You got time for tea?" Roxie asked at the door.

"Can I take a rain check? Made a big pot of chicken soup and need to deliver it to a couple of places. That flu has been hard on our residents. You hear that old Mrs. Goldson passed away from it a couple of days ago? Funeral is next week."

Roxie frowned in thought. "She was in her nineties, right?"

"Ninety-three to be exact. Seemed healthy as a horse." Amalia took the poster. "If you've got enough, why don't you give me another? I'll put up one at the garden store too. Got to stop there anyway."

"I can always print more. Thanks. See you at Annie's for coffee tomorrow morning? Usual time?"

Amalia nodded. "You back to regular walking?"

"Working on it."

Amalia leaned over to scratch Sir Charles behind his ears. "Such a good dog. Okay, see you in the a.m."

After posting one flyer at the garden store, she pedaled on home, parked her bike in the rack, and gathered up her packages. She pushpinned the poster up on the bulletin board in the entrance. Someone must have recently removed all the out-of-date ones since there was room for this one. She noticed a card about a cat needing a home. Darn, Ima Goldson's old cat, Jehoshaphat, needed a home. *Got to think on that*, she said to herself. She had assumed Ima's daughter would take the grumpy critter home to her house. For some strange reason, Jehoshaphat liked Amalia, one of the few people he tolerated, in fact. But did she want to be tied down again? Not that she planned on being gone for any length of time, but...

The fragrance of chicken soup greeted her as she opened her door. Which reminded her why she was hesitant about taking in Jehoshaphat. The odor of a litter box. All the ads claimed the newfangled ones had no odor, but while her sight wasn't as good as it used to be, her sense of smell made up for it. Hauling cat litter around on her bike might cause a bit of a problem. Of course, with Amazon, she could have both litter and cat food delivered right to her door. Was she trying to talk herself into or out of being owned by a cat?

The Crock-Pot fragranced the house anyway. She dug out plastic containers, most of which had had an earlier life containing cottage cheese or sour cream. Her Norwegian mother referred to them as Norwegian Tupperware. She had most assuredly passed on her frugal ways. This way no recipients felt obligated to return the containers. Once the four were filled, she had enough left for only two or three meals for herself. Perfect. She sealed them, then wrote instructions on the lid of the one for old Mr. Green. Usually she brought his down on a tray, ready to eat instantly. But with instructions, he could manage his microwave. She sliced and buttered the remainder of her sourdough-four-ingredient-bread-with-no-kneading, and slid each slice into a sandwich bag. Into two of the bags she added a recipe card with instructions on how to make the bread. Clara still liked to bake bread and Bess would manage this easy one. No kneading saved joints.

She tapped once on Green's door and entered just as he invited her in. "Brought you chicken soup even though you're not fighting the flu."

"Bless you, I was trying to figure what to have tonight. Just put it in the refrigerator, please. I can warm it in the container?"

"You can, but pouring it into a bowl with one of your small plates on top is safer."

"Okay. Any chance you can stay to visit a bit?"

"Need to deliver three others, two in bed."

He nodded. "Better see to them first. Thank you. If you hear any good news, I could sure do with some." He waved at the TV. "Not any more gloom and doom. You hear there was another shooting in a school? North Carolina this time. Sure hope they catch the ba— Ah, the shooter."

"What is this country coming to?" Amalia headed for the door. "You know to call me if you need anything."

"Yeah, yeah, go about your angel-of-mercy assignation."

"By the way," Amalia added, "I got a new book called *The Joys of Bird-Watching*. You might like it when I'm done."

"Print or ebook?"

"Print. Call if you need me." She waved to him and headed for the elevator. Earlier in the day she would have taken the stairs. She stopped at 216 and tapped on the door as she pushed it open.

"Brought you some chicken soup. Supposed to be good against colds and flu. You want to eat now or later?"

"Thanks," came a wavery voice from the bedroom. "I don't feel much like eating so just put it in the refrigerator."

Amalia shook her head and dug the tray out of the cookie sheet slot in the woman's kitchen. "You're eating now."

"I just can't."

"Agatha June Spencer, you are going to eat now if I have to feed you myself. You want to end up back in the hospital?" She poured the soup in a bowl, topped it with a plate, and turned the microwave to two minutes.

While the soup heated, she set up the tray. "What have you had to drink today?"

"I finished the pitcher of water you left." The voice was sounding stronger. How much was true flu, and how much was sheer depression? Agatha's son had died two months earlier and she'd been struck down by the grief, taking away all her will to live. Amalia finished setting up the tray and carried it into the bedroom.

"Good old remedy for what ails you, chicken soup and homemade bread. You want coffee, tea, or juice to go with this?"

"None, thank you."

"Okay, tea it will be. And I'll refill the pitcher. Good for you on your drinking today. Now, which will it be, sitting up in bed, the tray on your lap, or I'll help you move into that chair and set up the TV tray?"

"Amalia, you are not listening to me, I just do not feel like eating."

"Got it. We'll get you sitting up and I will feed you."

Agatha shook her head. "Can't you tell I just want to be left alone?"

"I know." While she talked, Amalia set the tray on the chair by the bed, pulled back the covers, and helped lift Agatha to sitting up, at the same time stuffing pillows behind her. She unfolded the bib she'd laid on the tray and snapped it around the neck that was looking more turkey-like every day. "You are not eating enough to keep a bird alive."

"You know birds can eat twice their weight in food every day."

"Well, at least your mind is working." She set the tray across her patient's lap and dipped a spoonful of soup.

Agatha rolled her eyes, but she opened her mouth and swallowed.

The eyes opened. "That is good."

"I know, you think I'd bring you something not good?" She held out another spoonful. *Lord, please bring life and joy back to this woman. She is too young to give up yet.* Granted she was in her mid-seventies, but until Andrew died and this bug attacked her, she'd been doing well. One of the group, you might say.

"I give up." She reached for the spoon. Part of the first spoonful hit the bib but she took a deep breath and tried again. This time her hand held more firmly.

"Try some of the bread, I think you'll like it. Come to think of it, dipped in soup might make it even better."

By the time the bread was gone, so was the soup. The pitcher was filled with water again, and Amalia brought in a cup of mint tea. "You didn't specify so this is what you get. The mint might help clear your head." She smiled at Agatha. "Now you drink this while I take Lily's soup to her, and I'll stop by on my way back. Did that home helper come today?"

"Was she supposed to?"

"Yes, to get you showered and change your bed, and she should have fed you lunch."

"No, another no-show."

"Did someone knock?"

Agatha wrinkled her forehead. "Perhaps. I don't re-member."

"But you didn't tell her to come in?" *I better talk with those folks again.* "The door wasn't locked?"

Shaking her head, Agatha sipped her tea. "I told them not to send her."

"I see. Did she call?"

Agatha did not look up again but she nodded.

"If someone can come tomorrow, I will tell them to stop at my place and I will bring her up and get her going." She sniffed. "It's beginning to smell like a sick room in here. Where are your air fresheners?"

"In the pantry."

"I'll be back in a while. You want the TV on?"

"No."

"Enjoy your tea." Amalia strode to the door, picked up her bag, and headed back out in the hall. One more to go.

Lord, am I doing what is best here? Agatha might need nursing care. When did she last see the doctor? Or did the visiting nurse come see her? All alone, Agatha was all alone.

She tapped on the door and pushed it open. "Supper is here." She stopped and grinned. "Well, look at you, up and sitting in the chair. How wonderful! And you used your walker."

Lily slapped a hand at the walker beside her. "When did that thing get so heavy? Felt like I'd walked half a mile just from the bed to here."

"Ah, but you did it, that's what counts. Now, can you eat in the chair, or do you need to go back to bed first?"

"I am so sick of that bed." She sent a glare at the bedroom. "Something sure smells good."

"Just call me the soup lady. Put this in the Crock-Pot this morning and the fragrance of chicken soup made it all the way into the hall before I got back." She went through the same procedure as at Agatha's and, while the soup heated, pulled the tray over in front of the chair. "What do you want to drink?"

"Too late in the day for coffee, so it better be tea."

"No decaf?"

"Nope. The cupboard is a'gettin' bare. Give me the herb tea, please."

Amalia smiled. "If you give me a list, I could pick up a few things tomorrow."

"Thank you, but it might be easier if I call the grocery and have it delivered."

"That place doubles their prices all because of their 'free' delivery. I'm sure MJ would shop for you. I'll write the list while you eat." Amalia set the plate with soup bowl and bread on the tray and pushed it up to the chair.

Lily bowed her head for grace and inhaled after her silent amen. "That smells like a bit of heaven in a bowl."

"Can you manage?"

"Slow but sure. Like that old turtle we talked about." Even though her hand shook, she got the spoon to her mouth and savored the flavor.

"Agatha dipped her bread in her soup. Might be easier. Oh, by the way, I brought the recipe along for when you are feeling better."

"Not easy to knead bread anymore." She flinched when trying to turn her wrist. "Blasted old Arthur. Never did like that name."

"I know. Arthur-itis wants to take up with all of us. Equal opportunity disease."

"That sure be the truth." She took another long sip.

"But the good news about this recipe, no kneading. You mix the ingredients one day, let set in a covered bowl, let it rise, scoop it into a pan, let it rest, then in the oven. I like to slash the top, sprinkle on coarse salt, and bake it in a hot oven. Can't fail."

"You serious?"

"Now, would I lie to you? All the instructions are on that card. My son gave me the recipe. He's baking bread all the time now. Folks think he is some kind of genius chef just because of that bread." Tell her about the UFO group or not? Amalia decided to leave it 'til later as she noticed Lily staring at the bowl as if her head was too heavy to hold up anymore. "How about I help you back to bed?"

"I—I think my get-up-and-go just ran out the door. My land."

"But you ate it all."

"Step in the right direction. Beginnin' to think I was never gettin' out of that bed again."

Amalia pulled the tray stand out and helped Lily to her feet. "The walker?" At the shake of her head, she put one arm around the woman's waist and held her arm with the other hand. "We can do this together. Then I'll park your friend there"—Lily snorted—"by the bed so you can use it at night."

"Got the potty chair right by the bed so should be good." Even her voice was fading.

"You call me if you need anything?"

"I will, I will. Thank you for comin'." Lily sank down on the edge of the bed. "You want to push in that night-light as you go out?"

"You have one in the bathroom too?"

"I do but the potty chair and I are becoming buddies." She collapsed on her side so Amalia lifted her legs and got her settled. "I'll dump the pot for you." Ignoring the stink, she did that and brought the rinsed pot back. "We'll get someone in to help in the morning."

"Thank you beyond measure. I prayed our Lord bless you and keep you strong. My daughter-in-law will be here Saturday and Sunday if I need her by then."

"Good. You've got your phone. Has it been plugged in?"

Lily fought to keep her eyes open. "Right there on the stand."

Amalia checked and plugged the phone into the charger on the wall. "You can still reach it, and you have your Life Line in case you need it?" Lily nodded. "Good, talk with you tomorrow."

Amalia rinsed out the dishes and left them in the drainer, then headed back to check on Agatha. Since she was sound asleep, even snoring, Amalia took the stairs back to her floor and apartment. Good thing she'd left the Crock-Pot on warm so her soup was hot. Perhaps she'd better make up another batch of that bread. She clicked her phone to Pandora, and the Celtic harp brought more life into her too-quiet apartment. While she ate her supper, she opened her latest novel and picked up where she'd left off. Shame she couldn't crochet and eat at the same time.

Were her eyes too tired for counted cross-stitch tonight? Her phone sang the "Hallelujah Chorus." Gracie checking on her. At least she had family who checked on her.

Chapter Three

"A UFO group? What in the world will you come up with next?" Ginny Clarkson asked, then smiled to herself and shifted her phone to her other ear. Roxie and MJ were amazing with their crazy ideas.

"Someone sighted an unidentified flying object over Wisconsin?" Her husband of forty years looked up from his morning paper and lifted his coffee mug in a silent request.

"Just a minute." She held the phone with one hand and picked up the coffeepot with the other. After filling his cup, she warmed her own. The timer went off on the oven. "Look, MJ, how about I call you back after breakfast? The muffins are ready to come out. Trying a new recipe that, if you are good, I might bring you later," She clicked off on MJ's chuckle.

"What was that all about?" Fred asked.

"UFO stands for 'unfinished objects,' you know, like those in your workshop and mine in the sewing room." At the arching of his eyebrows, she shrugged. "Okay, and the greenhouse, and the flower gardens, and the basement."

"Don't forget the barn." He returned his attention to the paper.

"That can go on your list. We started that together."

"Well, I can't go any farther until you make up your mind which style you want."

"Oh." She'd conveniently forgotten that. Sometimes it was nice to be able to blame undone things on "I forgot." Supposedly as one grew older, the memory lagged. His didn't. Hers did.

Fred's brow was puckered. "You know that chest of drawers I was working on? That's been sitting in the corner how many years? You're strong, but not strong enough to handle the frame while I dovetail the sides. Be nice to see that finished; the spalted maple drawers are such pretty wood."

"I agree." She turned off the oven and pulled out the pan of nicely browned poppy seed muffins to set on the hot pad on the counter. She put four in a napkin-lined basket and flipped the rest on their sides, still in the pan.

"You want eggs with this?" She set the basket on the table and slid into her chair. Her right hip grumped at her, a habit it seemed to be developing.

"What's the matter?"

"The hip again," she replied, "but too bad, I am going out to the greenhouse right after we eat."

"You going to do something about it?"

"The greenhouse?" she asked.

He rolled his eyes and reached for a muffin. "You know what I mean."

"I got a deal for you. I'll talk to the doctor about this hip if you will talk to him about that episode the other day, you know, the one where you had a pain in your chest."

"That was heartburn. I told you."

"Right. All I ask is that you stop self-diagnosing and mention it to the one who knows more about that kind of thing than you do."

"I told you, I'd get around to it after..." He glanced up, caught her over-the-top-of-her-glasses stare, and reached for the butter. "All right, you make an appointment for both of us and *we'll*"—he put the emphasis on the plural—"go. Just don't make it this week."

"I will check both our calendars, but if I make it, you have to promise to go." He'd been known to cancel for any number of reasons in the past, some of them a bit flimsy. But she had to admit, he was always busy. Not just on their place, but if anyone needed help, it was can-do-anything-that-needs-doing Fred to the rescue. She buttered her muffin and took the first bite. "Ahh."

"They are good. How about some yogurt to go with this and maybe a bit of granola sprinkled on top?"

She smiled. "And blueberries?"

"Now that is a fine idea."

"You sure you don't want bacon and eggs with that?" Another eye roll.

"No, thanks, honey. That will be fine." He was involved with the paper again. "Did you hear about that fire out by the park?" He read her the opening paragraph. "Can you believe that arson is a strong possibility?"

Ginny went to the kitchen, but on her way glanced at the bird feeder out the sliding glass door to the deck. She could hear a squabble going on. "The squirrel is back."

Fred slammed his paper down, pushed to his feet, and muttering imprecations, some more colorful than others, banged on the door as he slid it open. "Well, you..."

She knew the squirrel was long gone, usually with a flick of his tail. Somehow being flipped off by a squirrel incensed her usually placid husband. She wasn't sure which antics tickled her more—his or the squirrel's.

After they'd finished breakfast, he cleared the table while she loaded the dishwasher, another of those daily chores they had learned to divide up to keep life flowing more evenly.

"If you have any commitments next week, you need to give me a list because I am calling the doctor next." She added a hefty dose of firmness to her voice.

He was an expert at giving her disgruntled looks but only muttered as he retrieved his pocket calendar. Flipping through the pages, he finally said, "No mornings, but Tuesday, Thursday, and Friday afternoons are free."

"All right. Now remember, you promised."

"Just say I agreed. You know how I hate making promises."

"Nothing can push this out of the way," she insisted.

"Just do it and make sure you write it in." He handed her his calendar and headed for the bathroom to shave.

The brief conversation with her friend, Ann, the receptionist at the doctor's office, lengthened when she mentioned the UFO meeting. Business done, she hung up and wrote, *Doctor's appt., 2 p.m.*, on Friday, May 5, in both their pocket calendars, then went downstairs to her office in the walkout basement to write it on her desk calendar too. She huffed a sigh. That Friday was taken. Now she'd have to change her afternoon meeting to some other time, all because she'd forgotten to write the meeting in her pocket calendar. She could hear their son's voice: "Just use the calendar on your cell; you always have that with you." Right, easy for him to say. Fred had tried it for a while but said he could do it ten times faster with pen and paper. Especially since she did most of his bookings.

Back upstairs, she tapped on the bathroom door and opened it enough to lay the book on the counter. "Two p.m., on Friday, May fifth. Maybe we can go out for an early-bird dinner afterward."

"Why don't you call and ask MJ and Daryl if they want to join us. I need to talk with him about that kayak he's working on."

"Okay, I need to return her call anyway." *At the rate I'm going, I won't make it to the greenhouse till after lunch.* She tucked her phone in her pants pocket, grabbed a denim shirt, and, whistling for Spook, headed out the door. "Come on, you big lug. And no, we are not going for walkies." Their rescue Lab-Rottweiler cross grabbed his harness off the hook by the door. "No, we're going to the greenhouse."

"Spook can come with me," Fred said. "I'm going to Tractor Supply for more shavings for the chicken house."

When the dog heard his name, one ear perked up and his tail beat a tattoo against her leg.

"We'll be out in the greenhouse when you're ready. Come on, boy. Go find your stick."

Ginny paused on the step and lifted her face to the warming sun. How she loved spring, especially after the winter that seemed to last forever. Spook brought her a stick and she tossed it out in the driveway. He'd been known to tear through a flower bed in a shortcut so she was careful where she threw it.

Fred had stopped to open the greenhouse door when he'd gone to feed the chickens earlier but still the moist warmth welcomed her. Even in February when Fred had shoveled a path to the greenhouse for her, she loved every moment of greenhouse time. She started various flowers, finally finding the lace ruffled pansy seeds she'd seen once, and other old standbys. State Fair Zinnias for height, Thumbelinas for borders, and several colors of newer varieties. Visitors could always tell zinnias were one of her favorite annuals. She set two gallon-sized pots on the bench and poured potting soil in the bottoms, then transplanted the Romas, Early Girl, cherry, and yellow pear tomatoes to the bigger pots and filled them with soil right up to the leaves so roots would grow all the way up the stem. Next planting would be in the ground, but she needed to wait until the danger of frost passed by. Wisconsin was known for frosts into May and even June once in a great while.

"I'm ready. You want anything from Tractor Supply?"

"Not that I can think of." She wrinkled her forehead, supposedly to help her think better. "I had a list somewhere."

Fred threw the stick for Spook. "Okay, then we are out of here. Come on, dog."

She leaned out the door. "Did you get diesel for the tractor?"

"No. Thanks." He detoured by the garage for the gas can. "You interested in fried chicken for lunch?" he hollered back.

"I am always interested in fried chicken, you know

that." She grinned to herself as she returned to her transplanting. Oops, forgot to call MJ back. She punched in the numbers and hit Speaker so she could keep on transplanting.

After the greetings, she could hear Looper barking in the background. She added, "Before I forget, I have extra tomato plants here if you want to come out and get them. Other starts too."

"Let me ask Daryl. He's been wanting to talk with Fred."

"Fred wondered if you'd like to meet us for dinner after our doctor's appointments in a few weeks. But maybe we could all go to the Purple Rooster for an early-bird dinner this Friday instead." She could hear MJ and Daryl talking.

"Yes to the dinner and yes to the plants. How about later this afternoon to pick them up?"

"Good. Fred is on his way to pick up shavings for the chicken house. Sure is handy buying that in bales. See you later." Ginny set a variety of tomato plants on one of the flats, added some flowers, and turned to the matching pots that always stood beside the front door.

They had the Fondy Flowers nursery fill all their hanging baskets every year, a unique service provided by her favorite nursery in the whole world, right near Fond du Lac. They would pick those up as soon as the frost was gone. So many things hinged on that magical date.

While she planted and potted whenever she could, Fred religiously gardened according to the routine of the old-timers who planted by the moon and the calendar. The produce from his garden fed their son's family and half the neighborhood, besides all the two of them could can, freeze, and dry. Fred, especially, liked running the food dryer.

Like always, she totally lost track of time in the greenhouse, until she heard the truck drive in. Could it be lunchtime already? She stepped back to study the two big pots, nodding as she looked them over. When the grasses grew taller in the middle, the sweet potato vine trailed over the sides, and the coleus branched out, they should look about right. Every year she tried to add something different, and this year it was a new kind of coleus and the New Zealand begonias. She'd leave the pots in the greenhouse for a week or so to let the roots start growing, then harden them off in the shaded area under the elm tree. She grabbed her gardening diary, made sure the vents were open to keep the temp from climbing too much, and headed for the house. That same design would do well in the big pots by the church doors and she would have plenty of plants to do them. The thought of throwing growing plants away because she had no more room to plant them was anathema. But some years it happened. One year several of the tomato plants went ahead and grew in the compost heap when she tried to dispose of them.

Spook came bouncing out to meet her, as if he'd been gone for days. "I know, boy, you are sorry you deserted me, but face it, you would rather go for a ride in the truck with Dad than just about anything else." She took his proffered stick and threw it down the driveway. "Except that."

"Jason said to tell you hello and asked if you had any extra tomatoes." Fred was setting plates and silver on the table. "Unless you'd rather eat outside?"

"No, this is good, the table isn't washed down yet." She hung her gardening apron on the hook by the door. "And tell Jason I probably will. If he'd come and get them before I transplant them again, like now."

"I'll call him back after we eat."

She inhaled. "I do love fried chicken perfume."

"I got extra coleslaw."

"Smart man."

As soon as Fred said grace, they helped themselves. Fred ignored two phone calls since several years earlier they had agreed not to answer cell phones—they no longer had a land line—during a meal.

"I'm going to ask Sam if I can pick the kids up after school so Andy can come spread the shavings. You want Addy to help you?" Andy and Addy were their son's eleven-year-old twins, both of whom loved to be with their grandparents. Fred and Ginny had nearly raised them for the years their baby brother suffered from severe health problems so that their mom, Erica, could give Joey all the time he needed. When he went on home to heaven at three, the whole family suffered, as did their church family.

"Of course, need you ask? Hmm, I wonder what kind of cookies Addy will want to bake today." Although she was only eleven, Addy had already decided that someday she was going to have either a bakery or a coffee shop with home-baked goodies.

"You better have everything on hand. Think I'll ask for peanut butter. We've not had those for a long time."

"Let's see, that UFO meeting is nine days away. I think after the group gets going, I'll take Addy along; she wants to learn to knit."

"Surely she can't have UFOs yet."

"Hopefully not, but she has our genes and you know Sam has UFOs around. The kids come by it naturally." She watched ideas flit across Fred's face. Wagging her head, she rolled her eyes. "Get the idea out of your mind that UFOs are a female thing. Men just aren't as willing to admit they need help. What about that trailer you started how many months ago? 'Bout gardening time again. Would be handy for hauling stuff around."

"I'm thinking to build removable low sides for it. Need to get a new tank of acetylene to finish welding the frame."

"Why don't you ask Sam to help you?"

"He's got about all he can handle on his plate already." The closer the school year drew to a close, the more frantic that shop department, trying to get all the students' projects done by the end of the year. Sam taught shop, including welding and woodworking. He drew the line at automotive. Sometimes he gave continuing workshops both evening and some weekends for interested adults. More often, Fred was at the high school helping him.

"I'm going out to clean up my mess while you pick up the twins. Take Spook along or Addy will be on your case."

"Was planning on it. Come on, dog." Spook did not need a second invitation. He'd started his dance as soon as Fred took out his keys.

After she heard them drive out the driveway, she checked the peanut butter jar. Whoops. Should have done that before. Taking out her phone, she pressed his key. "Almost out of crunchy peanut better and bread too. Sorry."

"Okay, we'll stop. Anything else?"

She checked the freezer. "You might have told me you emptied the ice cream carton."

"Do we have bananas?"

"One."

"Think Andy and I are hankering for banana splits for dessert."

She frowned. "Along with peanut butter cookies?"

"What else are we having for supper?"

"I'm putting the lasagna in the oven now."

"I'll get French bread then too." He closed the line.

Back out in the greenhouse, Ginny breathed a sigh of delight. Inhaling the greenhouse perfume always made her smile. She had at least an hour. The flat of trailing petunia seedlings was next. Using the garden knife, she cut the flat into squares and dug out the first two to move to the four-inch pots all lined up in an empty flat. She used a pancake turner to slide under the squares and lift each into an individual pot. A quick press, add a bit more potting soil, and gently mist her babies. She set that flat on the shelf under the bench and pulled out another to repeat. She'd just finished her fourth flat when she heard the truck turn in the driveway. Petunias done. The peppers looked ready to do tomorrow. This was her first year to try eggplant so she had started only a few.

Although Fred's garden grew about anything they planted, she loved to try new things.

As soon as the truck stopped, both twins came running to the greenhouse to greet her.

Addy stopped at the door. "Grandpa said he wanted peanut butter cookies. What kind do you want?"

"I want cowboy cookies." Andy poked at her.

"Not today."

"I thought we could make some for the UFO meeting. We can keep 'em in the freezer."

"Can you keep Grandpa from the freezer?"

"Good point."

"What's a UFO group?" Andy gave his grandma one of his questioning looks. "I thought you didn't like *Star Wars*."

"This group is for people with unfinished projects."

"That doesn't make sense. Unfinished projects is UFP."

Leave it to Andy—things had to make sense for him. "It's okay. Grandpa is going to go too. You got any unfinished projects?"

"Yeah, his book reports." Addy poked her brother in the ribs.

"Schoolwork doesn't count."

"Why not?" She looked at her grandma. "You going to take Mom along? She has lots."

"I'll ask her." Ginny pulled off her gloves and stuck them in her apron pocket, then hung her apron on the hook by the door. "Let's go bake cookies."

"I'm hungry." Andy put on his *I'm starving* look.

"I know. There are sandwich makings in the refrigerator. Addy, why don't you call your mom and tell her to come here for supper. Andy, same for your dad."

"Oh, good. We won't have to have hot dogs again."

"Gee, that's what we have for snacks." Ginny put a sad look on her face.

"Graaan'maaaa."

"She's teasing," Addy picked up the stick and threw it as far as she could down the driveway. "Go, Spook."

Thank you, Lord, for these two. Ginny followed them into the house, where they took the stairs two at a time. Such boundless energy. What would they do without them?

Chapter Four

"What if no one shows up?" Roxie bit her lip nervously. She was wearing her plain gray tennis shoes today; she always wore them when she was nervous.

MJ grinned. "We are going to have SRO, you wait and see."

"SRO?"

"Standing room only. We better ask Anne if she has any more chairs."

"Ever the optimist." Roxie straightened the tablecloth on the table waiting for goodies. She opened the container and took out a lemon bar. "I never should have made these."

"Stress eating?"

"What else? I'll go ask Anne."

Anne was just putting the final touches on one of the trays they used in the diner to carry plates to the tables, now covered in cookies. She held both hands, flat out, in a quieting motion. "Easy, my friend." A knock at the diner door grabbed her attention. "See, people are starting to come. Would you please unlock the door and point them in the right direction."

"Of course. MJ wanted to know if you have extra chairs stashed anywhere else."

"I'll take care of that. You go to the door. Oh, and leave it unlocked."

Roxie turned the lock with one hand and pulled the door open with the other. "Welcome if you are here for the UFO meeting, and the diner is closed if you are wanting supper."

"The UFO meeting, of course." Three women filed in.

"The meeting room is straight through there." Roxie pointed the way. She thought that due to her years as a real estate agent, she knew everyone in town, but she didn't recognize any of them. She turned to greet two ladies from her church. "Welcome, meeting room is in the back, but you already know that."

"Were we supposed to bring our projects?"

"You could if you wished, but this is basically an informational meeting. Glad you could come. And here is Jeff! Good evening, Jeff."

A wizened old man grinned as he entered. Roxie happened to know he was a widower whose only son had recently married. She knew nothing more about him. "Good to see you, Roxie. The poster didn't say what kind of unfinished projects."

"All kinds. No restrictions."

"Good. Wait'll you see what I have." He walked on through to the back.

Amalia entered with a big smile. She was wearing a crocheted-and-starched floppy hat tonight with a long blue grosgrain ribbon. "Hi, Roxie. Would you believe I have three other hats that are not completed yet?"

Roxie laughed. "I sure would."

Ginny and Fred came through the door.

Roxie said, "So good to see you both! Fred, I can't believe you have any unfinished projects."

He chuckled. "Are you kidding?"

She lost track of the number of people she greeted, all the way from two college students to a granny with a walker, several with canes, and three other men who were not husbands of those attending. The back room was beginning to sound like a convention center.

"Told you so," MJ said with a chuckle. "Let the adventure begin."

The men were standing around the back of the room and several of the younger people were sitting on the floor when Anne's Gary brought in more chairs so the others could sit.

"This is it, no more room. You could sit around the tables out here." He motioned to the guys.

Three women stopped in the entrance. "We'll sit out here."

MJ tapped with a spoon on a glass. When that didn't work, she tapped louder and raised her voice. "Can I have your attention, please?"

Addy, who was sitting on the floor in front, put two fingers in her mouth and near to blasted the eardrums of those right around her.

People laughed but they did settle down.

"I hate to break up discussions like this but we do need to get the meeting started." MJ paused. "Thank you, thank you." When the hush finally won, she smiled at those gathered. "Welcome to the organizational meeting of our proposed UFO group. I will start with a confession. When Roxie came up with this idea—and it was her idea, not ours together—I was pretty skeptical. Let's face it, this is kind of a loony idea. But now that I see so many here, I am not the least bit skeptical. This is an idea whose time has come.

"Our goal is to assist each other with finishing projects that we already started. I get the feeling some of us have plenty of those and all of us have some. I was planning on going around the room so each of you could introduce yourself and perhaps one of the projects you would like to finish, but I never dreamed we'd have this many. Roxie, who was the greeter out there, was afraid it would be a bust."

Roxie nodded. "True. Glad to see you all. We promise we will have a larger room the next time we meet."

"How did you think this up?" someone from the group asked.

Roxie answered, "That's next on the agenda. MJ and I were talking one day about trying to get some things finished, when I said I'd heard about a group like this and followed up to learn more. That group sent me their guidelines." Roxie handed MJ the paper.

MJ muttered, "I thought you were going to present this."

Roxie shook her head. "You're doing fine." She liked that MJ had something to supervise again. What would Roxie herself do if she ever retired from selling houses?

After shooting her friend a dirty look, MJ continued, "First off, let me ask a couple of questions. How many have three to five UFOs at your house? Raise your hands." Most hands in the room went up. "I see. How about ten?" More than half the group again. "Okay, between fifteen and twenty?" Far fewer hands this time.

"Anyone with no idea." She raised her own hand and counted five others.

"I'd give some of mine away if someone else needs more to do," one of those women said. Laughter answered that one.

"I figured I'd have a contest and whoever guessed closest to the number I have would get to keep one of them," MJ said.

"Good idea but then you'd have to dig them all out and count them. Not me." More chuckles.

"You're right. Me either. So, how many have quilting projects?" A good portion of the room. "Knitting? Crocheting? Weaving?" The numbers were dropping.

"How about needlepoint?" Several raised their hands.

"Woodworking? Stained glass?"

"I've always wanted to do that."

"Uh-uh." MJ shook her head. "Remember, no new projects."

"Oh, that's right."

"Does anyone else do tatting?" one lady asked as she looked around the room for another who did. One more lady raised her hand.

One of the men, Jeff, piped up, "How about building an eight-foot peapod?"

MJ's mouth dropped open. "That's a lot of peas!"

"It's a boat—a little boat like a punt that you sail or row around in."

"I'll help you," Fred offered from the back. "If you'll help me with a big, heavy chest of drawers."

"Deal!"

"Hmm, hadn't thought of that as a by-product. Any others? Oh—painters?" Several hands went up.

"I do house painting; that might be a bit difficult to work on with the group." Ready chuckles skipped around the room.

"Well, as we said, anything goes. I can see we have a critical need for such a philanthropic group."

"We're going to need to meet more than once a month."

"That might be a good idea too. Let's review the other group's suggestions and see if we agree." MJ consulted the paper in her hand. "Now, the first premise is, we promise not to start anything new."

"Uh-uh, I'd never get to start another new thing in this lifetime." Anne shook her head. "I can't sign something like that."

"I agree. I still haven't started a baby quilt, and it is due in two months."

"This is our group; we can do what we want. I'm just going to read their suggestions." MJ glanced around the room for agreement. "Okay, they meet once a month; we might want to meet bimonthly, like the first and third Thursdays or some such. Even though we don't feel we want to sign something, we can still pretty much agree on the value of not starting anything new. Right?"

"Oh, yeah, it sounds good. But..."

"I know," someone ventured. "How about we take pictures of the finished projects so we all can celebrate."

Roxie bobbed her head. "Now, I think that is a good idea."

"Me too," Amalia, who'd been rather quiet, responded. "Any idea where we will be meeting?"

Roxie replied, "I was talking to Maureen at the Yarn Shop, and she has offered her place. Remember, everyone has to bring their own projects and supplies."

"I can't go in that store without buying some of her wonderful yarns."

"Ask her to close the cash register?" More chuckles.

"What do you think I am? Stupid?" Maureen herself asked from halfway back. "But I promise no sales hype."

"Just going in there is addictive."

"Glad to hear that," Maureen said with a smile and a wave. "If we are too crowded we'll have to find a bigger place, but we can start there."

"Great. Now what's next?" MJ studied her list. "Here. There will be no business meetings; we just show up and get started. We want to keep this as simple as possible."

"How about a list of names with contact information?"

"Good idea. Now, about the day to meet."

"Not on Wednesday night, like this one."

"I know, church night."

"What about Thursdays?"

Amalia wore her pondering look. "You know, people say they dread Mondays. Perhaps this would be something to look forward to." She nodded while she spoke. "I know I would."

"You look forward to everything, O bringer of sunshine," someone from the back added.

"Ain't that the truth?" This brought more chuckles.

"I'll take that as a compliment." The blue ribbon on Amalia's floppy hat swayed as she nodded.

"Meant it as one."

"She makes the best pies," another added.

"I know. Why, she brought me soup for a whole week when I was down with the flu. Saved my life."

Amalia rolled her eyes. "It wasn't that big a deal."

MJ raised her voice. "Let's get back to the topic. Amalia suggested Monday nights. Any discussion or other suggestions?"

One woman offered, "I wish we could meet in the morning or afternoon. I don't like being out after dark in the winter."

Several assents from around the room.

MJ looked at Roxie. "It's your meeting now." And she stepped back.

Roxie stepped forward. "I know driving in the dark is difficult for many of us, but if we meet at Maureen's shop, evenings would be better. If we meet after she closes, we wouldn't fill up her parking lot and block out paying customers. Besides, I know some of us work during the day; we aren't all retired."

Jeff pointed out, "In the summer, the sun rises in the north and sets in the north. Plenty of daylight. We could meet in the evening all summer and then change to mornings or afternoons when the days get short again."

"Excellent point!" Roxie said. "Anything we set up tonight can be changed; does anyone object to evenings until, say, September?"

Lots of head shaking, no frowns.

"Good. Let's agree on a day." Roxie paused. "Let's start with the two nights mentioned, Monday and Thursday. Those for Monday, raise your hands." She counted. Way more than half. "Okay, Thursday." Monday was obvious.

"Hey, you can't vote for both." Roxie stared at one couple.

"Why not, we are good for either." The two looked at each other and shrugged. "Made sense to us."

"Whatever." MJ looked at Anne, who shrugged back

at her. That couple had been married so long, they always thought alike, or at least it seemed that way. "Okay, Monday night it is, at least for the time being."

One of the men sighed. "Means no Monday night football."

"Tell your TV to save it for you. Hey, fall is months away."

The snorts around the room obviously came from women who could not care less about football.

"Good reason to have it on Monday night. How about first and third? Any dissenters?" Roxie paused. No one spoke up. "Then that will be our night. One good thing is that this is our group—if something isn't working, we'll change it."

MJ studied the calendar Roxie handed her. "So we meet at the knitting store a block down the street from six to nine next Monday for our first working meeting."

"If some of you want to come early, the door will be open and the coffee on," Maureen amended.

Addy raised her hand. "Can I bring cookies? Grandma is going to teach me to knit."

"Sweetie, you can bring cookies to my shop anytime."

Amalia reached over and patted the girl's shoulder. "I just had an idea. You and I need to talk."

Ginny looked between her granddaughter and her friend. "Uh-oh. Be careful what you agree to, Ads."

Jeff's voice from the back asked, "How can I bring my peapod to Maureen's?"

Maureen grinned at him. "Out in the parking lot under the roof where I park my car. Be cold in the winter but perhaps you'll have it done by then. You give us a challenge, we will work it out."

"All right, are there any more questions, discussions?" MJ nodded. "Good, then, the beverages are on the first table out the door along with the cookies and bars. Anne, anything you would like to say?"

Anne stood. "Just thanks for coming and hope to see you again soon. By the way, lattes are on special for the next two mornings, until noon. Prices at the cash register. Omelets are the breakfast special for tomorrow. Now come help yourself; I put Addy's name on the tray of cookies she baked. Addy, stand so they see who the whistler is."

❀   ❀   ❀

A half hour later, MJ closed the door behind the last attendee. "Well, our project is on the way."

"I'd say; what a turnout!" Anne picked up the coffeepot. "Even if half these people show up..."

"For sure." Ginny handed her trays to Addy and picked up the iced tea and lemonade pitchers. "I better get this kid home before her dad scolds me for keeping his daughter out late on a school night."

"So Jeff wants help with his peapod. That will be good." Fred joined several others in setting the room back to rights. "This won't take but a minute. Hey, Amalia, you want a ride home? I can throw your bike in the back of the truck."

"Thanks, but it is still light enough out."

"Thank you all for your help cleaning up." A few minutes later, Anne jangled her keys by the door. "See some of you in the morning."

"And you start baking muffins at...?"

"I know, morning comes early." She locked the door behind them, and she and Gary turned off the lights as they made their way out the back door to where their car was parked.

❋   ❋   ❋

MJ and Roxie met at the gate to the white picket fence the following morning. They let the dogs go through the normal doggy greeting before striding out to get their mile in. Both dogs trotted on ahead at the ends of their leashes, knowing full well where they were going.

"Talk about a perfect spring day." MJ raised her face toward the sun. "What did Loren have to say about the meeting?"

"You know her, never does look too excited about something but she was trying to decide which project to get back to first. I said the most recent start, she figured the oldest one. She decided on the set of Christmas placemats because those are the closest to done."

"I see. Ever practical. And she has how many to choose from?"

"Somewhere around ten, I guess." Roxie tweaked Sir Charles's leash. "Just because Looper gets sidetracked, you don't have to."

"The day I see ten again will be a miraculous day of celebration." MJ heaved a sigh. "Come on, I am needing coffee more each second."

Roxie suggested, "Let's go the long way around so we don't decide to head on home after Annie's. In fact, perhaps we could stop by Mona's quilt shop."

"You're not starting another project, are you?"

"I wouldn't dare. I found a project I had tucked way back, a crib quilt for my niece's first baby. She's having her third baby in three months." Roxie shrugged. "What can I say?"

MJ giggled. "Better late than never."

At the quilt shop, Mona was displaying her new summer fabrics, gorgeous flower percales, and rich, swirling prints. While Roxie bought quilting thread and double-fold quilt binding, MJ stood with her eyes squeezed shut and her ears covered, going, "La la la la la la..."

Roxie took her purchase and change. "It's safe now. We're leaving."

A bit later, after several more shoulder jerks, they panted their way into Annie's.

"That bad, eh? Ready in a moment." Anne greeted them with a commiserating smile and a rapping of the used espresso grounds on the edge of the container. "Hey, you still want the used grounds for your compost?"

"Of course. I'll tell Daryl it's time to pick up. Our roses love coffee grounds."

"He doesn't compost it all?" While she talked, Anne steamed the milk and poured the latte together, taking that extra moment to make a heart on the top of the full cup. "Here you go. Roxie, you have that pondering look. What's your pleasure?"

"I think I'll have mine iced. Getting hot out there."

"Okay, you realize my phone's been buzzing all morning?"

"About the meeting last night?" At Anne's nod, MJ snorted. "My phone started at seven forty-five. If three-fourths of everyone who says they're coming show up, we either need a bigger place or to have two groups."

Roxie suggested, "We could do a daytime and an evening group. I know I'd rather do evenings. I need my mornings in the office."

"But you show houses in the evenings."

"I show houses any chance I get. This way I could do one or the other." She glanced at her watch. "Speaking of which, I have an appointment in an hour. Good thing we are on the homeward stretch."

MJ frowned. "What about that couple you showed the house to a few doors down from me?"

"If the counteroffer is accepted, it's a go. You'll like them as neighbors." Roxie swirled the ice in her latte. "Let's get moving. You got any ginger cookies, my friend?"

"I do, Gary started early this morning. One lady last night ordered three dozen to be picked up on her noon break."

Both women nodded. "That's great."

"Yup, and a couple others asked if they could meet here for lunch and bring their knitting along. Can you beat that? That back room might get to be real popular. A couple of writers are back there now. One said my whole-wheat cinnamon rolls are the best she ever tasted."

"Well, that's only because they are." Roxie pushed back her chair.

"Grab a doggy treat as you go."

"Yup. We're going to make Annie's Fountain City Cafe the most favorite coffee spot in Fond du Lac."

"I hope the house sale you set up goes through." Anne waved them out.

"From her mouth to God's ear." Roxie leaned over to pat Sir Charles's shoulders and unhook his leash. "Come on, boy, we gotta hurry."

"Let me know how it goes," MJ called after her. Now, what to attack next?

Chapter Five

Amalia's nose told her she was at the animal shelter even if she hadn't seen the sign. She didn't really mind mild animal odors, but this was too much. She entered and crossed to a shabby desk, bringing Ima's cat carrier. "The daughter of Ima Goldson, recently deceased, brought you her mother Ima's cat. I would like to adopt him."

"No you don't."

"Yes, I do, that's why I came."

The receptionist stood up. "Come, please," and led the way through two sets of doors to the cage area. She waved her arm at a battery of small cages. "We have some beautiful cats here in need of adoption. Many of them are kittens. Sweet, lively kittens. What color would you be interested in?"

"Gray. I want a very old, fixed, gray Maine coon cat with a black smudge on his nose. A ragged left ear would be perfect."

The woman studied her. "That cat bites, and it is very old. It is mean, really not a good fit for anyone who likes cats."

Amalia kept her annoyance hidden. Probably. "That's quite all right. I don't like cats."

"You'll have to pay for shots and registration."

"The cat is up to date with all his vaccinations. Here. Ima's daughter gave me his medical history booklet signed by his vet."

The woman was not about to give up so easily and argued for another ten minutes, but finally, Amalia walked out into sunshine, away from that horrible stench, with Jehoshaphat in the cat carrier.

The old gray puss did not like riding back to the apartments in Amalia's bike basket. He hissed and meowed and, before long, howled. *This is ridiculous! Stupid. Why in the world am I doing this?* All the way home Amalia berated herself. So did Jehoshaphat.

She locked up her bike and carried the cat box to her door, set it down, and let herself in. "Welcome to your new home, Jehoshaphat. I have a dish of cat food waiting for you, and clean water, of course, and a nice cat bed scented with catnip or something. The salesgirl said it's an aroma cats love. I'm going to set the pet carrier beside your food dish and let you get used to the kitchen. Then I'll let you out. You'll notice also that you have a fancy litter box that is guaranteed not to stink."

Jehoshaphat was not impressed. He continued to wail.

The phone chimed. Amalia answered.

"It's Loren here. I have your books. May I drop them by at five?"

"Excellent. But, Loren, you know I could come to the library and get them."

"I know, but it's on my way. I'm happy to."

"Thank you."

"Amalia, do you have the TV turned up too loud? What am I hearing?"

"Not the TV. My cat. I'll be waiting out front at five."

＊   ＊   ＊

"Hey, you want to celebrate with me tonight?" Roxie asked her daughter.

"Sure, why?" Loren replied, her voice coming through brightly over the phone.

"Offer has been accepted and they are on the fast track for closure since both parties want that to happen, and they already have approval for the loan, which isn't surprising, since they are putting fifty percent down."

"Good for you, Mom! How about going by the furniture store afterward and looking at that rug for your office again? Be just the thing to tie it all together."

"Loren, you are a girl after my own heart. Grand way to celebrate." Roxie grinned to herself. "What time are you done there?"

"Should be home by five. Hey, we've heard the buzzing about last night even here at the library. I think I'm going to put up a display of craft books and we'll post a sign about the new group meeting. Keep in mind that we could host the group here if you outgrow the Yarn Shop." Loren always sounded so upbeat.

"I'll mention it to MJ. See you when you get here. Or if you're too hungry, I could come by there and we can throw your bike in the back and head out sooner."

"Thanks, but I'll ride. I have some books to deliver to Amalia for one of her shut-ins."

Strange. Amalia had seemed just fine. "She okay?"

"Yes, I just said I'd do this for her."

"Later, then." Roxie clicked her phone off and laid it back on her desk. Leave it to Loren. No sense planning supper for early. If only she would meet a good man in her heart errands. Her incredible shyness made meeting new people so difficult for her. But she seemed to be thriving at the library, being in charge of the displays.

Between the phone calls, the never-ending paperwork, and Sir Charles pleading for her to come throw the ball, the afternoon disappeared.

On my way, Loren texted at five.

"Oh, good grief, already," Roxie muttered as she headed into the kitchen to refill her glass of water infused with cucumber slices and mint leaves from the refrigerator. Ever since she'd purchased the pitchers with an infusion tube, she'd drunk more water. Maybe she'd mention that in her weekly newspaper column. Back at her desk, she jotted down the idea on the list she kept right beside the desk calendar. The deadline was tomorrow. The afternoon had flown by, just like the week. Her weekly hints column kept her name and picture in front of the reading public better than any paid advertisement. They didn't pay much but she didn't pay at all, so she figured it well worth the time and effort.

The phone again. She glanced at the unfamiliar number. If this was another telemarketing call.... She'd had two already today from the same number. She picked up the whistle she kept handy and answered, whistle at the ready.

"Can I speak with the lady of the house, please?" A man's voice.

Roxie blew the whistle sharp into the phone and

clicked it off. "There, that should do it." So far, it seemed so, since no one called back.

While the ideas were fresh, she started her column with, "We have a new organization in town. The first meeting was last night at Annie's Fountain City Cafe, where SRO took on a new meaning. From standing room only, the meeting took over half the dining area also. UFO has taken on a new meaning too, from unidentified flying objects to unfinished objects, or rather, projects. Obviously there are many of us with this tendency to not finish all the things we start. We're meeting again on Monday night, the first of May, and plan on meeting bimonthly at Maureen's Yarn Shop. Everyone who needs help to cure this syndrome, come on by.

"My other hints for this week are also extremely practical." She went on to write about drinking more water due to infused water always at the ready and finished up with: "For those of us who are mosquito magnets, I read of an antidote. Drink a glass of water mixed with one teaspoon of apple cider vinegar. Bragg's is the best. I know I've mentioned other uses for the all-purpose vinegar but I tried this one, and voilà, I came home bite free. A first.

"And with that I am off to celebrate many things: good business, great friends, living in the best town anywhere, new ideas, and the best dog in the world. Sir Charles and I thank you for reading our column."

She reread it, made a couple of changes, and hit Send. One more thing crossed off the to-do list. When Sir Charles scrambled to his feet and tore out of the room, she knew she'd spent more time than she'd planned on. His happy yips announced to anyone within hearing distance that his Loren had come home. Now his pack was all together, as they should always be.

"Mom, where are you? Go get Mom, Sir Charles."

"Just leaving my office, sorry."

"But you told me to hurry."

"I know but I got my column finished and I will be ready in ten minutes. Feed him and Juno, will you please?"

"Where's Juno?" Loren appeared in the doorway to her bathroom, where Roxie was freshening her makeup.

Roxie shook her head. "I have no idea. Did you call her?"

"She always meets me at the door, like Sir Charles. How long since you've seen her?" Juno, their faithful fluffy orange-and-white cat, never missed a meal, and you could tell by the look of her.

Oh, now what? Lord, where is our cat?

"Could she have gotten out?"

"If she did, she'd have been yowling at the door." Roxie dropped her mascara back in the zippered bag. She paused to suck in a calming, hopeful breath. She closed her eyes to help trigger the memory. The cat had greeted her and Sir Charles at the door after their walk that morning. She'd been rushing around to get ready to leave for her appointment. Did the cat get out while she was carrying the box she needed to deliver to the office? Possibly.

"Mom, we have to find her."

"I know. Let me think."

"What if she got hit on the street? She has no street smarts." Loren was always quick to worry.

"Okay, did you check the garage?"

"She would have answered me by now."

"Humor me."

Sir Charles perked up his ears and headed back down the stairs.

"You think?"

"He could hear something we can't. Follow him." Together they pelted down the stairs. "Sir Charles!"

His yip announced he was in the kitchen. They found him wagging his tail on the front of the door to the garage. When they didn't hurry enough, he scratched at the door and whimpered.

"Good dog." Loren opened the door and Sir Charles barreled through it, heading for a stack of both full and empty boxes.

No cat to be seen.

Sir Charles nosed boxes that had obviously fallen from the pile.

A disgusted feline expletive came from somewhere in the stash. Both Loren and Roxie pulled boxes out, all the while calling Juno. They found her caught in a box that was crammed between several others. The two looked at each other and snorted, shaking their heads in disgust. As soon as they'd dislodged the offending box and pulled open the flaps, Juno hissed at them as she scrambled free.

"Hey, it's not my fault, dodo bird, you got yourself stuck, you know." Loren started restacking the boxes. "Why do we keep all this junk here?"

"Because I've not had time to sort it and obviously you haven't either."

"I thought cats were supposed to be smarter than this." They both looked to where Juno grumbled at the door to the house. "I know, you need a drink and food." Loren turned the handle and pushed open the door. Tail rigid and straight in the air, Juno stomped into the laundry room, where her dishes awaited.

"This was all I needed." Roxie headed for the sink to wash her hands. "All that dust in there." She caught a sneeze against her inner elbow. "I say on your next day off, we take care of that disaster waiting to happen."

"I thought we were going to work in the yard."

"After this, even if we have to get up early. All we need is a fire or something."

"I am off day after tomorrow."

"No idea what is on my calendar but nothing happens before nine anyway."

❖   ❖   ❖

"So what went on at the library today?" Roxie asked after they'd placed their order at the restaurant.

"I spent most of the day on the bulletin boards and tomorrow the display cases. I'm setting up displays of homemade items next month so I requested samples with a brief history. I'm hoping for some unusual crafts. The woman who grows and paints gourds is a good example. That peapod boat intrigued me but it's a bit hard to display. We've done some good collections too."

The waitress set their salads in front of them. "Pepper?" She raised the pepper grinder. After cranking it a couple of times over each salad, she smiled. "Your dinner will be up shortly."

"Their salads are always so fresh." Roxie bowed her head. "Thank you, Lord, for crisp vegetables, a good dinner, and time together with my daughter." She squeezed Loren's fingers. "Amen."

Roxie savored every bite of her rib-eye-with-the-bone-in steak. "How come I can never make steaks come out like this?"

"Too impatient?"

"Guess I use up all my patience on people."

Loren cut herself a piece of her steak. "But you love to see people happy with their new homes and do everything you can to make sure that happens."

Roxie nodded. *Now if only I could help make the most important person in my life right now happy.* But she had learned that nothing set Loren off faster than her mother meddling.

She spread her napkin over the remains on her plate so she wouldn't keep picking at it and drank her iced tea instead, both elbows propped on the table. "That was delicious. You want dessert?"

"Not really."

"Good." She signaled for the check. "Rug shopping, here we come."

"If they still have that one, we can be in and out pretty quick."

Roxie liked the furniture store in the strip mall. They set up beautifully appointed display rooms as well as groups of things, like all the lamps.

"Good evening, ladies, how can I help you?" The young man who greeted them paused, studying. "Loren?"

"Yes." She stared at him. "I know you, don't I?"

"You graduated from North High?"

"Yes." Loren sneaked peeks at him, still not smiling.

Smile at him, for pity's sake, it wouldn't cost you anything. Roxie willed her daughter to respond.

"So did I. I think we were in the same American history class." His smile widened. "You always sat in the front row, I hid in the back." He held out his hand. "Nathan Owens."

Loren hesitated, then shook his hand. "Loren Gilburn."

"You're not married." He released her hand with what Roxie thought of as some reluctance.

"No. Ah, we came to find a rug for my mother's office."

Oh, Loren, wake up. You can at least smile.

"Sorry. Of course, come this way." He dropped his salesperson mask back in place and motioned toward the rugs hanging on frames on the back wall. "Did you have something particular in mind?"

Good man. Roxie silently cheered him on. And kept her mouth shut—a bit difficult to do, but he'd looked at her daughter with interest. A bevy of questions bombarded her mind. He was not wearing a wedding ring but that didn't mean a lot in this day and age. Millennials were a whole different breed of cat than earlier generations. *Please, Lord, let the rug be gone, anything to keep us here. What else could we be looking for?*

Loren turned from looking over the rugs. "I don't see the one we wanted, Mom."

"Perhaps if you describe what you were looking at, I could help you?"

Loren glanced at her mother, who sent it back. Ah, the telepathy of mother-daughter glances. Loren rolled her eyes and turned back to Nathan.

"What were the colors and the size?" he asked.

"Square rug, geometric pattern, shades of burgundy, dark blues, and gray."

"Ah, yes. Sorry, that sold the other day. I could order another one. It will take about three weeks. What size did you need?"

Loren looked at Roxie. "What, eight by eight?"

Roxie nodded. "Do you have anything else that is similar?"

"I think so, let me bring a couple of things from the back." When they both nodded, he left through the door between the rug racks.

"What, you don't want to wait for an order to come? We could just order it and leave."

"I know but perhaps there is something I'd like better."

"And you've been looking for a rug for how long?"

Roxie shrugged. "He seems really nice."

"He sure isn't the same round geek I remember."

"People have a way of changing, growing up, you know?"

"I guess." They turned as Nathan rolled in a dolly with several rugs on it. He lifted one off the pile and spread it on the stack by them.

"This has similar colors."

"The blocks are bigger." Roxie studied the rug. "Now I wish I had the other to compare with."

"This one has tan rather than gray and the burgundy is more rust." Loren flipped through the pictures on her cell phone to the one she'd taken. "See?"

Roxie nodded.

They both shook their heads at the next one he flipped out. "Too busy."

"So what have you done since high school?" Nathan asked.

"Associate's degree in library science and now working at the library."

"Will you go on for more?"

"I don't know." She turned to her mother. "What do you think? Look at more or order?"

Oh, Loren. Ask him a question. At times Roxie felt like shaking her daughter—and now was one. "I think order. That other one is too perfect."

"So, what have you been doing since high school?" she asked Nathan since her daughter didn't.

"Got my degree in business so I could be a better help for my dad." He led the way to the counter.

"Your dad owns this store?"

"Actually, we have a chain of four stores around the area. I manage this one, my brother manages the one in Green Bay, Dad the one in Madison, and my sister the one in De Pere."

"That's great, a family-owned business that has grown well."

"My grandfather started it back in the forties. He and a friend of his made furniture and needed an outlet. No one's made the furniture since then, but we make sure we have good quality at a decent price." He pulled out an order form. "Name?"

Roxie handed him her business card. "This is easier." While he filled out the form, she nodded at Loren. "See that lamp over there?"

"Unusual."

"I know. How do you think that would fit in the living room?"

Loren shrugged. "I like the one we have."

Nathan laid the form on the counter and showed Roxie the information. "How would you like to pay for this?"

"Credit card." She drew out her wallet and extracted the one she used for much of their living expenses, then paid off before it came due. She had another one she used for her real estate business. She had been the money manager in the family from the get-go although Greg, her husband, had been equally money conscious. Money had never been an issue between the two of them. Surely there had been areas of conflict between them, but these years later, he had been burnished with hero qualities. She'd never cared to find someone to take his place. He was too hard to measure up to.

Except for her children. Good thing her brother had taken on the role of strong male in their lives. The two older ones were off and growing their own lives, but little Loren, the baby, had yet to find her niche in life. Or to really want to, or so it seemed to Roxie. She brought herself back to standing in front of the counter at the furniture store.

"I'll call you as soon as they notify us it's shipped." Nathan was nodding and smiling. "Now, is there anything else I can help you with today?"

Roxie bit her tongue to keep the words from tumbling out. *You could fall in love with my daughter and help her build a happy life.* She cleared her throat. "Not that I can think of. Oh, by the way, do your stores ever work with Realtors in staging homes for sale?"

"I know I don't, but I can ask the others."

"Is there a reason you don't?"

"Would you believe I've never been asked?"

Roxie smiled. *Aha!* "Might you be amenable to such an idea?"

He nodded as he looked at her. "We could talk about it."

"Good. I'll be in touch. Thank you."

"Good to see you again, Loren." He paused. "Excuse me, I need to get this." He answered a call. He waved as they turned to leave.

"Mother, what were you doing? You have never encouraged staging." Loren put a down twist on the word when they reached the parking lot.

"Who knows, perhaps there will be a property that would be enhanced with that." Roxie slid behind the wheel. "Thanks for coming with me." And who knew where this might lead?

Chapter Six

Amalia picked up the phone and punched in numbers she knew by heart. One ring. Two. Ginny answered.

Amalia got right to business. "So do you still have more tomato plants?"

"Amalia, where are you going to put in a garden?" Ginny asked. "I thought Maple Reach wasn't going to have a community garden this year."

"*They* aren't. So I am going to do pots on my deck. Two tomato, one cucumber, a lettuce basket, and some flowers. I can do the tomatoes and cukes on trellises; I have the sweet peas on one now. So what kind of tomatoes do you have?"

"How about I give you either a yellow pear or a sweet grape and say either a Roma or Early Girl? I have pickling cucumbers and lemon cucumbers started. One of each in that pot might work well. I'd put marigolds in the pots to help ward off the bugs."

"Sounds perfect."

"I can either bring them to you or Fred can pick you up on his way and you can come for lunch."

"Lunch. You know me, I never turn down food." Amalia reached out and slid her door to the deck open.

"Are your sweet peas blooming?"

"Yes, they are scenting my whole apartment now that the door is open. Any idea when Fred will be here?"

"Soon."

"'Kay, tell him I'll meet him at the side door." Amalia clicked off and stepped out on the deck to sit down in the one chair in the shade. Mornings like this made waking up a delight. She'd already had her breakfast sitting at the round metal table, with bright floral cushions on the teal chairs to match the table.

Jehoshaphat came wandering disdainfully out onto the deck and flopped down beside her chair. His ragged ear tipped toward her, the only acknowledgment he made of her presence. He raised his ragged gray head to sniff and look about. A hummingbird swooped into the feeder. The cat gave it a passing glance and settled onto his belly, his paws tucked under his chest.

Amalia had been afraid the first time he came out on the deck that he might leap up on the rail and escape. Were he to get out into the world, he would die quickly, unable to hunt or defend himself, because Ima had never allowed him out of the house. For his own good. But no problem. He was too old and too arthritic to jump up on a chair, let alone the rail.

On days like today, she missed her yard and garden at the farm so badly she had to breathe carefully. Yes, moving here had a been a wise choice, yes, she was pleased most of the time, but with no grass to go barefoot in, no chickens clucking, birds singing in her trees, somehow digging in her pots did not equal digging in the earth. She had yet to find angle worms in the pots. Her garden soil had been full of worms and compost and years of loving care. Perhaps she should dig some out at Ginny's, just for the good of her pots, of course.

Memories flooded her of raising her two daughters and one son to appreciate homegrown fruit and vegetables, and eggs from their hens, the beauty of God's amazing earth, and that if you wanted to eat, you had to do the work. And now they were all living too far away to have daily or even weekly visits. Thank God for the Internet so they could all keep in touch, even if it was not face-to-face. True, the kids had invited her to live with them, but so far, she had resisted.

Her youngest lived in an apartment out in Seattle. She didn't mind the rain but Amalia shuddered at the thought of all the gray days. The son lived in Madison now, and who wanted to ride a bike in a busy city like that? And Marie...no. Just no. There would be too much friction.

Marie still harbored hard feelings about her selling the homestead. Not that relatives had homesteaded the land or anything, but somehow through the years, "the homestead" stuck. This was the second year Marie's girls could not come spend summer weeks with Grandma on the farm.

A grumble snort caught her attention. She glanced down to see the now-relaxed cat beside her.

"I know, Jehoshaphat, my mind took off all by its lonesome. Got sad news for you—time for me to get myself downstairs to meet Fred. You behave yourself, hear?" She picked up the monster-sized cat, set him on the sofa back in the living room after closing the screen, debated closing the sliding door, and opted for the fresh air instead.

Picking up her basket, which held her cell phone, her current ball of yarn to add rows to the lap robe for the senior center, the recipe she'd promised Ginny, her sunglasses, the small pack of licorice for Fred, biscuits for Spook, and her ever-present bottle of water, she bade Jehoshaphat behave himself and clicked the door behind her. She had made sure she had the door key in her pocket, just like she automatically lifted the current hat from the rack beside the door and clamped it on her head. That the doors locked automatically was not a selling feature to her. Hers was propped open with a painted rock most of the time she was home.

"Attractive hat," Fred said by way of greeting as he held the truck door open for Amalia.

"Thank you, kind sir. Nothing like an immediate change of plans, eh?"

"You know, you are not a change of plans, but family." He went around the front of the truck, shaking his head as he climbed in. "You'd think I never washed this the way the bugs are sticking to the grill."

"Aww, face it, that's your way of decimating the blooming bug population. That's one thing Wisconsin grows well, bugs." She dug in the basket on her lap and handed him his licorice. "Hard to find the good stuff, other than at the Scandinavian store."

"I just don't understand how Ginny cannot like licorice." He backed up the truck and waited to turn on to the street. "You need to stop anywhere?"

"Nope. Did you go over and help Jeff with his peapod?"

"I did. Still a lot of work to do on it, but he hopes to sail it this summer. Better be a long summer."

She chuckled as he rolled his eyes. "How's Sam doing with his end-of-school craziness?"

"Counting the days."

"I have a project for him when he has time."

"Has time?"

"I know, poor wording. When he can take time."

"He promised Erica and the twins that they would hightail it up to the lake for a couple of days the first week off before beginning the summer madness." Fred turned onto the road to their place.

"I thought summer was supposed to be relaxing in the sun with a good book, swimming, fishing, you know, those kinds of things."

He snorted. "Right. Gardening, canning, freezing, landscaping, helping Grandma and Grandpa, playing ball, attending ball games."

"And completing UFOs."

"That too. I think we need to do a christening when that peapod is finished. Be a good reason to celebrate."

"And Daryl's kayak. You think he'll ever use it?"

"Hard telling."

Spook waited for them in the middle of the driveway, announcing their arrival.

"He figured he should go along but at least he doesn't pack a grudge. Ginny is in the greenhouse, I 'spect."

Spook greeted Amalia with his usual exuberance, sniffing at her basket, his doggy grin making her smile too.

"You crazy dog. You know I always have something for you." She pulled out the paper-towel-wrapped doggy biscuits. "Ah-ah, you know the rules." She held them until he parked his hindquarters in front of her, then she flipped him the first one. "Sorry, poor toss, but you got it." As soon as he'd crunched that one, he sat down again, barely controlling the wriggling. He caught that one on a flying leap. "You are quite the athlete." She headed for the greenhouse, stopping to admire the newly transplanted starts. "My word, Ginny," she remarked from the entrance, "You have enough to provide for half the county."

"I know. Would rather have too many than not enough." Ginny beckoned Amalia into the richly fragranced, humid air. "Come see my latest babies." She motioned to a flat of seedlings. "Got these seeds from a seed swap. I gave some of my crocosmia bulbs and got these. The swap is for seeds we harvest from our own plants. Always a gamble but fun."

"These are?"

"Snapdragons. Talk about tiny. I had to sprinkle them on white paper and brush them onto the flat with a soft brush. Almost needs a microscope, but they sprouted."

"Hey, you promised us lunch when we got here," Fred called from the garage.

"Coming," Ginny called back. "Hope you feel like grilled ham and cheese sandwiches. I have a lettuce salad too, you know, with that yummy dressing I got from old Mrs. York. Be ready as soon as the griddle heats up. All we have to do is pour the dressing on the lettuce. I love new lettuce like this." She unsnapped her apron and hooked it on the post by the door, leaving her gloves in the pocket.

Fred escorted them inside. "You want to take some eggs when you go?"

Amalia nodded. "I can always use more eggs. Made

a frittata the other day with leftover ham, green onions, and asparagus. Reminded me how much I miss my garden out on the farm."

Ginny snorted. "Fred will grow enough vegetables to feed half the congregation, and that is after we and Sam get all we can use. Of course, Sam has his garden too."

Amalia put her basket on the counter. "You want some help with canning this year, I will gladly volunteer. No sense canning for one. I couldn't resist strawberry freezer jam, however. Gave small containers away at the home."

"And they thought you'd given them gold." Ginny washed her hands at the kitchen sink after turning the dial on the rectangular electric griddle. "Hand me that platter of sandwiches on the bottom shelf, please."

Fred said grace a few minutes later when they sat down to eat. "Now, help yourself, Ginny made enough for two teenage boys." He passed her the platter.

Amalia took one bite and closed her eyes in bliss. "Homemade bread."

"I felt a need to make bread yesterday. Now I promised Fred I would make cinnamon rolls for breakfast one of these day."

Fred hinted very broadly, "Tomorrow would be a good time. You could keep some of the dough and make fry bread for the twins. They'll be here for the weekend."

"I hope you realize how lucky you are to have the grands so close." *And a house big enough for company.* She thought of the times her little ones had come to the farm until they moved away—and she sold the farm. Children could visit her at the home but not for long.

Rules forbade anyone from moving their families in to stay with them.

Now it was easier for her to go visit them.

Amalia caught a pained look on Fred's face. "You okay?"

"Yeah, just gas. I forget and eat too fast. All Ginny's fault."

"My fault? How did that get to be my fault?"

"You're too good a cook, that's how." Amalia shook her head. "I could see that one coming." A movement out the big window caught her attention. "There he is again."

Fred shoved back his chair and headed for the door. "Dang varmint. Dad-blasted squirrel." He muttered imprecations as he grabbed the broom handle and brandished it.

The squirrel was nowhere to be seen.

"I'm not sure who has the most fun, Fred or the squirrel."

"The squirrel by a long shot. He was thumbing his nose when I saw him. Acknowledged by a squirrel. Fred is some privileged." Amalia raised her glass in salute.

"We could take our iced tea outside and watch the birds. Let Fred dish up the ice cream; he made it last night. Still have a few of Addy's cookies too. I hid a couple of containers in the freezer."

Amalia groaned. "You should have warned me. Let me clear the table first."

"Fred's turn."

"So I can give Fred a break."

"You know him, he likes the dishes just so in the dishwasher. He wants to take care of dishes, I let him." She slid the glass door open. "Oh look, the grosbeaks are here."

Amalia paused to watch the striking bird with the scarlet chest and his mate take over the feeder, managing to scatter seeds down for the ground-feeding birds. Another pang of homesickness hit her. Must be the day for it. Tears did not come easy for her, but she could feel them burning at the back of her throat.

"Are you all right?" Ginny asked softly.

"Yeah, or I will be." She looked around for her iced tea and nodded when Ginny raised it from the small table between the two recliners. Instead of sitting down, Amalia leaned on the wooden railing around the deck. A large basket of fern on one side of her and trailing arbutus on the other. Crossing her arms, she heaved a sigh. "Your hostas are growing well."

"Once they came up. I was beginning to be concerned. Fred pulled the winter mulch off them after the frost left the ground, but we didn't see any green until the hens started scratching in the beds."

Feeling more under control again, Amalia settled into the bright floral cushions and picked up her glass. Spook flopped down between them with a sigh. The song of a purple finch came from one of the maple trees leafing out behind the house. She picked up her ball of yarn from the basket beside her and studied the lap robe to see where she was to knit or purl and set the needles to clicking.

"Do you ever just sit and enjoy?"

Amalia shrugged. "Probably not. I don't miss out on the enjoyment by knitting. My hands do that all on their own. And then I don't feel guilty for sitting down."

"What are you going to bring to the meeting on Monday night?"

"Oh, a piece of cross-stitching. I put it away and just found it again. I thought of that rug I have on the coffee table, you know the hooked one? But it's too big to haul around. Besides, the cross-stitching is a true UFO. I think I started it on the farm."

"Oh, my goodness. I guess that does qualify." Ginny sipped her iced tea, wiping the moisture from the glass on her pant leg.

"And you?" Amalia asked.

"You remember when I started the ribbon embroidery?"

"A couple of years ago, right?"

"I found that bell pull all neatly packaged in one of the zippered bags bedding comes in nowadays, at the bottom of the trunk. Hope to send it to Josie for her new apartment."

Amalia looked up at the sound of the sliding glass door opening. Fred set the tray he carried on the end of Ginny's lounger. "Fred, you ever hear of small dishes of ice cream?"

"Those are small," Ginny answered with a head shake.

"How do you two keep slender with all this delicious food?"

"Hard work." Fred passed out the bowls, then the cookie plate, and settled into a recliner he dragged over. "First time I tried this recipe. Used coffee and then drizzled the chocolate syrup over the top before I froze it again. The recipe called for smashed chocolate-covered espresso beans but I didn't have any and didn't want to make a trip to town, so used almonds instead."

Amalia closed her eyes, the better to savor the flavor. "You could open an ice cream store. You'd have to beat the customers away."

"Na-ah, I'd have to make big batches and that sounds too much like work. This is experimenting. That home ice cream freezer Sam got me for Christmas is the perfect toy. This way I can make the kids' favorite flavors." Fred raised his bowl. "More?"

"Fred, you trying to corrupt me or stuff me like a Thanksgiving turkey?"

"Nope, just don't want you to go home hungry."

"Fat chance." She set her bowl and spoon on the tray. Glancing at her watch, she huffed. "Speaking of which, I need to get something in the oven for tonight."

"How many are you still feeding?"

"Only Agatha. If I don't bring something, she forgets to eat. This way I know she gets at least one good meal a day."

Ginny frowned. "I thought she was on the Meals on Wheels list."

"She was. Not sure what happened there, but you know, she can have some bad days. I just ignore them."

"How much longer can she live there?"

Amalia set her dish aside. "Good question. If that son of hers would research assisted living like he said he would. You know, some people just can't deal with a mother who is slipping like she is. I'm just filling in. I'm sure we're going to need to call Social Services pretty soon."

"But then she goes for a while more like her old self?"

"That's it. And then she is so grateful. At least so far, he is paying her rent and making sure she has money when she needs it."

"Like for groceries and stuff?"

Amalia nodded and glanced over at Fred, not having heard from him in a bit. As she suspected, he'd fallen into his post-dinner snooze.

"We'll give him a few more minutes; he usually wakes up on his own. Let's go out and put your plants in a flat and in the back of the truck. You tuck the eggs into your basket. How about half a loaf of bread too."

"I do not turn down homemade bread."

Out in the greenhouse, Ginny handed her several four-inch pots. "The pegs say which is which. Now, when you plant these tomatoes, bury them so deep that the dirt reaches the first leaves. Then new roots will grow all along the stem and the plants will be really robust. They've been hardened off, but I'd still plant them in the evening and shade them the next day or two." She handed off a six-pack of marigolds, the cucumbers in round pots, one of each kind, and two others. "These are sweet basil and spearmint. I use the mint leaves in iced tea. The more you clip both of these, the better they grow. You have clay pots?"

"The big ones"—she held out her arms to show sizes—"and saucers for underneath. One fits in a round metal stand."

"How about a coleus or two?"

"I'm running out of space."

"Surely you can fit these in; the colors of the leaves are so rich. With your southeast exposure, you can do about anything."

"I know, that's why I chose that one." A hummingbird buzzed by her to drink at the feeder. "They're here. Good, I'll get my feeder out." She set her plastic flat in the pickup bed and looked up when she heard Fred call Spook.

"Hope you don't mind if he comes along."

"Not at all."

"See, I told you." Ginny set a larger pot in the back. "You need some pink too for the hummers."

"Maybe I better get some of those holders that hook over the railing." Amalia thought a second and nodded. "That's what I'll go do. You ever done one of those hanging baggy things that lets the tomatoes grow hanging upside down? I could put one of those hooks in the ceiling."

Fred raised a finger. "We have some good hooks. Be right back."

Amalia and Ginny grinned at each other. "Bring a couple of them," Ginny called. "We'll use every elevation and get a write-up in the gardening column in the paper."

Fred slid back under the steering wheel. "You do have a stepstool, don't you? I could go get mine."

"No, I have one."

"Good."

Amalia waved out her window, Spook barked once as if to say see you later and Fred honked the horn.

By the time he left Amalia's place for home, Amalia had pots, the plants, and a bag of Fred's own potting soil he had thrown in to keep the pots from sliding toward the back or sides. Two strong hooks, one on each side, were embedded in the ceiling and he had promised to weld her a couple of sturdy pot holders for over the rail, not like the cheapo ones found at local stores.

"You ought to go into business, Fred of all trades, available to make your life easier."

"Then I'd have to set up appointments and such, I'd need a secretary and a bookkeeper, and before you know it, I'd be back in business again. Don't you know I'm retired and I want to stay that way? I should have them done by tomorrow. One good thing about a wooden deck rail, the pots are more easily attached. Just set 'em on top and nail 'em down."

"True. Thanks for the help and the amazing ice cream."

He smiled and nodded. "What's your favorite flavor?"

"Probably blueberry."

"You'll get some when the blueberries are ripe."

"Or peach." She waved him off. "What can I give you in exchange?"

"I'll think about it." Spook barked, he honked, and away they went.

Amalia stared after them. What would they ever do without Fred? Good thing he was healthy.

Chapter Seven

W e're going to need another table." MJ looked to Maureen, owner of the Yarn Shop.

"At least one. Going to be pretty crowded. I'll get two, and we'll have to use folding chairs."

The back room, which had looked vast when they were setting up, seemed more the size of a storage closet now. Maureen had used it as a gathering spot for knitting lessons, putting a cookie-and-coffee table in the middle of the room and a few clusters of easy chairs here and there, some with arms (for crochet) and some armless (for knitters). She had once talked of inviting in the mah-jongg players when they lost their gathering room at the senior center, but they moved to the basement of the branch library. She had spoken of getting a bridge club going, but it hadn't happened. The room had never been filled up before. It was now.

Roxie duct-taped down the last of the extension cords that brought electricity to the power strips serving a sewing machine table. She stood up. "Quite an operation; bigger than I envisioned. Do you think we can squeeze one more table in if necessary?"

Maureen shook her head. "I already moved the

coffee station out into the other room to make more room for worktables. And I see right now I'm going to have to get more folding chairs from somewhere."

"From the Lutheran Church on Fifth," MJ suggested. "They bought new stacking chairs and put their old ones in their basement. I bet they'd love to see them find a good home here."

As several more people, carrying baskets or bags with their projects, filled the last two tables, the noise level had risen. Those who'd arrived earlier had their coffee or drink of choice and had already begun work on their projects. MJ went around the room, greeting people and handing out stick-on name tags. "Just your first name is fine," she repeated—and repeated. "And make it big enough for others to read." She smiled at Roxie, who was on her way to refill the coffeepot. "Who would have thought it?"

"I told you we were filling a need. There is hot coffee in those two carafes while I get this one going again."

When arrivals trickled to a stop, MJ stood and clapped her hands. "Can I have your attention? Hello!" Someone else yelled, "Quiet!" and that worked. "Welcome, everyone, and I hope you will get to know some of the people around you. Obviously we had no idea we would have so many in attendance. We've outgrown our space before we've even begun." Chuckles sprinkled the group. "So someone suggested we set up a daytime group too. Can I have a show of hands how many would prefer a daytime UFO meeting." She counted and Roxie called out, "About half. That would be more manageable. Anyone have a suggestion as to where a daytime group could meet?"

"Would we have to come to one or the other or whichever works best for that time?"

MJ shrugged. "This is not a membership group, but a service really. We set the places to meet and you attend when you can."

"How about attending both? I want to get these things done."

"If that suits you. One thing I want to see happen is that we celebrate every project that is finished. We'll take pictures and post them on that bulletin board." She pointed to a three-by-four corkboard on the wall. "And while we are not signing a contract—"

"Good thing," someone muttered, causing more laughter.

"Remember, the goal is finishing something, not starting something new."

"Could starting new things be described as an addiction?"

"You mean like a fabri-holic or yarna-holic?"

"Something like that."

MJ raised her voice again. "As soon as we have a daytime location finalized, we'll let you all know. As for tonight, let's go around the room and everyone say your name and what number one is for you. I'll start. My name is MJ Bronson and I am working on a crewel embroidery picture."

"When did you start it?" someone asked.

"I stand on the fifth amendment." Then rethinking, she shook her head. "No, must be at least five years ago." She motioned to the lady beside her.

The woman raised a large and beautiful crewel depiction of two big sailing ships being loaded at a wharf. "I started this when we lived in Baltimore near the naval shipyard. But then we moved here and I sort of just put it aside."

Roxie cooed, "It's going to be spectacular when it's finished."

Grinning, Jeff raised a half-finished boat oar high. "I'm getting excited about my little peapod again. I can add a keel and spritsail and sail it as well as row it." He frowned. "Adding a keel isn't considered a new project, is it?"

Roxie laughed. "Let your conscience be your guide."

Fred was sanding the parts of a drawer for his chest. Roxie displayed the afghan she was working on. Even Maureen had a UFO, a lovely teal sweater she had started the year before.

When everyone had been introduced, MJ reminded them, "The doors will close at nine thirty so Maureen can go home and get ready to reopen with her knitting group in the morning at ten." She sat down and started sorting through her bag for her thread card and a packet of needles, along with the lighted magnifier that fit over her head.

"Well, shoot, I can't find my scissors," said the woman across the table and two down.

MJ passed her scissors across the table and went back to searching the card for the right yarn. Good thing she had set this up correctly all those years ago, including enlarging the instructions.

"Here, you can keep them. I have an extra pair." One of the other women handed hers over.

Conversations filled the air as people started getting to know each other.

"What are you working on?" Roxie asked the woman knitting next to her.

"A baby sweater and hat. The baby I started it for is now in first grade."

Roxie burst out laughing. "Oh, good. I have a baby quilt to do and my niece is in junior high. I should teach her how to finish it."

"Maybe you'll have it done by the time she has a baby."

"No, that's the next project. I brought this table runner tonight so I could do the hand stitching on it. That way I can claim I finished something quickly to encourage myself."

"Good idea."

A sharp "Aaak!" broke the background hum of chatter. "I don't have any more sewing machine needles. Well, rats."

"Here." Paula stood up and crossed to her. "These are universal, supposed to fit any machine. What size?"

"Twenty or twenty-one. I'm working on a quilt block."

"There you go." Paula handed her a needle.

Roxie poked MJ. "There's an additional benefit of working together."

"I guess this really is a service rather than a club. Or a ministry." MJ finally had her needle threaded with the wool yarn and, locking the thread on the back, started the long and short fill-in stitches on the leaves. Her stitches looked clumsy at first but by the second leaf she'd settled back into the rhythm.

Some left about nine, always thanking Maureen for the meeting space, and the rest trickled out as they put their handwork away and stood, many of them rolling their shoulders and stretching.

MJ heard someone mutter, "I know better than to sit for that long, but the time flew by."

Another answered her. "Next time I am bringing my own chair, one of the plastic high-backed outside ones. Lightweight and good for my back."

"Good idea, think I'll do the same."

Several stopped to thank MJ and Roxie for getting the group started and others for realizing a daytime group would be good too. "I just don't like driving in the dark anymore," one of the older women commented. "Fine right now but when the nights get longer again? Daytime group for sure."

Maureen bade MJ, Daryl, and Roxie good night as she locked the door behind them. The three stood on the sidewalk.

"I thought you and Loren came together," MJ said to Roxie.

"No, she has an early morning meeting and she knew I'd stay until the door closed. She said to tell you thanks and good job. You walking in the morning?"

"Of course. Besides, I bet this is the topic of choice at Annie's in the morning."

Roxie asked, "Weren't you surprised to see that man, hmm, what's his name?"

Daryl answered her. "There were four men. You probably mean Hudson, the one who is knitting an afghan."

"Yes, well, I know you and Fred, and Jeff."

"Fred went over and helped him on the peapod oar."

"Right. Did Hudson say how he got into knitting?"

Daryl nodded. "His mother had started an afghan before she died, and when he was laid up with a badly broken leg, his wife challenged him to finish it to honor his mother. Said he finds it very relaxing so he kept on.

Says he has several started but they got put away when
his wife was sick and he took over with the caretaking."

MJ stared at her husband. Learning this much about
someone else was not like him. Perhaps starting this
group might be good on several levels. One of the older
women had told her thank you because this got her out
of the house for a change.

The three of them, with baskets and bags, walked up
the street, past Annie's, and toward home. Instead of
turning in at the yellow house, they kept on walking.

"You don't need to walk me home," Roxie said.

"I know, but it feels good." Daryl grinned at her. "MJ
here is always after me to get out and walk more."

"As you said, it feels good. Such a perfect evening.
Listen: crickets."

"You want to come in for coffee?" Roxie asked when
they'd reached her house.

"No, thanks," MJ answered after a quick check to see
if her husband wanted to. "But I'll see you in the morning, eight?"

"How about seven thirty, I'm showing a house at ten
thirty."

MJ and Daryl wished her good night and turned back
for home.

"Good, we'll be home in time for the news." Daryl
picked up the pace. "I heard Looper howl when we
went by."

"He could hear us talking, I suppose." They could
hear him clearly when they turned in at their gate. "You
go watch your TV and I'll take care of him."

Short though they were, their basset's legs had springs in
them when Daryl and MJ came in the front door. Yipping

and whipping his white-tipped tail in a circle, the dog darted from one to the other, whining and whimpering.

"You goofy dog, we have not been gone for days, you know, just a few hours." MJ set her basket down. "Come on, go outside?" Looper tore off to the back of the house and danced at the back door. She heard the TV come on and knew Daryl was settling into his recliner. MJ reached back inside to the canister holding the doggy treats and, biscuit in hand, sank down onto the bright floral lounger. She heaved a sigh and looked up to see the stars. Thanks to the city's light pollution, she could only see the big ones but the arch of light-dotted indigo above that faded to rosy gray in the west brought peace seeping throughout her body. Shame she didn't do this more often.

"Oof." Four big feet and fifty pounds of basset landed on her thighs. "You big horse, what do you think you are doing?" She handed him his treat and waited while he crunched it away and searched for another. "No, just one or you'll be fat as Murphy."

Murphy lived one street over and he was so fat he could hardly run. She had volunteered to walk him for the owners but the offer had been met with a shrug and an excuse. Shame to see a dog so out of shape, but then so were his masters.

Daryl was sound asleep in front of the TV when she went back in the house.

✿   ✿   ✿

"Been hearing all kinds of good comments about the meeting last night," Anne said in the morning by way of greeting.

"Glad to hear that," Roxie said. "Oh, and just black this morning."

"No latte?"

MJ stared at her, then shrugged and turned back to Anne. "I'll have the usual. I could smell the cinnamon rolls down the street."

Roxie took her coffee with a smile. "And yes, before you ask." They moved over to a table and sat, Roxie dumping in her usual creamer and one packet of sweetener.

"So much for black."

"This is my black." Roxie propped her elbows on the table and sipped her coffee, held by both hands.

"So Loren said you ordered your rug."

"Yep, finally. Did she tell you about the young man there?" She gave her unblack black coffee another stir.

"Loren?" That didn't sound like the shy Loren to MJ.

"Yeah, I know. But the manager there is a really charming young man and he recognized her from high school. Reminded her of a class they were in." She leaned closer. "I think he was definitely interested and glad he saw her."

"And Loren?"

"Said he sure didn't resemble the fat geek with big glasses she remembered."

"And?"

"Hey, that's a start. He has my contact info so he can get ahold of her if he wants to."

"And how do we encourage the *want to*?"

"MJ, for Pete's sake, this was just last week."

"Well, we can pray about him, that's for sure."

"I have. I really want her to find a good man and get married. To be as happy as Greg and I were. I mean, she has really good memories of her dad."

"As do you."

"I sure do. Enough to last a lifetime."

"Here you go." Anne set their plates and the latte in front of them.

"Amalia been in this morning?" Roxie asked.

"Nope, but she's usually later. She ordered cinnamon rolls for a couple of residents at the home, so I know she is coming."

"Does she do that often?"

"Only on the days we make the rolls." Anne waved at a call from another table.

Fred's truck was at the curb in front of MJ's house when they got back. Roxie waved good-bye and had to tug on Sir Charles's leash when he wanted to stay with Looper.

"Good luck with the house showing."

"I have a tour of four places planned for them so it's not just this one. They are just starting to look so I'll show 'em all I can."

MJ shut the gate and took the lead off Looper. "Go find Dad." The dog yipped once and headed off around the house. She followed him to find Fred and Daryl sitting on the deck, a flat of plants on the grass. "I see you come bringing treasures, Fred. Good morning."

"Good morning. We seem to have more than we can possibly use..."

"That's nothing new. Ginny come with you?"

"Nope, she's working on planting our pots today." Fred swilled from his water glass.

MJ asked, "You guys want a refill? Or iced tea?"

Fred pushed back his chair. "Thanks but no. I'll go get that other flat and be on my way."

"Hey, is Ginny coming into town today?"

"She has a meeting at three," Fred replied. "I think at the library. You need something?"

"It'll wait." MJ turned to her hubby. "I'll be down in my room and I am not turning my phone on."

Daryl nodded. "Fine by me."

"Help yourself to lunch out of the refrigerator. There's soup in the green container, sandwich fixings in the cheese drawer, and leftover enchiladas in the flat one on the second shelf."

"What's for supper?"

"I have no idea, it's not even noon yet." She pushed back the screen to the sliding glass door and, inside, poured a glass of iced tea and headed downstairs. Her quilt was going to be ready to machine quilt by the end of the day. She had already layered the underside, the filling, and the top on the four-by-eight table Daryl had built that folded up against the wall when she was not using it. It had not been put away for some time because she'd not gotten back to it for several weeks. This next step of pinning the layers was going to be done today. Therefore, the phone was off.

She looked up at the round clock when the bird call signaled two. No wonder she was hungry.

"MJ, you down there?"

"Coming right up, Ginny." She jogged up the steps.

"Tried calling, but with no answer, I figured you'd turned your phone off."

"I did. Want some iced tea? I'm just taking a lunch break."

"Thanks, but I just stopped to say I've had a bunch of phone calls raving about the meeting last night."

MJ pulled her cell phone out of her apron pocket. "A

bunch of messages." And dropped it back. "I am incommunicado today."

"I know, the meeting last night inspired you to finish something else too?"

"How did you know?"

Ginny grinned. "I hooked on that rug for an hour and a half this morning, you know the one on the coffee table in the family room? The woman next to me said she got a rug done by making herself hook one or two rows every morning. I thought it was a good idea."

"But an hour and a half?" MJ did not mention how absorbed she had just been in her quilt project.

"I got carried away. Going to make sure I stay with two rows tomorrow. Three of the callers said the meeting inspired them to do the same."

"Well, I'll be...Never thought something like this would happen." She pulled a bag of mixed greens from the produce drawer. "You sure you don't want some salad?"

"No, thanks. I'm out of here." Ginny headed for the front door. "See ya."

MJ took her salad and a refilled iced tea out on the deck, watched the birds at the feeder as she ate, offered Daryl iced tea, which he turned down, and then returned to her quilt-pinning.

Ginny and Fred, she and Daryl, two couples so close, so comfortable with one another. She remembered reading somewhere that a woman will be lucky to find one true soul mate in her life. MJ had four, for there was Roxie too.

Chapter Eight

"Fred, where are you?"

Nothing. A crow answered her from the top of a pine tree.

"Where's Dad?" Ginny asked Spook, who was usually with Fred when he was home. His truck was here so that meant that someone had come and picked him up. But who and for what? There was no note on the counter, no message on her phone.

This was not like Fred, but someone must have had an emergency and he took off in a hurry. She checked through the house once more, then walked out to his shop. Door shut, but no Fred.

She punched the speed dial for Sam. "Is your dad with you?"

"No, he was earlier but we got all the kids out of the shop and he headed home. Both the twins had something at school so he said he was going home."

"The truck is here, Spook is here, but he's not answering his phone. This is so unlike him."

Sam suggested, "He must be in an area that has no cell reception."

"True, but who with? You know him, someone has an emergency and he'll be there."

"One of the neighbors?"

"Planning to call them next."

"Have him call me when he gets back."

"I will." She clicked off and went in the kitchen to turn the oven on for the goulash casserole she had in the fridge. Whenever he got here, he would be starving. Unless someone invited him for supper, but he would have let her know. He was so good that way. "Come on, Spook, let's go look for Dad." He wasn't in the greenhouse, the shop, the barn. The tractor was in the machine shed; he wasn't working on that, maintenance always being high on his list.

"Fred, this isn't like you but you could call and let me know where you are." Concern slipped into anger. All she had to do and here she was on a fruitless search because someone else needed him right at that moment. Back in the house, she went to his desk to check his calendar. Nothing.

She called the three neighbors with whom he often swapped labor. Nada. No one had seen him. Nor had Daryl Bronson, Jeff, or their pastor.

"What's going on?" MJ asked when she called back. "Daryl said you called."

"I did. I can't find Fred. I've been calling all around but no one has seen him since he left Sam at the school."

"But the truck is there."

"Yes and Spook. No note, no call. Something like this hasn't happened for a long time." Years earlier he had been more focused on his own schedule until that time she got stuck in a snowbank and had no way to get through to him. He learned what frantic meant and insisted they both keep the other informed. Life had been much easier after that. Cell phones helped a lot too. Cell out of power? Not likely—he was obsessive about making sure the phones were charged.

Well, he couldn't be stuck in a snowbank but something was wrong. *Lord, You know where he is. Could You please prompt him to let me know? And yes, I am trusting You, with my mind anyway, but my stomach is not in agreement.* Good old acid reflux snaked into her esophagus. She headed for the kitchen and a glass of water, stopping by the bathroom for an antacid. *Please, please, please, Lord,* beat with her steps.

She never had liked waiting. Especially when she didn't know the outcome. She dug her phone out of her pocket. Sam. "No, nothing yet," she told him.

"Do you want me to come over?"

"No, you have plenty to do there. I'll call you as soon as I know anything, or he will call you. I know this is something we'll laugh over down the road, but right now..."

Right now I am about into panic mode. She sucked in a deep breath, held it, let it out slowly like she'd been trained to do when the panic attacks threatened.

"Call me if you need me." Sam hung up.

Another call rang the chimes. She hit the button. Was it Fred?

No. "Mike Raymond. I hear Fred is missing."

Pastor Mike! "It's good of you to call."

He asked, "Could Fred have fallen when he was out hiking in the woods? Simply that his cell is not functioning?"

"That's what's so frustrating. Any number of things could have happened. Innocent things."

"We're praying here and I can be there in fifteen—"

"I know, thank you, but...it's not like he's been gone for hours. Just that this isn't like him."

"It's getting dusk. You sure you don't want help?" Mike's concern was genuine, Ginny could tell.

"Let me know."

"Okay, thanks." *You and all the others. This will be so embarrassing. Fred, how could you do this to me?*

Do something, anything, to get my mind off this. Greenhouse? No. "Oops, forgot to put the casserole in." Spook padded beside her into the kitchen. When he went to stand at his dish, she got the message. Casserole in the oven, she poured the kibble into his bowl, added the warm water, and set it on the counter for a couple of minutes. To stall him, she tossed him a chicken jerky chew. Setting the timer, she clicked Fred's number again. What kind of an accident could have taken out his phone? Was he lying out in the woods, unconscious? Why would he go out in the woods without Spook? She set the dog dish down and Spook dug right in.

"Soon as you're done, we'll go shut the chicken house door, 'kay?" Good thing she had the dog to talk to; she wasn't liking her own inner conversation. Mad was on the slippery slope to frantic fear, at the moment the two jockeying for first place.

Lord, what do I do next? I am praying, my heart is crying out to You. Are You there? Or am I choosing to worry instead of trust? I don't want to do that but where is Fred? Where can he be? She ignored the tears that blurred her vision and the fire that gripped her throat.

What to do? An inner suggestion reminded her what needed to be done next. Close the chicken house door so that nothing could get in to destroy them. There were plenty of predators who had managed that through the years. But Fred had spent much time and money animal-proofing the henhouse. Since the house was under the trees, she took a flashlight along. "Come on, Spook. We can at least make sure the chores are done." She stopped at the barn and dumped grain into the steers' boxes. Both were waiting patiently. Now some for Addy's pony. A soft nicker welcomed her. Every night Fred brushed both Magic, the pony, and Smoky, the donkey.

"Sorry, not tonight." She handed each of them one of the biscuits Fred kept near the grain bin.

Spook ran ahead of her and waited at the closed main door to the chicken coop.

"Spook, you know you don't go in there."

Spook looked over his shoulder and pawed at the door.

"Stop that, you silly dog, you'll scare the flock." Hmm, the latch wasn't on. Fred always left the latch in place. She pulled open the door and Spook squeezed through, whimpering. "Shh, you're going to cause a riot." She stepped into the dark house. The chickens were scolding for being disturbed.

Spook whimpered and whined.

The beam caught the dark figure lying flat on the floor, Spook nosing at his hand.

"Fred!" Ginny almost dropped the flashlight when

she knelt beside him. "Fred, honey, wake up! Fred!"
Her wail set Spook to howling. She felt Fred's neck for
a pulse. Nothing. No breath. His hand was stiffening.
Oh Lord, how long has he been like this? Call 911. She
whipped out her cell and obeyed the voice, answering
the questions the dispatcher asked without really thinking. She couldn't think.

"Ginny, this is Georgia, hang on, honey. They are
on their way. You said you were down in the chicken
house?"

"Yes."

"We have an ETA of nine minutes. When you hear
the siren, go outside and wave your flashlight. Turn right
off the drive, correct?"

"Yes."

"I can't keep the emergency line tied up. Just a moment." She clicked off. Moments later, Ginny's cell rang.
She thumbed it on.

"Georgia. Maybelle is manning dispatch for me. Oh,
Ginny, I am so sorry. Have you notified Sam yet?"

"No. I just called 911." She hiccupped a sob. "Georgia, I think he has been gone for quite a while."

"Maybelle is calling Sam. Stay with me. Is that Spook
howling?"

"Yes, he—he came in with me. I was just coming to
close the chicken door. I'd been calling everyone to see
where he had gone."

"Did he have any heart problems, stroke problems?"

"Possibly. I made him an appointment with the
doctor for this Friday. I finally got him to agree to
go."

"Sam is on his way. Five minutes, Maybelle says."

Sobs racked her from her toes on up.

"Ginny, are you going into shock? Ginny, answer me!" Her voice was stern. "Breathe! Ginny, breathe!"

"I—I am." She inhaled again, blinking and trying to respond. "If I turn the light on, the chickens will fly all over."

"Okay, leave the light off. Is the door open?"

Ginny looked over her shoulder. "Yes. I can hear the siren."

"We told Sam we would keep you on the line."

"I—I can't quit crying."

"No, of course not. Will Spook let them in?"

"Oh, I don't know. He's lying right here with his muzzle on Fred's leg. At least he quit howling." She listened. "Sam is here."

"Mom! I'm leaving the truck lights on for them. They are turning in now, both the ambulance and the fire truck."

Spook growled, deep in his throat.

"Easy, Spook, it's Sam."

Sam blocked what little light was coming through the door. "Easy, Spook."

Ginny took his collar. "If he is growling at you, what will he do when they get here?"

"I'll put him in my truck." But when he leaned over to take the collar, Spook snapped at him. "Is there a rope anywhere around here?"

"In the barn. Hanging by the halters just as you go in the door."

Sam took off. The flashing red-and-blue lights lit the outside world. He returned in less than a minute.

"Hey, Sam, in here?"

"Yes, but I gotta get the dog into the truck. He's gone into guard mode."

"Maybe he'll let Ginny get him out of there. Or we have a tranquilizer."

"Please, just go back to the truck. And tell the paramedics the same."

Ginny recognized the voice of the Fire Chief Adam Brunsfeld, one of their friends from church. Sam handed her the rope. She tied it through the collar loop and stood up. "Come on, Spook, there is nothing you can do here." She tugged on the rope but he sank back on his haunches, front legs rigid. She cupped his furry face with both hands. "Come on, boy, we gotta let them do their work." She stepped back. "Heel, Spook, heel now." She tugged gently on the rope. "Heel, Spook." She slapped her thigh and turned to walk away. Whining, Spook obeyed the command he'd learned so long ago.

"Good boy. Come on. Come." Tears streaming down her face, she led their dog out to the truck, opened the door, and ordered him in. Spook leaned back on his haunches again but, at another command, leaped up on the seat. She threw the leash in after him and slammed the door shut. The dog scratched at the door and set to howling again. The mournful cry made her stagger as she turned.

"Adam, douse your lights or we'll have chickens flying all over the place. Just bring the stretcher." Sam spoke softly. "He's been gone for a while."

"I have to check him."

"I know. But how about using flashlights?"

Adam took his bag inside and knelt by the body. "Aw, Fred, it shouldn't have been this way."

Ginny leaned against the wall outside, fighting to keep her knees from buckling.

"You better sit down, Ginny." Eva Donaldson, their only paramedic and female firefighter, wrapped an arm around her former Sunday school teacher. "Let me help you. Hey, bring a stool over here, quick."

Ginny leaned against her as if she had no choice. Even though the voice seemed to come from far away, the strong arm was right there.

"Breathe, come on, breathe with me. In deep, exhale. Good, the stool is here. I'll move you over a bit and sit you down. You with me?"

Ginny nodded, or at least thought she did.

"Good, now put your head down between your knees."

A gentle hand pressed against the back of her head. She could hear Spook howling, men talking in the chicken house. She breathed in and huffed out. "I think he's been gone for some time. I hunted and hunted and I couldn't find him. I should'a looked down here."

"Why should you have? Ginny, listen to me. You did everything right, you did all you could. Now just let us do our jobs."

Adam stepped out the door. "We got the call, a smoke alarm is going off at your house, Ginny. Did you leave something on the stove?"

"Ah, no. Wait, the casserole in the oven."

"We better take the truck up there. Come on, Tim. Let the other crew take over." He ran for the truck and started it up. Tim grabbed on the back and around the circle they went, back to the upper drive and to the house.

"How many hours has it been in the oven?"

"Since five. What time is it?"

"Ten."

"How can it be? Please, Lord." The darkness crept back in.

"Head back down, easy, just breathe. Let them deal with the house."

Sam stopped beside them. "They need you in there. I'm here, Mom." He leaned over and hugged her close.

She could hear the tears in his voice and felt them dropping on her arm. She should be comforting him. She was his mother. The remaining fireman said out the door, "No flames, all smoke. They're opening all the windows and tossed the baking pan out the back door. He just wanted you to know, Mrs. Clarkson, Sam. No fire."

"Thanks," Sam answered. "Did you hear that, Mom?"

She nodded. She could hear them moving the gurney, giving orders, all speaking softly.

Sam stood, keeping one hand on her shoulder. She leaned into him. When the doors slammed, Eva came back and knelt beside her. "I'm going to take your blood pressure, don't want you going out on me. How are you feeling right now?"

"Still woozy but better, I think." The cuff pinched and deflated slowly.

"What's your normal?"

"Oh, between 120 and 130 over 75 to 80, I guess."

"You're up but not dangerously so. Pulse high but not dangerously so."

"What will happen now?"

"You have any history of strokes, heart, breathing problems?"

"No, no, and asthma but not for a long time."

"Do you have an inhaler?"

"Somewhere."

"Back to your question. We'll take Fred to the hospital but there is no need for you to ride along. We will have some papers for you to sign in the morning. Do you have a funeral home that you prefer?"

"I—I can't think." She clamped on to Sam's hand. "I . . ."

Sam said firmly, "I know where the papers are. Can we let you know in the morning?"

Eva's voice beside Ginny's shoulder said, "Yes. Look, Ginny. I am going to let Sam take you up to the house. Oh, shoot, the smoke."

Sam replied, "The basement should be clear. We can use the bedroom down there."

Ginny warned, "You're getting far away again."

"How can I help?" Pastor Mike loomed beside Sam.

"Oh, good. I didn't hear you drive up." Eva kept her hand on Ginny's other shoulder. "If you and Sam can take her up to lie down, I think that might be best." She nudged Sam. "But if you see any change with your mom, you call, hear me? Even if she says no." She squatted beside the stool. "You heard me, right?"

Ginny nodded. "Long as I don't have to walk up there." She sucked in another breath. "We can go in the sliding glass door so no steps to climb." Just talking took every bit of stamina she had left.

"Come on, Eva," the ambulance driver called. "We need to get back online. There's an accident out near Bowers."

"Don't worry about us, we'll take care of things here."
Pastor Mike took charge.

"Get some fluids in her." Eva called from the ambulance. It roared away up the drive.

Ginny tried to keep her eyes open but the tears seemed to have glued them shut.

"Hang on here and I'll bring my car close."

"Erica took the kids next door so she'll be here any minute. I told her to go to the house and warned her about the smoke."

"Let Spook out of the truck." Ginny felt woozy.

"No, I'll get you in Mike's car and then drive the truck to the house and bring Spook inside." He sniffed. "Anyone else you want me to call?"

"I—I—sorry, I can't think."

"That's okay, Mom, we'll take care of things."

Mike stepped in front of her. "Okay, me on one side, Sam on the other. Just let us help you."

"Did someone shut the chicken house door?"

"I will," Sam answered. "On three, we lift and we'll let you get your feet under you. Unless you want me to carry you."

"Carry me? I don't think so." With total concentration, she managed to put one foot in front of the other and sank down on the car seat. Sam lifted her legs and swung her in. "I'll be right up. At least you can't fall down now."

She leaned her head against the seat back. "How did you know to come, Mike?"

"Georgia called me. So did Erica. Said Sam was on his way over and 911 had been called."

"Oh." She felt the uphill drive, turning the corner and

stopping. It was as if she was sitting in the backseat, watching what was going on. Surely all this was happening to someone else. "When am I going to wake up from the nightmare?"

His warm hand clasped her ice-cold one. The fog was creeping in again, dense and dirty.

Chapter Nine

"If someone can give me a ride, I can spend the night with her and stay for however long she needs me," Amalia said into the phone. She turned off her alarm clock.

"Thank you, Amalia," Pastor Mike replied. "I'll be right in. Ginny is sleeping, and this will allow Sam and Erica to go back home."

"Good, I'll be packed and meet you at the side. Thanks." Amalia mopped at her tears again. She knew so well what Ginny was going through, even though her valley had been fifteen years ago when Aaron died. Although it was not unexpected since he was some years older than she, one can never be prepared. And for poor Ginny, there had been no preparation. Amalia dug out her small suitcase, folded in the things she would need for the next few days, and zipped it shut. She made sure her knitting and a couple of other projects were in her bag along with the necessary supplies, and she watered her plants well. Stacking Jehoshaphat's food dish high, she told him, "I'll ask Pastor Mike to make certain you're fed. I'll give him a key." Who knew when she might be back? It all depended on how Ginny was doing.

Earlier, she had called a friend in senior services to take over her senior-living-home chores and now, hat on head, she shut the door behind her, making sure the little sign on her door said GONE VISITING, so the woman who checked every door every day would not panic when she hadn't turned her tag over.

Dear Lord, she prayed, *comfort all of us, but especially Ginny and her family. Fred will be sorely missed here on earth but I know You gave him a grand welcome up there.* Then she thought, *Bet he was surprised to go home so abruptly. Collapsed in the chicken house. I sure do hope it was a swift journey so he didn't lie there and suffer—all by himself. Somehow I don't think chickens count.*

When Pastor Mike pulled up to the curb, Amalia picked up her bag and case and, heaving a sigh, stepped outside. Automatically she checked her watch. One a.m. Good thing she was not one to sleep heavily or she might have missed the call.

"Thank you for doing this." Mike held the car door open for her.

"I'm glad I can. My sister did the same for me when Aaron died. But that was a waiting game, not a blindsided surprise, or rather, a shock. Do they know the cause of death?"

"Preliminary suggests a major heart attack that just dropped him."

"Poor Ginny, yay for Fred."

"I know. At times like this, if I didn't believe there is more life after the body dies, I could not—"

"He was your friend too, wasn't he?"

"Fred was everybody's friend. If there was any way he

could provide help, he did, to whoever needed it. And on top of that, he was just plain fun to be around."

"I can see and hear the angels and all the saints welcoming him home. What a party!"

"And so we help Ginny and the kids through this."

"I know. Sure brings back lots of memories. So grateful we lived on the farm and there were so many things that had to be done....I found that keeping real busy made grieving easier."

"She depended on him for so much, like he depended on her. What a pair they were." They rode in silence, except that she asked for someone to look in on the cat. Already that cat was crippling her ability to just go.

Pastor Mike assured her the cat would not pine away. He stopped the car at the path off the driveway. "You want me to carry that in for you?"

Amalia smiled as she scooped up her bag. "No, thanks, you go on home and get the rest you need. Give that wife of yours a howdy from me."

"I will. She said to tell you, the coffeepot is always on."

"Thanks." She shut the door behind her and walked the flagstone path to the patio and sliding glass doors. The upstairs was all dark. She tapped at the door and opened it before Sam could get there. She sniffed. "Is something burning?"

"Not now. Mom had a casserole in the oven, and five hours later, the house was filled with smoke. The guys on the fire truck came up to check it out. Good old smoke alarm did the job."

"Ginny sleeping?"

"Like a log. I hear so many people say they couldn't sleep. I think she just crashed."

"That's good." She lifted her case. "Where shall I put this?"

"They said to not use the upstairs until tomorrow when they set up some exhaust fans and the smoke should be cleared. The guest room down here has twin beds. Mom is on one, you take the other."

"I can sleep on a sofa or wherever."

"Why, when there is a perfectly good bed?"

"Whatever. Are there any doctor's orders for her or just take one minute at a time?"

"Eva said to push fluids, so when she wakes up, hand her a glass of water. If there is any change, BP a bit elevated but understandably so, to call for help. You drive, right?"

"Yes, I just opted to no longer have a car since I live right in the middle of town. My driver's license is still current and I will probably maintain that. Good ID."

Erica stepped out of the room where Ginny slept. "No change. She's not running a temp or anything."

"Okay, you two go on home and hug those twins of yours. They will sorely miss him."

"As will we all." Sam shook his head. "I think I'm in about as great a shock as Mom is. And to find him like that. How horrible." His sigh carried the weight of gallons of tears. "The chicken coop is locked up. I'll be over in the morning to do the chores."

"If you need anything, call me." Erica rubbed her forehead. "I hope the smoke doesn't bother you. Oh, I put a bottled water by her bed. There are more in the fridge in her office."

"Thanks. Glad they caught it before the house ignited."

"I know, me too." Sam slid open the door and ushered Erica ahead of him. "Night."

Amalia carried her case into the bedroom and set it on the chair. Spook thumped his tail from where he was stretched out alongside Ginny's legs. His eyes begged her to leave him there, so she did. She had no idea if this was permissible behavior but too bad. Today was not a permissible day. They'd deal with that later. She changed in the bathroom and, after standing to watch Ginny in a log state, slipped under the covers. The smoke smell was not severe here but she could guess about the upstairs. Oh, well. If the fire department didn't exhaust the upstairs, they could call one of the cleaning services in the morning to bring out their huge exhaust fans to clear the air. In reality, everything might need to be scrubbed down to free the house from the nose-biting odor. Knowing the horrors ahead of all the paperwork caused by a death, she figured she could run interference for her friend. Fred most likely had all the info in folders in one drawer of the file cabinet or, if there was a safe, some things in there. That was the way Fred did things.

She drifted off with her usual adaptability, waking every time Ginny made a noise. Once she was sobbing in her sleep, but didn't respond to any questions. At six, Spook wanted to go out, so Amalia slid the glass door open enough for him to leave and come back. Go back to bed or...Back to bed won out, but an insistent phone soon trumped it. Since it was now eight a.m., she grabbed it before it could ring again.

"Morning, Amalia, everything still all right there?" Sam asked.

"Yes, your mother's still sleeping. What time do you plan to go to the hospital?"

"I just called in that I won't be at school today so that is next on my list. Eva said there would be papers to sign."

"There are always papers to sign. Mike is planning on being here about ten unless we call and set a different time. So you want to go to the hospital after that?"

'That will be fine. By the way, I was over there early and did the chores so you needn't worry about that."

"Thanks." She clicked off the phone.

"Sam?" Ginny's voice was more croak than talk.

"Yes, he said he did the outside chores early this morning. He'll come back in time for the meeting with Mike. If you tell me where the dog food is stored, I'll feed this hungry beast and start some breakfast. You need help getting up?"

"Why? I'm not an invalid."

"True. Just offering."

"What if I never want to get up again?"

"Uh-huh, feels that way right now. You have quite a few messages on your phone. You want me to screen them?"

"I don't know. What I want doesn't matter." She paused, the back of one hand across her forehead. "I keep hoping I'll wake up and this is all a horrid nightmare."

"If only we could set the clock back." Amalia rose. "I'm coming, Spook."

Ginny croaked the instructions. "In the pantry, the tubs are marked. He gets a cup and a half of kibble, add warm water, and let it sit a few minutes before you give it to him. For some strange reason, I cannot make myself move."

"You can have a few more minutes. Holler if you need anything." Amalia followed the dog bounding up the stairs. Instead of heading to the kitchen, he tore down the hall into their bedroom and came out, head and tail down.

Amalia felt herself tear up. "You were hoping to find him, weren't you, fella? I'm sorry. Come on, let's find you some kind of treat. *Peeuw*, it stinks up here."

Spook made another round of checking every room and returned to wait by her side. When she set his dish on the floor, he ate some, made another round of the upstairs to check for Fred, finished his breakfast, and went to stand at the door to the garage. She watched when she let him out. He put his front feet on the car door, looked inside, did the same thing with the truck, and stood sniffing the air.

Despair radiated off him in waves as he lay down on the concrete apron.

"Yeah, I know just how you feel." Amalia descended into the daylit basement and asked Ginny, "What would you like for breakfast?"

Sitting on the edge of the bed, Ginny shook her head. Slowly, as if even that took more energy than she had. "I'm not hungry."

"I know. That's not what I asked you. How about toast with cheese on it? Get some protein in you, or I will fix eggs any way you want them."

"If I eat, I think I will throw up."

"Toast then. Coffee?"

"Fred wants his coffee first thing. He would have set

the coffeemaker on the timer." Tears started again, her whole body drooping. She sniffed and reached for the box of tissues on the nightstand between the beds.

"A shower might help you feel better."

"No. I'll go upstairs and get dressed."

"Your clothes will probably smell of smoke."

"Who cares?"

"Who do you have your homeowner's with?"

"Why?"

"Smoke cleanup is covered under most homeowner's insurance policies. Either Sam or I can call them and get the cleaning process started."

"I don't remember who I have. What a dumb move that was."

Amalia decided to ignore that comment. "Does Sam know?"

"I suppose." She levered herself upright and stood for a moment.

"You dizzy?"

"Just for a second. I always stand and wait like that for my balance to catch up with me. PT taught me to do that."

Habit can be a good thing. "I am going up to scramble some eggs. Maybe you could eat a few bites. I'll make the coffee too, just in case. Unless you'd rather have tea."

She heard Spook at the door and went to let him in on her way upstairs. Her phone, set on vibrate in her pocket, caught her attention. "Good morning."

It was MJ. "How is she?"

"Up and getting dressed. Sam will be here any time. Mike is coming at ten."

"Can we bring you anything?"

"Not that I know of. Going to try to get her to eat a bit."

"How bad is the smoke?"

"Air is clear but the odor needs cleaning, I'm afraid. I need to take care of that. I'll get the insurance called to start as soon as possible. I'm sure everything needs to be scrubbed down or commercially cleaned."

"Did she sleep?"

"Didn't want to wake up."

"Don't blame her. I think we are all in a state of shock. How will we handle all the food that people will want to bring if you can't use the upstairs?"

"No idea. Hadn't thought about it. Let me know if you come up with a plan." She smiled as she said it. MJ always had a way to do things. "Talk later. Thanks." She clicked off.

Ginny's phone chimed again. Amalia let it go to voice mail. She was tempted to turn it off. She'd see what Sam wanted to do.

Upstairs she ignored the stink and set about fixing breakfast. When she didn't hear any activity, she went down the hall to the master bedroom. Ginny was half dressed and lying on the bed.

"You need some help?"

"Can you bring Fred back?"

"Sorry, my friend, sure wish I could."

"I know. Stinks in here."

Amalia picked up the blouse Ginny had pulled off the hanger. "Here, stick your arm in." Ginny did as told, but when it came to buttoning, her hands stayed braced against the comforter. Amalia buttoned the shirt, put shoes in front of her feet. "Slide your foot in those, then go wash your face and brush your teeth, comb your hair."

The tears dripped off Ginny's chin.

Amalia took a couple of tissues and mopped her friend's face. She picked up her hand and pulled her upright, then steered her to the master bath. "Can you manage? I can comb your hair and wash your face but you have to brush your own teeth. Oh, my dear friend. I know everything feels like too much. We'll get you through today and then one day at a time."

Ginny propped herself, arms rigid on the sink counter, her head hanging. She sucked in a deep breath and, being careful not to look in the mirror, got out the toothpaste and brush.

From below came, "Mom?"

"Sam's here."

She nodded and started brushing.

Amalia reminded her, "You need help, I'm in the kitchen."

Another nod. The tears continued to drip.

Chapter Ten

I always thought this room was cavernous," MJ commented as they looked out across a churning crowd of crafty people working on UFOs. "But it seems too small now."

Roxie nodded. "I never dreamed this many people would be interested."

"And listen to the chatter. It's a great social occasion too. I just wish the room were bigger."

Roxie pointed. "It doesn't help that Jeff brought his peapod inside. There's eight feet of floor space right there."

"But look at the progress he's making in such a short time." MJ leading the way, the two wandered over to Jeff. He was stroking white paint on the bulging sides.

MJ saw from the label that the paint was marine primer. "Do you have a name for her yet?"

Jeff grinned. "Sure do. Remember the baby in the old Popeye cartoons?"

Roxie laughed out loud. "Swee'Pea! Perfect!"

Jeff got serious. "I want to thank you two. I was just dawdling along with this thing and thinking maybe I'd never get it finished. But with this UFO party, I got excited about my peapod all over again. I'll be sailing her out on the lake pretty soon. And it's because of you."

MJ smiled. "I'm very glad."

They checked on a few other workers and paused by the door.

"Have you heard anything from Ginny?" MJ asked.

"No, but I'm sure that now that the memorial and everything are over and the kids have gone home, this is really hitting her."

MJ agreed, in spades. "I stopped by a couple times but she was napping. Amalia says she sleeps a lot. On the positive side, I had a nice long chat with Amalia. Would you believe she rescued a cat? You know she's not a cat person."

"I'd believe every word. She'd rescue a hyena if the hyena needed it. I tried calling but no answer. Her messages are full. Maybe I should call Sam."

"He and Erica and the twins are up at the lake," MJ said. "He said he tried to talk his mom into coming with them but she was adamant."

"So she is at home by herself now?" Roxie frowned.

"She insisted. He gave in. At least the house is all cleaned and the smoke stench gone. After all, she's a big girl now and knows what she wants, even if it's not what we want for her."

Maureen joined them. "The lady in the corner there is knitting a stuffed lamb, but she didn't have any stuffing. So I opened up the front to sell her some. And you'll notice I got the storefront spiffed up."

"I noticed. New paint and hanging baskets. They're beautiful. It's all beautiful." Roxie leaned back against the wall.

"Fred delivered the baskets the day that he died." Maureen blinked several times. "There are memorials to him all over town, in pots and gardens. Ginny's flowers are blooming and his veggies will soon begin producing. Every day someone mentions something he did for them and how they miss him. I've not seen Ginny. Is anyone checking on her?"

"Off and on. I know she has her phone turned off." MJ tipped her head back.

"Guess I don't blame her. Please say hi to her when you see her." Maureen walked off to get another chair as a new crafter came in.

"I'm out that way looking at a house," Roxie said. "I'll go by and bust the door down if I have to. I'm glad that Sam and his family are up at the lake. The kids said they wished they could have stayed longer, but they have lives too."

"Amalia offered to stay with her but Ginny insisted she just needed to be by herself." MJ shook her head. "So, who is taking care of the chickens? I don't know how she would be able to go in that chicken house."

"One of us should have gotten a key." Roxie pulled out her cell phone and hit Amalia's number. She shook her head. "No answer, and she's not here tonight." Waiting for the voice mail prompt, she said into the phone, "Amalia, did you get a key to Ginny's house in case she has locked the doors? Thanks." She clicked off.

Roxie looked up Sam's number and tapped it in. "At least someone is answering. Hey, Sam, Roxie. I'm going out to your mom's tomorrow. If she has locked the doors, is there a key anywhere?"

Sam's voice was strong, so he had good cell service wherever he was. "Third pot from the steps by the front stoop."

"Good. Thank you. Oh, do you know anything about their chickens and animals? Is someone there to take care of them?"

"Mom said she would be okay. Chores were not a problem. Why, do you know something I don't know?"

"I—I just don't know how she can go in that chicken house. I don't think I would have been able to."

"There are automatic waterers for all the animals and…I checked on everything before we left. I think you are worrying needlessly."

"How long since you've talked with her?"

"Ah, yesterday. I've left messages on her phone but you know her and that cell phone and keeping it charged."

"I know." Roxie felt super-sad all over again. "Fred took care of that. I'll make sure her phone is plugged in."

"Besides, she promised me she would be all right; she didn't want us changing our plans."

"Yup, that's Ginny. Thank you, Sam." She closed the line.

"You want me to go with?" MJ asked.

"Not necessary, but I will call you."

The next morning, Roxie prepped for her house appointment as Sir Charles wiggled his butt and tried to look cute enough to be taken along.

"Sorry, Sir Charles. Not this morning." She chose rust linen pants, an off-white silk blouse, and some of her funky jewelry, refilled Sir Charles's water dish, gave him a treat, and made sure she had all the appropriate paperwork in her briefcase before heading to the car. The ringing of her phone made her pause. The furniture store.

"Mrs. Gilburn, this is Nate from The Fond Furniture. I just wanted to tell you that your rug is here and ready for you to pick up."

"Marvelous. I'll see if we can come in this evening."

"I could deliver it."

"Ah, okay, would after six work?" Loren would be home by then, maybe…

"I will make it work. See you then."

She clicked off and turned on to the street of the house she was viewing, thinking about the phone call. For some reason, she felt really good about Nate's delivering the rug. Surely he could stay for coffee.

After punching the address into her GPS, she headed out of town. All the while she drove north, her mind kept running ahead to Ginny, then going backward to when Greg died. She had been devastated, even though she'd known it was coming. Known on one hand and kept praying for healing on the other. Those months she'd cared for him, driven him to doctors, then specialists, then radiation. He'd done his best to fight it, but the tumor in his brain had metastasized from a spot on his lungs that had been growing undetected.

Yes, she knew how Ginny was feeling. But at least for Roxie, Loren was still living at home. She had been finishing high school then and going into the University of Wisconsin. Having another body in the house to provide for, talk with, even cook for helped. That was when she decided to go into the real estate business and got her license a year later. Studying for the certification had helped her too, the demands of assignments, and the tests. So many times she had wished she'd never started, but she finished.

*   *   *

An hour later, she and the owner had signed the agreement for her to list the house, after he did what she suggested—repaint the front door and the shutters, spruce up the yard for curb appeal, pack away much of the clutter of living in one home for twenty years, and get an inspection. She was fairly certain the house would sell quickly, in today's market.

She reset the GPS for Ginny's, although once she was back on the main road, she knew where to turn off. The corn in the fields along the road was leafing out bright green and the alfalfa was on the way to a first cutting. The lovely day buoyed her spirits, until she turned into the driveway.

She blew out a breath and blinked back tears. The lawn needed mowing. The flower beds, which were normally immaculate, really needed attention. This early summer was always weed season. How would Ginny ever keep up this place without Fred?

One thing she knew, she would encourage Ginny not to make any major decisions for the first year and preferably two. She knew too many widows who regretted major decisions like selling a place, or moving, or marrying again. There were gold diggers, gigolos out there who preyed on grieving women, milked them dry, and moved on. Or lived off their new wife.

She could hear Spook announcing her arrival from inside the house. She found the house key under the third pot from the steps as Sam had told her and knocked. With no answer, she let herself in the door to a dog overjoyed to see her.

She dropped her purse on the floor and petted and calmed the dog. "You want to go outside?" Spook immediately put his nose to the screen door. "Good boy." She let him out, and set her purse down on the sofa. "Ginny? Ginny, are you here?" With no answer, she checked the master bedroom. Empty, the bed made, and everything spotless. Fred's office and the guest room were the same. "Ginny, where are you?"

She found her downstairs in the twin bed she'd slept in because of the smoke. The other bed was all made up as Amalia had left it. Sitting on the edge of the bed, she laid a hand on Ginny's hip. "Ginny, it's me, Roxie." She shook gently. "Come on, I know you can hear me. I let Spook out. Did you feed him this morning? What about the chickens and the animals? Ginny, if you can hear me, you have to respond or I will call 911."

"I hear you." Her voice was scratchy. "Now go away."

"No, I'm here and you're stuck with me. Remember, I've been in the same position you are. Like Amalia. We do know how you feel."

"Just leave me alone." Ginny sniffed and snagged a tissue from the mound between her and the wall. "Please." Her voice broke on the "please."

Roxie fought the tears, then gave up and reached

for the tissue box. Empty. "Where do you keep your tissues?"

"Bathroom."

Roxie patted her friend's hip and fetched another box from under the sink. Better a big box than the small square ones. Pulling one out for herself, she set the box on the nightstand. "Have you had anything to eat today? Drink?" The water bottle on the stand was empty. "Where's your recycle? No, I'll just go fill this one." Another trip to the bathroom. She could hear Spook at the door upstairs. "I'm coming." Up the stairs, let the dog in, refill his water dish, coffeepot was empty, no grounds in the basket so she went ahead and started coffee. How much easier a Keurig was. She'd have coffee to take back down immediately.

Instead she poured some orange juice out of the pitcher and took the glass back downstairs. She'd get fluids into her friend one way or another.

Ginny had not moved.

Forcing cheer into her voice, Roxie set the glass of juice on the nightstand. "Okay, my friend, roll over here and let's talk."

"Go away."

"Sorry. I'm here and you are going to sit up and drink the juice or the water or both."

"Now you sound like MJ." Ginny rolled on to her back.

Roxie grabbed the pillow off the other bed and stuffed it behind her friend. "There. Now, here." She held out the glass.

"In answer to your question, I opened and closed the

chicken house door, I fed the pony and donkey, and the dog and the cat."

"Did you pick the eggs?"

"No, I—I can't go—" She shook her head and gave in to the tears.

"I wouldn't be able to either." Roxie reached for her and Ginny leaned into her arms to sob against her shoulder. Roxie let her cry it out, her own tears running down her face. As the sobs and shaking abated, Roxie mopped her eyes. "So much for waterproof makeup."

Ginny sat back against the pillows. "You look beautiful even with raccoon eyes."

"Thanks." Roxie handed the glass of juice back. "Ginny, my love, you have to drink or you'll be in the hospital with dehydration, all loony, and need an IV, at least. We really can't let that happen. Crying can dehydrate you, you know."

"I do *not* want to go to the hospital."

"I know. So drink. I started the coffeepot. Would you like a cup of coffee?"

"Maybe later."

"Fine, now, how long since you had anything to eat?"

"I don't know."

"We probably need to go through your refrigerator and decide what food is still good. But in the meantime, how about I fix you eggs and toast?"

"I—I can't."

"Okay, do you have any applesauce?"

"In the pantry."

"Good. I will make you toast and a dish of applesauce; both are easy on the stomach. Now, while I am doing that, how about you coming upstairs to eat with me?"

"What will you have?"

"Something. I'll see what is up there."

Ginny heaved a sigh. "All right."

As Roxie climbed the stairs, she kept a hand on Spook's head as he followed her up. *Thank you, Lord. A step in the right direction—I hope.*

Chapter Eleven

N ate is going to deliver the rug tonight," Roxie announced on the phone.

"So?" was Loren's response.

Roxie glared at her phone. "So, I thought perhaps we could invite him to stay for a cup of coffee, or iced tea." *You know, so we, meaning you, could get to know him better.* Her daughter could be so obtuse.

"If you want. Perhaps you should ask him to move the furniture too."

"Oh, good idea."

"Mother, I was being sarcastic."

Roxie smiled to herself. She knew that. "Oh. Look, he offered."

"Sorry. I'll see you shortly after five. Just working on another design."

"Okay. I'm on my way home from Ginny's."

"How is she?"

"Tell you when I see you. Oh, and the house I looked at, it's a go. They have some work to do but nothing major, that we know of. They've not had an inspection yet."

"Good, Mom. Later."

When she got home, Roxie changed clothes and dug

out the vacuum. When her entire office was vacuumed and dusted, she rolled the chair out in the hall. "Well, Sir Charles, once we put the rug down, I will need an office mat to roll the chair around on. One more thing. What do you think?"

Sir Charles lay down in the doorway, chin on his paws.

"I know, you want me to come throw the ball." The pooch raised his head and pricked his ears. "Go find your ball."

He took off down the stairs and was back before she could turn around, grungy yellow tennis ball in his mouth. He dropped it at her feet. She tossed it down the stairs and followed him down. At least she got Ginny to drink and eat some. If only she would let Amalia come back and stay with her. She called Amalia, rather than waiting for her to return the last call.

"I know, I was about to call you. I'm ready to go whenever you want to take me out there. When I show up and set my suitcase on the bed, what can she do?"

"You think there is a reason she has not moved up to her own bedroom?"

"Can't stand the thought of Fred not there."

Roxie suspected as much. "So, how can we help with that?"

"We can't but no big deal."

Roxie checked her watch. "I need to be back here by five. Can we do that?"

"Sure, just give me long enough to get out of the car."

"No, I was going to throw you out at the end of the driveway. Thanks, Amalia. I think we will all be relieved that you're there."

"All but Ginny."

"Right." She whistled for Sir Charles and lifted the hatch on her SUV. "Come on for the ride, big guy." He jumped in, panting in delight. He loved to ride in the car. He also loved to run the farm with Spook, but not today. On the way to pick up Amalia, she had two phone calls, one looking for a house and one with another possible one to list. She agreed to show the buyer around in the morning and made an appointment with the seller late that same afternoon. She drove back in her driveway right at five o'clock, and went in to make sure there was plenty of iced tea. If coffee was the drink of choice, the Keurig would take care of that, even letting Nate have his choice of flavors. She took a plastic container from the freezer to let the cookies thaw before she stuck them in the oven just long enough for the cookie fragrance to perfume the house.

Then she picked up the phone and called MJ. "I have a favor. Call me back when your phone rings once."

"What?"

"You heard me."

"All right but you have to tell me afterward what is going on."

"I will."

Sir Charles put his nose to the door into the garage, his feathery tail whipping back and forth. When Loren opened the door, he went into his usual yip and bounce and whirl and cry of delight. Loren was home.

"What a welcome, Sir Charles boy. Let me put my pack down." Loren swung her backpack to the chair and gave their dog the rib-thumping, ear-fluffing, nose-kissing greeting he expected, all the while talking to him in their special language. When he calmed down, she took a puppy treat from the canister and tossed it to him. Sir Charles never missed a catch. "So what time is the rug coming?"

"Nate said six," her mom replied.

"Good." Loren reached in the fridge and pulled out the iced tea pitcher. "What flavor do we have here?"

"Peach."

"Oh, good. Someone brought mango-flavored to work today. That was really good."

"Did you ask what brand it was or where they got it?"

"I will. You want some?" Loren gestured with the pitcher.

"Sure. Then let's go out on the deck. I want to kick back and put my feet up a bit."

"I'll take yours out. Want to bring some of those cookies? What are we having for supper?" Loren talked over her shoulder as she pushed open the left side of the French doors.

Roxie held the door for the cat and stepped out on the deck. Several birds were eating at the feeder on one corner, and two house finches splashed in the birdbath that took up the opposite corner. "It is so peaceful out here." She settled down on the chaise lounge and sipped her tea. "Are you hungry?"

"Well, yes."

"I thought we'd order pizza in after the rug comes."

"Have you called it in?"

"Nope. After the rug."

Sir Charles leaped off the deck and tore around the house, barking up a storm.

Roxie stood up. "Shoot, I should have told him to come down the alley. You go show him in, please."

Loren gave her a one-eyebrow-raised look, but did as asked. Roxie followed Loren through the house. As she walked out the front door, Loren had a firm grip on Sir Charles's collar. "Come on, Sir Charles. Don't worry, Nate, he's all bark. Sir Charles, come with me. Now!"

Nate leaned over and patted the red head. "Sir Charles, are you? What a good boy."

Sir Charles waltzed in a happy little circle.

"Okay, now you see the real Sir Charles. You need some help?"

"No, thanks, just making sure this is the right place." Nate went around to the back of his paneled truck, the name of their furniture company emblazoned on the side. He pulled the paper-covered roll from the back and slung it over his shoulder.

Loren held the door open. "Come on, Sir Charles, let the man get in without tripping over you."

"Where shall I take it?" Nate paused in the doorway.

Roxie's phone chirped and sang.

"Upstairs. Mom, you coming?"

"I'll be there in a minute, just got a phone call."

Loren half shrugged. "You want me to put another shoulder under that going up the stairs?"

"I got it. Something sure smells good, chocolate chip cookies?"

"Mom was hoping you'd stay for coffee or iced tea and cookies—if you can take the time, that is." Loren started up the stairs. "This way."

"I'd like that. I'm done for the day at the store."

Roxie, her phone to her ear, watched as they reached the top of the stairs and Loren went ahead, motioning the door to the left. They disappeared into the office.

"Thanks, MJ." Roxie pocketed her phone and took her time walking upstairs. She waited. She heard the roll thud to the floor. When she finally arrived at the office doorway, Nate had cut the plastic bands and rolled up the paper cover. He tossed the paper out into the hall as Roxie reached the office door.

Loren asked, "Can we lay it out and move it around to see what looks best?"

"Sure. Nice hardwood floor." Nate gave the carpet roll a push with his foot.

"Oh, my, that is even more perfect than I thought." Roxie stood in the doorway. "It certainly brightens up the room."

"Now how do you want it positioned, Mrs. Gilburn? Centered exactly? Diagonal?"

"First of all, please call me Roxie, and secondly, what do you suggest? I thought laid square in the middle but now I'm not sure. Come on, Loren, you're the one with the design sense."

"Let's try it both ways so you can see. Centered." He picked up a corner of the rug and pulled it diagonal. Then stepped back.

"I like it either way or both ways, whatever." Roxie looked to Loren.

Loren waved a hand around. "Me too, but this seems more appealing. I like the floor showing this way."

Roxie nodded. "So do I. But we need to lift up the file cabinets to slide the end under."

"They won't be as solid as they were, if that is impor-tant," Nate warned.

"It shouldn't matter."

So Nate leaned against first one file cabinet and

then the other as Loren and Roxie straightened the ends out.

Nate smiled and nodded. "Shall I lay the chair mat down?"

"Was this part of the contract?" she teased him.

"Nope. Just want to see happy customers."

When it was all put back, including the accessories, the three stood by the door.

Roxie wrapped her arms around herself. "I have always liked my office, but now this room is perfect. So inviting."

"Looks like you are a real reader." Nate motioned to the bookshelves covering one wall.

"We both are. Thank you for helping lay this. Can we reward you with coffee or iced tea, and the cookies must be cool enough now to eat." Roxie stepped backward into the hall. Nate and Loren followed, so she led the way downstairs.

"I haven't had homemade chocolate chip cookies for I don't know how long," Nate commented.

"Loren baked them."

"You like to bake?" He looked at Loren. She nodded. "My sister does too. But now that she has kids, she doesn't share with the rest of us as much."

Roxie waved a hand. "You two go sit out on the deck and I'll bring the tray. Do you want coffee or sweetened peach iced tea?"

"Iced tea, please. I drink coffee only in the morning."

"Wise man." She watched the two of them sit down at the table. He held her chair for her. *Oh my gosh, real manners. What is this world coming to?* Glasses, pitcher, and plate of cookies. Oh, napkins. She bumped the screen with her foot to make it slide back and stepped out on the deck. She could hear someone's lawnmower in the distance, but other than Sir Charles's toenails clicking on the deck and the birds twittering, heavenly peace. Setting the tray down, she paused for a moment. *Thank you, Lord, for such a place and time as this.* "Help yourselves."

Nate rose and pulled out a chair for her. "Thank you for the invite. How it can be so peaceful here right in the middle of a busy neighborhood...amazing."

"I know. We should have a grand sunset tonight too. Just enough clouds." She pushed the plate of cookies his way. "Please, don't be shy."

"Please don't tell me you took time to bake these this afternoon."

Loren laughed. "She would be lying. They were in the freezer."

"An old Realtor trick. Put cookies back in the oven just long enough to release the flavor and the fragrance. I tell my clients to do this or bake a loaf of bread before the showing. I even give them a package of frozen bread to bake the day of their open house. It helps visitors think of the place as a home and just might be one of those things that encourages a buyer. I've learned that small things count big."

"My mom is one of the top Realtors in Fond du Lac." Loren pushed the cookie plate closer to him.

"I'm not surprised." He leaned back in his chair, glass in one hand, a cookie in the other.

"So, did you go directly out of college into your father's firm?"

"I really started working at the store in Racine when

I was in junior high. I broke my leg playing baseball one summer and went to work dusting, polishing, general cleanup to keep from being bored. I'd read about every book in the library, and for some reason, I've never been much interested in video games. Dad had always encouraged us to want to be part of the company, but you know, every boy dreams of playing professional ball."

Roxie asked, "You said each of you kids now manages one of the stores?"

"Three of us, four stores, Dad has the fourth but one of our cousins is just finishing college and has been working each summer at a different store. They all have their own personalities, the stores, I mean. Dad tailors the store to the needs of the community."

"Unusual, isn't it?" Loren asked.

Nate nodded. "It is. But none of us were coerced into the family business."

"And you all are the third generation?"

"Right."

Roxie smiled. "Fascinating. I've always been interested in family businesses that go down through the generations. If I were ever to write a book, that would be the topic."

Loren gave her a surprised look.

"I know, not much chance I would sit down long enough to do that, but it is a good topic."

"We sell furniture, you sell houses, and you once said something about staging a house. Does that mean arranging temporary furniture in it?"

"Exactly."

"There is probably some way we could work together." He flashed her a guilty grin as he reached for the last cookie. "Mom always said never take the last of something when you're a guest."

"There's more in the cookie jar," Loren said. "And I can always bake more on Saturday."

He looked at Loren. "You work on displays at the library?"

"I do. And bulletin boards. I love to display people's collections, especially those of historical value."

"My aunt collects thimbles. Her mother, no, her grandmother, started the collection over a hundred years ago. Thimbles. When you think of collections, you think of stamps or coins, but thimbles?" He grinned and shrugged.

"Really? Would she mind showing them to me? Has she ever put them on display anywhere?"

Here was the real Loren, Roxie thought happily, not the one who hid behind her shy mask.

"I will ask her and get back to you, or have her contact you."

And Loren actually smiled a little. "So many kinds of antique collections get shown at the Register House historic landmark, and that's great, but more people use the library. We've had collectors get together after a display with us."

Roxie ignored the rumbling in her belly, then before she realized what she was doing, she asked, "Nate, have you had supper?"

"Ah, no, and now that I think about it, I'm not sure I had lunch."

"We were planning on ordering pizza in, you want to join us?" She didn't look at Loren, just in case she was sending her that *Oh, Mother* look.

He thought no longer than a moment. "Yes, I would like that, if you really mean it."

Loren sniffed. "Mom never says something she doesn't mean. What kind of pizza do you like? I'll go call it in."

Nate replied, "My favorite is everything and anything."

"Good, we agree. Thick or thin crust and we like extra cheese."

"Whatever, I like them both."

Loren pushed back her chair. "One giant enough?" She looked at him, then Roxie. "Salad?"

"Not for me, thanks," Nate answered. "Hate to mess up a good pizza with too much green."

Roxie rolled her eyes and Loren gave her mother one of her looks.

"I get it. No salad tonight." Roxie raised her hands in surrender.

"That's very nice of you to ask me," Nate said to Roxie as Loren went back in the house.

"This way it's more of a party; we can celebrate the new rug. Not that we need a cause to celebrate but..." She drained her glass and held it up. "More?"

"Please. But I can get it."

"No, tonight you are a guest." She brought the pitcher back and refilled all their glasses, then sat down again. "My, but this feels good. About time our weather lets us use the deck again. Three weeks ago there was six inches of white out here. I was beginning to think winter was going to hang around forever."

Loren returned. "Twenty minutes."

"Who is delivering tonight?" Roxie asked.

"MJ's grandson, Brian. He's a good kid." Loren sipped from her glass.

"He can drive already?"

"Mother, he's a senior this year."

"Oh. How time flies."

"So when you're not working at the library," Nate asked Loren, "what do you like to do?"

She shrugged. "Take Sir Charles for bike rides or walking, especially out to the lighthouse and around the lake. When we're at the park, the trick is keeping him out of the water."

"He's a beautiful dog."

"And he can get real smelly. He acts like you are abusing him when you hose him down or give him a bath. Do you have a dog?"

Nate nodded. "I did but he's living with my dad since I moved into an apartment here in town. No pets."

"Big dog? Little?" Loren asked.

Roxie winced. *Please don't say a yapper. Loren really does not like yappers.*

"Guess he would be considered a big dog. Part Lab and a mixture of some kind. Got him from a rescue."

A bit later, Sir Charles scrambled to his feet and leaped off the deck, announcing a visitor.

Roxie dug the cash out of her pocket and handed it to Loren. "Tell him no change. I'll get the plates and forks."

Loren hastened inside.

Nate frowned. "Isn't it a rule that you eat pizza right out of the box?"

"Thank you, a man after my own heart. Do you like extra spices on yours?"

"Nope, just the way it comes. The pepperoni takes care of that."

Loren returned, set the box on the table, and opened the lid. "Ahh."

"That first smell is divine." Roxie passed the stack of napkins. As soon as Loren sat down, her mother said, "Grace?" On the amen, she smiled at their guest. "Help yourself, company first."

When no one could eat the last piece of pizza in the box, Roxie invited, "Cookies and ice cream for dessert?"

"Please, don't be offended," Nate said, "but I have no room for one bite of anything more."

"Me too." Loren closed the box. "Sir Charles would love to have this, but sorry, fellah. Pizza is not on your diet."

"How can you ignore that look?" Nate ruffled the dog's ears.

"Hard willed."

Nate pushed back his chair. "Thank you so very much for this unplanned evening. All I did was deliver a rug. I hope I can see you again, and perhaps next time, I can be the host."

"That would be lovely." Roxie gave Loren the look that said, *See the man out.*

The nod said she got it.

"Again, thank you." Nate extended his hand. Roxie shook it with a wide smile.

Loren told Nate, but she was looking at her mother, "I'll let you know when we're baking cookies."

"Great."

"Let's go around the house." Loren led the way.

Lord, I sure do have a good feeling about this. Roxie

picked up the pizza box, stuffed it in the trash, and took the tray, including the last piece, into the house, humming as she went. She wrapped the pizza in aluminum foil, the glasses went in the dishwasher, and she was just refilling the pitcher when Loren and Sir Charles wandered back in the kitchen.

"Nice guy," Roxie said.

"He asked me and Sir Charles to go biking around the lake on Sunday afternoon."

"Really?"

Loren rolled her eyes. "Yes, Mother, I agreed to go." But Loren was not wearing the leave-it-to-my-mother look. She actually looked interested. Roxie floated up the stairs to her bedroom. Maybe, just maybe, this was the first step to another answered prayer.

Chapter Twelve

"Y ou got everyone contacted about the morning UFO group?"

"Yes, sir." Roxie snapped a smart salute.

"Come on, you don't have to be sarcastic."

"Then easy on the orders." Roxie rolled her eyes and shook her head. Some days MJ was more sergeanty than others. "Just reminding you. This is an all-volunteer organization."

"What got into you?" MJ jerked to a stop as she did so often, her basset at the end of his leash, tail whipping as he nosed out something. "What did you find now?" She yanked a plastic bag out of her pocket, ready for cleanup. "Oh, no. No, Looper, leave it." She stooped down and pushed the dog's nose away. "Looper, leave it."

"What did he find now?"

"A baby bird. Must have fallen out of the nest." She looked up into the tree but the new leaves hid a possible nest.

Sir Charles nosed his friend and sat down to wait it out.

"Is it alive?"

"Barely." She cupped the half-naked little one in her hands. "What can we do?"

"If Loren were home, she'd take it in." Roxie looked around. "No mother birds dive bombing us. They say leave the babies and let the parents find them and care for them."

"I don't think this one will last that long. Doesn't the mother bird know one of her babies is missing?"

Roxie took off her hat. "Put it in here and we'll take it with us. Better than a pocket."

Looper braced his short front legs against MJ's thigh and yipped his suggestion.

"He thinks it's his."

"I know. He'd probably eat the poor thing."

Roxie nodded. "Bassets are like that. Here, give me Looper's leash so you can carry the hat."

They set out again, Roxie with the two leashes. "Never a dull moment."

"What do you have there?" Anne asked when they came in, MJ cradling the hat.

"A baby bird. Looper found it. Can I have a napkin to wrap it in? At least we can keep it warm."

"Hey, Paula," Anne called to a woman seated at a table in the corner, "your daughter takes in orphan animals, doesn't she? Think she'd take on a not-even-near-fledgling bird?"

"What day is it?"

"Wednesday."

Paula came over and looked at the nestling. "I hate to tell you but I seriously doubt that baby bird can be saved. She's in class. I'll leave her a message."

"Do you have a box we can nest it in?" MJ asked.

"Do we have boxes? We always have boxes. I'll get you one." Anne returned with a small box and a couple of napkins.

MJ took it. "We can put it near the oven to keep it warm."

Anne rolled her eyes. "The health department does an inspection and we're toast."

Paula assured her, "I'm sure Lacey will stop on her way home and pick it up. I'll bribe her with a latte."

"The things we do for our friends." Anne handed Roxie her latte. "Any rolls or...?"

"Cinnamon buns are tomorrow, right?"

"And orange glory on Friday. I could make you cinnamon toast on bread Gary baked last night."

MJ blew out a puff. "And here I thought I was going to get by with just a latte." They took their coffee to their usual table under the big painting of a woman wearing a red dress. "So, when you informed people that the morning group is meeting tomorrow, did any say they were coming?"

Roxie nodded. "A few. I didn't keep track, but enough, I think. Perhaps we should try to at least get it started."

Anne delivered the cinnamon toast, a serving for each of them. They both inhaled deeply, letting the wonderful aroma caress them.

MJ took a bite and paused, savoring. "I was planning on it. You heard from Amalia?"

"Ginny wants to sleep all the time or at least hide out in bed."

MJ shrugged. "Can't say as I blame her, but not healthy after a while."

"I guess Sam and family come home tomorrow, and he told Amalia that now that school is out, they'll take over. I think she'd rather go to the daytime group."

"Mm-hmm." MJ sipped her latte. "If we both go..."

"I think the little bird is gone." Anne handed back the box.

"Well, we tried." Roxie shook her head. "I remember Loren crying for hours when some creature she tried to save would die. Each one had a funeral service and burial in the backyard. She has always been so tenderhearted."

"Takes after her mother." MJ said it in a kindly way.

"Hey, did you find yourself working on your project or at least wanting to this week?" Anne finished with another customer and came over to the table. "I see the toast did not last long."

"How could it? Like eating a memory. My mother used to make cinnamon toast for us," MJ replied. "Regarding the project I brought—yes, and I put the latch hook rug up on the coffee table in the family room. Anyone who sits on the sofa has to latch hook a few stitches. I have been doing a row every morning while Daryl has the news on." She half shrugged, her head tipping slightly. "Strange, isn't it? You, Roxie?"

"Twice. You should come see my new rug in my looks-like-new office. Really brightened it up."

MJ's eyebrows went up. "You got it up the stairs all right?"

"Well, the delivery man carried it up. None other than Nate Owens, store manager, and I believe he is interested in Loren. He remembered her from high school and invited her biking Sunday. He is a delightful young man."

"Well, I'll be. They're going biking on Sunday af-ternoon, eh. We will all pray for good weather." MJ checked her watch. "Better be getting home. I promised Daryl I'd help him with his kayak. Something about stitching gunwales."

"And I have a new client who wants to see some houses today, so we are out of here." Roxie headed out the door.

"What about the bird?" Anne called. "Wait. Never mind, I'll take care of it."

"Good luck with your showings," MJ said at her gate. "You want to bring Sir Charles over while you're gone? Looper loves to have company."

"Thanks, maybe I will, although I'm sure all he and Juno do while I am gone is curl up in a sun spot and sleep." She patted his head. "Come on, big dog, let's get home."

❂   ❂   ❂

The next morning, three people were already in the room when MJ and Roxie arrived at the UFO meeting place, the senior center. They shared a grin and set their bags down on the table.

"Welcome, everyone." MJ stepped in to be the greeter. "Glad you could come. There is coffee and tea on the corner table."

"And I brought cookies," Maureen's daughter Josie announced. "Can't have a meeting without cookies."

"Hey, I didn't know that was a law." Roxie smiled at her. "And knowing you, they are homemade."

"How embarrassing to bring store-bought." Josie

pulled the lid off her plastic container, releasing cinnamon oatmeal fragrance.

"Are they even cooled yet?"

"Oh, yes, took the last batch out of the oven at eight, so please, everyone, help yourself."

Roxie set out a Sharpie and a deck of HELLO–MY NAME IS labels. "So, here are name tags, just in case we have people we don't know." She saw Maxine, a recently widowed retired schoolteacher. "Maxine, what are you working on and the magic question—when did you start it?"

The unashamedly gray-haired woman held up a variegated rust cable-knit sweater back. "Let's just say that the grandson I started this for is now a football player at the high school."

"And that is size...?"

"Oh, six or so. I'll find someone to give it to. Thought of unraveling it but the back is finished; this is the front, and the sleeves will go quickly, no cable there."

"I love that I'm not the only one," Roxie sighed.

They had one crocheter, halfway through a baby afghan, and a painter who was setting up her easel. "I want to give this to my daughter for a wedding gift in a month so I really need to get on it."

"Any of you find that our first organizational meeting spurred you to working on your number one after the meeting?"

They all nodded. Roxie turned when she heard the door open. "Ginny." She leaped to her feet. "Oh, I'm so glad to see you."

Ginny smiled weakly. "You can blame Amalia. She said I had to get out."

Right behind her, Amalia looked up toward her hat brim. Her hat today was the straw boater.

"If you are trying to look angelic, it isn't working." MJ's smile nearly burst open her face.

"Oh, well, we are here and we have things to work on so...Is that oatmeal cookies I smell?" Amalia sniffed the air.

"Josie is going to get wealthy bottling that perfume." Maxine commented. "Ginny, I am so sorry."

Ginny blinked. "Thank you." She held up a table runner she had quilted. "Down to the handwork and it's been waiting since last winter."

"You going to make napkins to go with that?"

"Years ago, I made napkins for my house for every season. Hand-hemmed them all." Several groans. "But I took them everywhere—to meetings to work on and avoid talking and volunteering for anything."

"Did it work?"

"It did. Now I just claim age." She drew her counted cross-stitch out of the bag. "Found this in a box in a closet. Who knows when I started it."

"Ginny, I heard you had some plant starts needing a garden."

Roxie watched her friend struggle. "I did. Let me check when I get home and call you."

"I know several others who want to come to this group but couldn't make it this week," Josie said.

"When I was deciding on which project..." one lady said, "I realized how much yarn I have stashed away. Maybe we could do a yarn swap or something. Or if any of you know who could use more yarn."

"The women over at St. Paul's are knitting and

crocheting baby blankets or blankets for the less fortunate. You can drop yarn off there anytime."

"Thank you. I wonder how many garbage bags I could fill."

The others snickered.

"My daughter said my fabric stash is out of control. I've sworn off fabric stores," Maxine averred.

"Are you going through withdrawal?" Josie snickered.

"I think so. I drive faster when I see a fabric store. The other way, I mean."

When the clock neared noon, they put their things away.

Maxine commented, "You know the evening group is meeting twice a month; what about this one?"

"I'm sure they will let us use a room here more often. I'll check and let you know." MJ nodded. "Thanks."

Later, when they were leaving the room, Roxie murmured to Ginny, "The first time for anything is always the hardest. Good for you for coming."

Ginny nodded and blinked fast several times. "Thanks. Not sure if I am happy with Amalia or not, but she can be mighty persuasive when she tries."

Amalia giggled. "I twisted her arm, gently, of course. I wouldn't want to leave a bruise."

MJ asked, "How about the four of us go have lunch?"

"I—I…" Ginny was shaking her head.

"Good idea." Amalia stepped in. "A chicken Caesar salad sounds good to me so how about the Ritz Café?" She leaned closer to Ginny. "Then we'll go back to your house and I won't bother you until supper."

"Promise?"

She nodded. "I promise. Unless, of course, you need

to show me how I can help out in the greenhouse. With all the work you've put in out there, I hate to see the plants die from neglect."

"What if I cry? Seems that's all I do."

Roxie assured her, "Never fear, you are with your friends who love you, crying or not."

The Ritz was nearly full, but they found a table in a fairly quiet corner. Service there, as always, was excellent.

Ginny did all right until a woman stopped by their table to extend her sympathy. "We all miss Fred so much. And the service was lovely, so well done." Her voice was cloying as she patted Ginny's hand. "If I can do anything for you, please let me know."

"Thank you, I—I appreciate that." She held it together until the woman and her friend moved on. Then the tears broke over the dam and she dug in her purse for a tissue.

Amalia handed her one. "It's okay, you handled it very well."

"I'll get the checks," Roxie whispered. "We'll see you later." She and MJ watched the other two head for the car. "My heart hurts so bad for her." She rolled her lips together. "And all she can do is get through it."

"I wish I knew a way to help her more."

"I know. Don't we all?" She tucked the tip under one of the glasses. "The best thing we can do is listen, let her talk it out and cry it out."

"It's just not fair." MJ slung her purse over her shoulder. "Just not fair."

"Notes and cards are a real comfort. I can remember one friend, and every week, I got a card from her for

several months at least. The best cards were those that
shared a memory they had of Greg. I kept them all in a
scrapbook." She half smiled. "I've not looked at that book
for a long time, but it was a help when I needed it."

MJ paused, apparently to think. "Perhaps we could
help respond to all the cards and donations?"

"Now, that would be a good idea."

Out in the parking lot, where their cars were parked
next to each other, MJ paused again. "What are you doing this afternoon?"

"Paperwork. Have a proposal to put together and
clean up on several others. The paperwork is enough to
drive Realtors out of business. What all is required with
a sale now takes two trees, all single-spaced, and legal-
size reams."

"Better you than me."

"You want to get paid, you do the paperwork. And I
like my lifestyle. You know that old saw, make hay while
the sun shines."

"Or, it never rains but it pours?"

"That too. See you later."

Driving, Roxie's thoughts turned to Loren. Nate had
called nearly every evening since he'd delivered the rug.
He invited her for coffee on Saturday morning. So much
for help getting the yard work done. She found herself
humming as she drove her convertible into the garage.

Saturday morning when Loren got back from coffee,
she found her mother in her office.

"Did you have a good time?"

"I guess. Nate said his father invited us for barbeque
at his house tomorrow afternoon, you know like for early
supper?"

"And you said?"

"I'd ask you."

"Do you want to go?"

Loren half shrugged. "I guess."

Well, don't act too excited, my girl. Roxie swallowed her comment and nodded. "Should I call and ask what we can bring?"

Loren shook her head. "How should I know?"

"We'll just take a hostess, er, host gift. Do you know his wife's name?"

"The father's not married. Divorced years ago."

"Oh."

"You want to go work in the backyard now?" Loren asked.

"Sure. Before it gets too hot."

"No, before it rains. You can feel it on the wind."

A barbeque tomorrow. As Amalia so often said, *Life changes in an instant and we have no control over it.*

Chapter Thirteen

"Grandma, we left you alone." Addy wrapped her arms around her grandma.

Ginny held her close, tears dripping down on her head. "I wasn't alone, Amalia has been here. And besides, I think this was a good thing." *Liar. Nothing has been good since you found Fred.* "But you know what, we sure missed your cookies."

"But people brought lots of cookies and pies and cakes and everything," Addy protested.

"Probably there are lots in the freezers, both here and at your house. But fresh are better."

"I don't want to make peanut butter ones." She lifted her tear-stained face to Ginny. "I don't ever want to make peanut butter cookies again."

How to answer this? Ginny smiled. Or tried to. "Grandpa liked them a lot. Someday we might want to make them as a tribute to him."

"We could change the name on the recipe to Grandpa's Peanut Butter Cookies."

"That's a good idea." Ginny smiled again on the outside.

"Andy didn't want to come."

"I understand but I thought that one night when nei-ther of you have something going on…"

Addy sounded weary. "It's summer vacation, Grandma. We don't have homework, you know."

"True, but you both have ball practice and games…"

"Games are on Saturday unless we do a tournament on Saturday and Sunday. You're coming on Saturday?"

The last thing in the world I feel like doing. "Wouldn't miss it. Want some lemonade?"

Addy looked around. "Is Miss Amalia still here?"

"I think she is down in the garden."

"The flowers or Grandpa's?"

"Grandpa's. You go tell her to come up for lemon-ade." Ginny checked her watch. "About dinnertime. I'll get something started while you go get her. You rode your bike over?"

"Yep. Dad said to ask if you need help with the chores tonight. I can do them."

"How about I call your mom and invite everyone here for hamburgers and something out of the freezer?"

"Good. Can I spend the night?"

Oh Lord, what do I say? What if I start to cry and I can't stop? I don't want to frighten her. "Don't you have ball practice?"

"At three. You could take me."

"Let me talk to your dad. See what their plans are." Ginny checked her watch again. Fred always wanted to eat at noon, a holdover from his growing up on the farm. The tears made her sniff.

"We'll make cookies after we eat?" Addy asked.

"Yes. Take Spook with you."

"Maybe he wants to stay back."

"We'll see." Spook had been staying close beside her much of the time. As if he was still grieving too.

Addy called, "Come on, Spook, let's go to the barn."

Spook wagged his tail but, instead of scrambling up, looked to Ginny.

"It's okay, boy, you go with Addy." He looked from Addy to Ginny. She nodded and said, "It's okay, you go."

Addy slapped her thigh and pushed open the door. When she leaped off the steps, Spook leaped with her.

In the kitchen, Ginny opened the refrigerator. Amalia had made lime Jell-O with cottage cheese. Probably to keep the cottage cheese from going bad. The idea of grilled tuna sandwiches made her nod. She pulled out the mayo, sweet hamburger pickles, and half an onion in a plastic storage bag. A couple cans of tuna from the pantry and she set to fixing it. As she drained the tuna at the sink, she paused to watch two hummingbirds at the feeder hanging from the eaves. The feeder was full; again, it had to be thanks to Amalia. Things had not suffered around here due to this faithful friend. Tears of gratitude didn't feel a whole lot different than those of grief, but they stopped a lot sooner and didn't leave her feeling as beat up as a washer tub at the end of the cycle.

She chopped the onion fine and added it to the tuna and mayo, then the pickles not so fine. She found a loaf of bread in the freezer and laid the slices out on the counter. Three pairs would be enough. How would she ever learn to cook for one? She remembered their early years, the difficulty of learning to cook for two rather than for six like at her home. While her mother and father both worked, she, the eldest, and the other kids did the small farming chores, mostly 4-H animals. Now her parents were milking three cows, had three steers in the pasture, Duroc hogs for another brother's project, and her chickens. Shame they all lived so far away now. Actually, she was the one who'd moved when she married Fred.

She set out the griddle and turned the dial once she heard their voices.

"Grandma, can we eat out on the deck?"

"Of course. Come get a cloth to wash the table off."

"What do you want me to do?" Amalia turned the cold faucet on and dumped a load of leaf lettuce in to wash. "The radishes are wormy but they still taste good."

"Fred always put more seeds in where he pulled something out."

"That's a fine idea. Where does he keep the seeds?"

"In the garden shed, in a plastic tub on the counter." Ginny buttered one side of the sandwiches and laid them on the hot griddle, then buttered the tops.

"Ice in the glasses and lemonade and iced tea pitchers on the table," she answered to Addy's questioning look.

"You want small bowls for the Jell-O?" Amalia asked as Addy carried the glasses outside.

"Please."

"You all right?"

Ginny swallowed and reached for a tissue. "The tears just sneak up on me. I could hear Fred say, 'Any chips?'"

"Well, are there? Or better yet, do you want chips out?"

Sniff, blink, mop. "If we have some. Addy likes chips."

She stared up at the ceiling, the tears quit, and she

took paper plates out of the drawer. After cutting the sandwiches in half on the diagonal like Fred had wanted, she handed a plate to each of them.

"Are you okay, Grandma?" Addy wore her worried look.

"I will be. We just have to get through the tears."

Amalia smiled at Addy. "I can promise, they don't last forever, and don't you worry, Addy, your grandma just needs us here to help her through the nows."

"That's what Mom said, but it makes me cry too."

"Oh, honey, I'm so sorry, but everybody tells me this is just the way it is." They sat down at the table, where a slight breeze tickled their hair and kissed their faces. "Addy, do you want to say grace?"

"Dear God, bless this food and help Grandma get through the tears. Dad too, I guess all of us. Please take good care of Grandpa. We sure miss him. Amen."

Ginny half smiled through her tears. "Thank you, sweetie."

"Oh, look," Addy said. "The prince is on the feeder."

"The prince?" Amalia followed the pointing finger. "Oh, you mean the male cardinal?"

"Yeah, the prince. He's so bright. There were a bunch of them here through the winter. Andy got some neat pictures of them against the snow."

"Andy is our budding photographer in the family," Ginny explained.

"Takes after you?"

"I guess, but Fred was no slouch either. He encouraged Andy by giving him a good camera last Christmas. He and Andy were taking pictures at the basketball games. Got some good action shots."

Addy added, "He wants to take pictures for the high school paper when we get there."

"You're twelve now?" Amalia asked.

"We turn twelve in June."

"So, tell us about your time up at the lake."

Addy shrugged. "Mom and I went hiking, and Dad and Andy went fishing. We played games sometimes in the evening and all day the days it rained. No TV or Wi-Fi up there so it was pretty quiet. Oh, and no cell phone. We went to town a couple of times so Mom and Dad could get messages." She looked to Amalia. "Andy and I have phones that can call home, but we don't get real phones that do all the other stuff until we turn fifteen. My parents are really strict."

Amalia looked at Ginny and snorted. "I'd say they have their heads on straight."

"Miss Amalia!" Addy's jaw dropped. "Did your kids have cell phones?"

"When my kids were teenagers, there was no such thing as cell phones. I made sure they always had change for a phone call if they needed to call home."

Ginny nodded. "Makes you wonder at times how we got along without them but we did."

"Mom says things have changed more than we'll ever know these days." Addy bit into the second half of her sandwich.

"You remember the Dick Tracy comic strips and that watch he wore? Nowadays half the country has one of those. Computer and everything right on your wrist." Amalia shook her head.

Addy brushed her fingers off. "Can we bake cookies now?"

"What kind do you want to make?"

"How about snickerdoodles and we can all roll the dough in a ball. Double batch."

"I've been hankering for molasses ginger cookies. You roll them in a ball too."

"Or drop by spoonfuls and mash with a glass, the bottom dipped in sugar."

"Can we do it the right way so they look pretty too?" Addy gathered up the plates and dishes and took them in the house.

"She is one good kid."

"They both are. We're, er..." Ginny stumbled and corrected herself. "I'm so proud..." She sniffed and rolled her eyes upward. "Please, I don't want to cry again." She sent Amalia an imploring look. "Will this go on forever?"

"Feels that way right now, but no, it won't. The crying bouts will get farther apart, but still, there will be times you get blindsided and they strike again. But they don't last as long. Often, when you least expect it, something will trigger the waterworks again. It can be a memory, or something you see or hear or even a smell." Amalia shrugged. She patted Ginny's hand. "Let's go make cookies."

"I need to call Sam. You go ahead." Just then her phone sang. "Hi, I was just going to call you." They swapped the normal beginning stuff before Ginny asked, "You all want to come here for supper? Thought we'd do hamburgers on the grill and something out of the freezer. Amalia brought up lettuce for our favorite salad so we're a go with that. Addy and Amalia are starting the cookie baking. I think Addy went through withdrawals while you were gone."

Sam replied, "If you want. No ball practice this afternoon so how about six? You have hamburger buns?"

"I have no idea if there are any in the freezer or not. You better bring some and ice cream to go with the cookies for dessert. She wants to know if she can stay here tonight."

"Up to you."

Ginny leaned against the deck railing. *It would give Amalia a break but what if I go into one of the crying jags or cry or shout in a dream? I seem to be doing that. And waking up crying. I don't want to frighten Addy. And that means I should move back into my bedroom so she and I are not sharing the downstairs bedroom. Like Amalia and I are.* She heaved a heavy sigh. It was as if someone had pulled a plug in the bottom of her foot and all her energy had drained out.

"We don't have to do this, Mom, if it is too much for you."

"I know but I want you all around. I want to catch up on your lives again, I've missed you." *When I was coherent enough to think of someone else.*

"Up to you."

Ginny yawned. "I might have to lie down for a while." A euphemism for falling down the well again.

"Look, we'll bring Addy home for tonight. Supper is enough for the first time."

"Okay. I'll get the patties out of the freezer and one of the hot dishes. I have onion and lettuce for the burgers but no tomatoes to slice. No chips, as if we need them."

"Sounds good. And, Mom, actually you sound more like your old self."

"Good. Later. I love you, son."

"And I you." His voice choked as she ended the call.

She made her way into the kitchen. "I hate to do this but do you mind if I go lie down for a while?"

"You okay, Grandma?" Addy turned from cracking eggs into the mixing bowl.

"I will be."

"You've done well." Amalia was measuring flour. "We'll call if we need you."

"Addy knows where everything is. I'll get the stuff out of the freezer. Addy, you want to come carry it up here?"

"Sure."

Ginny lay down on the twin bed that had been her hiding place as well as her sleeping place. For a change, she fell asleep before a tear attack.

When she felt someone sit on the bed beside her, she climbed toward the round bright hole at the top of the well.

"Grandma, Miss Amalia said I should come wake you. She said you wouldn't hit me."

Ginny felt a snort coming on. "She did, did she?"

"I told her you wouldn't hit anyone, but you did swat me once when I was being a brat."

"That was a lot of years ago." Ginny heaved a sigh and sniffed. "I smell ginger cookies."

"Yup, we made a double batch of those too. You got out of making cookie dough walnuts."

"What a pity." She forced her eyes open and reached up to pat Addy's cheek. "What a nice way to wake up."

"Should I run up the stairs crying that you slapped me?"

"Oh, the things you think of. Such a creative mind. What time is it?"

"Three fifty. Miss Amalia said it's too hot in the greenhouse so she's sitting back on one of the loungers on the deck. She says to come join her, the iced tea is sweating."

"Well, we can't have that." Ginny swung her legs over the edge of the bed to a chorus of creaks and groans and not from the bed springs. "*Uff da.*"

"You haven't said that for a long time."

"Really." She slid her feet into her sandals. "*Uff da* is a useful expression, good for any occasion. I learned it from a Norwegian woman who used to live next door to us before we moved out here." When she stood, she paused before moving, the way her doctor advised her. Less chance of getting dizzy that way.

"Where's Spook?"

"Up in Grandpa's leather recliner."

"He knows better than that."

"I think he wants to be closer to Grandpa. The chair smells like he did."

"I'm surprised after they cleaned the smoke away from everything."

"Dad said that could have burned the house down."

"Don't I know it?" Together they climbed the stairs. Spook leaped off the chair as soon as he saw her.

"Hey, Spook, that's all right for now." She ruffled his ears. "I know you miss him too. I think even the chickens miss him. They give me the stink eye."

"Grandma, you're making that up." Addy headed for the kitchen. "I'll bring cookies out."

Ginny pushed the screen door open on the sliding glass doors. "Now if you don't look comfortable."

"I got several more rows done." Amalia held up about

eighteen inches of afghan all in varied colors. "Trying to use up all the leftovers and I have plenty."

"If you need more, I can send some with you."

"Sam called to make sure I wanted to stay longer. I assured him that was not a problem. I love being out here. And my grumpy, sociopathic house pet seems to be perfectly happy living alone."

"Maybe the cat doesn't miss you, but everyone else would sure miss you at the home, since you take care of half the residents."

"Only a few and not permanently. Just helping some get back on their feet so they can stay there. When I'm not there to do it, senior services sends volunteers around. But senior services is overworked and underpaid, so I'm glad to help out when I can."

"I'm happy to hear that." Ginny smiled. "I was afraid the other people you help would be neglected."

Amalia waved her crochet hook. "Oh, and your phone sang several times, but I let them all go to voice mail. One was MJ, so she called me to make sure you're all right."

"Did we have a good time at the UFO the other day?"

"We seemed to. You didn't get a lot done on your project, but that's okay. The evening group is on Monday night."

Addy set the plate of cookies on the table between them and sat cross-legged on the deck, leaning against Ginny's lounger. Spook sniffed her face and licked one cheek before lying down with his head on her thigh. Addy leaned over and whispered in his ear, "Where's your ball?" That made it twitch. He shook his head and got up, searched the deck, and waited at the door for her to open it. Then he cased the upstairs, pounded down the stairs, and returned with it in a couple of minutes. "Boy, you must have hidden it well. Come on." She tossed the ball over the railing and away he went after it.

Amalia announced, "Before I came out here, I made the salad dressing for tonight and set up the tray for the hamburgers. The scalloped potato casserole is in the oven with the timer set to start at five."

"You are a godsend."

"I can only sit still so long before I get the heebie-jeebies."

"Right."

Spook left the ball chasing and loped barking down the driveway.

"They're here." Ginny tried to blow out the tears that immediately clogged her throat. "Here I go again."

"What triggered it?"

"Fred isn't here to grill the hamburgers. He never let anyone touch his grill, said they might take his job away." She blew her nose but the sobs only worsened. "I don't want them to see me falling apart again." She rose from the lounger and headed for the bathroom. "I'll be out as soon as I can."

Chapter Fourteen

"What did you say his name was?" Roxie checked with her GPS to see how far before the turn.

"Richard Donald Owens, he goes by Rich." Loren stared at her mother. "What's with you? You meet new people all the time, why is this any different?"

Because this is the father of the man I believe you are going to marry in the near future. The end of that thought caught her by surprise. Interesting how her hunches went at times.

Roxie said accusingly, "You got sunburned this morning."

"I know, haven't had to use the sunscreen yet this year and didn't even think about it. I put the aloe vera on."

"Your skin is so much like your father's. He was close to a redhead; you both got the translucent skin." She slowed down and turned to the right as per Lola's instructions. Roxie had named the woman on the GPS so she could yell at her in a more personal way. Sometimes even Lola made mistakes. "Will there be a lot of people there?"

Loren shrugged. "How should I know? Nate offered to pick us up but—"

Roxie finished the sentence for her. "In case things got uncomfortable, you wanted a way out."

"How did you know?"

Roxie rolled her eyes. "I'm your mother. A mother learns things by the time her youngest child is twenty-six years old." Good thing. Well, if Mr. Richard Owens was anything like his son, this would be enjoyable.

"You have reached your destination on the right," said Lola mechanically.

"Must be right on the lake." The paved driveway wore the manicured look of a good yard service. She turned in and clicked off the GPS. "Take a nap, Lola."

Loren snorted. "You have a love-hate relationship with that GPS system. It's just a device."

"Looks like a park." A pond off to the right caught her attention. "Look at that gazebo. You'd think we were in New England. Quaint."

One more curve and the house came into view. Roxie's years in real estate quickly estimated the value, the architect, and the taste of the man who was hosting them. Looked like he had done very well for himself or he was in debt up to his eyebrows. She had a strong feeling it was the former. She mentally clicked off the business side of her brain. She was here to enjoy herself, not to help the owner sell.

A huge fluffy white dog came bounding across the lawn, followed by Nate. Both were wearing wide grins.

"Welcome, glad you made it all right." He opened Roxie's door for her and went around to open Loren's. "Meet Sophie. Believe it or not, she is still a puppy." He laid his hand on her head. "Easy, girl, you needn't scare the company." Roxie climbed out and stood straight to look around.

Loren let the puppy sniff her hands, up her arms, and kiss her chin. She cupped her hands around the jawline and snuggled her nose into the fluff. "Oh, you are something else. What a beautiful girl." She grinned up at Nate. "I think she likes me."

"How could she not?"

Roxie nodded inside. She was right; he was hooked. Line and sinker hooked. *Oh Lord, thank you for answering another of my many prayers.* In church that morning, the sermon had been on gratitude. She felt it overflowing and kissing everyone around her.

Now she was glad she had decided to wear a floral summer dress with a cropped pink crocheted jacket and floppy straw hat. Since the top was down on the convertible, she picked up her hat from the backseat, grabbed the bottle of wine in a hand-painted sleeve, and came around the car.

"Good to see you, Nate."

"Don't you look lovely?" He shook her hand and tucked it under his arm. "Dad is out on the deck. He says we should not waste such a glorious day inside."

"Are you expecting a lot of people?"

"Nope, just us and Mom might be coming. Her house is right up the road." At the look of confusion on her face, he added, "They were divorced when I was in grade school and, as soon as they weren't living together, got along famously. Made it a lot easier on us kids."

"There are four of you, right?"

"No, three. Dad oversees the home store with my cousin growing up into managership there."

Roxie pointed. "Oh, that crabapple tree is stunning. You have some landscaper."

"Actually, Dad laid out all the plans, working on a different section each year. We were a lot of the slave labor. He says gardening is his relaxation, as is the sailboat. Do you two go sailing?"

Loren shook her head. "I've been out once or twice. My dad used to have a boat but with a motor, not a sail. When he died, Mom sold the boat, since none of us were really interested in it."

"That must have been rough."

As they came around the house, Lake Winnebago glittered in all its blue glory before them. Sails dotted the lake, along with sailboarders in wet suits, because the water was still icy cold from winter.

Roxie paused and caught her breath. "What a view."

"I was hoping for a day like this. Hey, Dad."

The man on deck, wearing green shorts and a lighter green T-shirt with deck shoes, waved and came down the four stairs to the ground level. "Glad you could make it."

"Roxie, this is my father, Rich Owens. Dad, Roxie Gilburn and her daughter, Loren."

"Good to meet you. You sold a house for a friend of mine and he raved about what a professional job you did. Got him more money than he had hoped too, which made everyone happy, I'm sure."

He was already tanned, with crinkles at his eyes that were surely smile lines. His dark hair was long enough on top for the curls to show. But his smile was what made him such a good-looking man. Wide and genuine, with a dimple in his chin. While his handshake was firm, it was not overpowering.

"I'm glad to meet you too. You have a fine son, and I can see where he got his good looks."

"Hey, a woman who speaks her mind. Come on, drinks are on the deck and umbrellas too. Loren, looks like the sun snuck up on you today. Nate said you two had a good bike ride. Roxie, are you a bike rider?"

"I am, but my bike doesn't get used as often as Loren's."

"She's off showing houses much of the time," Loren explained.

"That's what it takes to be good at what you do." He motioned them up the steps, making sure Sophie didn't mow them down. A smaller dog, obviously part Lab and probably shepherd of some kind, met them with wagging tail. "This is Abner, Nate's old dog. He had to come live here when Nate moved into that apartment in Fond du Lac. Shame so many condos and apartments, well, most rentals, have a no-pet policy. Everybody needs a dog or a cat in their life. Nate said you have both a dog and a cat."

Loren nodded. "The cat, Juno, rules the house, and Sir Charles, our dog, guards the house and the outside is his, or so he thinks."

"Sounds about right. What can I get you to drink? We have lemonade, iced tea, Arnold Palmers, and sodas in the cooler."

"An Arnold Palmer sounds good." Roxie sat in the chair he pulled out for her, looking directly at the lake. "Oops." She pointed out across the water. "A sailboarder just got dunked." She watched, amused, as the fellow squirmed back aboard. He was amazingly nimble.

"What would you like, Loren?" Nate asked. "Oh, we have strawberry-flavored lemonade."

"That sounds good."

"You said you like strawberries." Nate's hand patted her shoulder as he gave her the glass.

Roxie made sure the chortle in her throat did not get heard.

"Is Mom coming?" Nate asked when they all had their drinks, chips, salsa, and guacamole in the center of the table and were seated.

"Nope, Norm had some family thing they were going to. I'm sure she would rather have come here, but you know your mother." He spoke easily, as if they were good friends.

"How long have you lived here?" Roxie asked Rich.

"My father owned the property, and after Mom died, he decided he'd rather live in town, so I took this place and had this house built. And been working on it ever since. Kind of a home in progress. The view is enough to make me want to stay here."

"It sure would." Roxie knew how property values had skyrocketed as people migrated out of cities and wanted lakefront property. "And your father started the furniture store business?"

"Yes, to sell the furniture he and a friend made. I have a couple of his pieces in the house. Whoever dreamed it would turn into four stores, all of which buy pieces from local artisans whenever possible. Right now I'm looking for someone who likes to make chests. I demand good wood and good workmanship, none of the typical assembly-made stuff on the market today."

"Hm-mm, I know of a couple of woodworkers. I'll see what they're doing. One of them had a dovetailed box that was beautiful."

Rich sipped his drink. "I've been to the local wood-workers meeting, but so far, most of them are carving, not building."

Roxie nodded. "So many of the real craftsmen are dying off—the joiners and furniture makers—and no one is taking their places." She glanced over to see Loren and Nate with their chairs close together so they could talk more easily. A fluffy orange cat was curled on her lap and Sophie lay between their chairs.

"Do you like sailing?" Rich asked.

"I guess, though I've not been out on the water for years. Loren and I were going to take up kayaking, but I never got around to it."

"Do you canoe?"

"Same story. We have a man at the UFO group who is building a peapod and another with a kayak."

"UFO?" The puzzled look he gave her made her laugh.

"I know what you're thinking, but we are not into extraterrestrials. UFO means, in our case, unfinished objects. Or projects. We had a big group the first meeting and now we've started a morning group also. We meet again tomorrow night."

"Intriguing. I always thought that someday I'd like to follow in my father's footsteps and build special things, perhaps sculpture or...I don't know, just been too busy to follow the dream."

She smiled. "I see things sometimes in the houses I tour that I would like to incorporate into my house or yard. I love the gazebo on the edge of your pond."

Nate stood up. "Thanks. Dad and I built it together. Can I get you a refill?"

Roxie held out her glass. "Yes, thank you. And that guacamole is really good. Not too spicy."

Nate disappeared behind her.

"Thank you, my secret recipe."

"You cook too?" she asked him.

"Sometimes," Rich said so casually she couldn't tell whether the answer was yes or no.

Nate came back with the refilled glass and handed it to her. "Don't let him fool you, he's an excellent cook. Taught all of us to cook too. Said we needed to be able to take care of ourselves because we most likely would be living on our own at some time. He was right—we all did or are."

"And you do the displays at the library, Loren?" Rich asked.

"I do and sometimes at the jewelry store down the street. I kind of fell into it."

"Really? Your degree isn't in design?"

"Library science, because I love books. They asked me to do a bulletin board one day and it turned out pretty good. Our woman in charge of that was moving away so I kind of stepped into her position. I learned a lot about old books and displays when I volunteered out at the YMCA camp during the summers."

"Old books." Nate nodded. "We have interesting history in this region. I donated some of the things passed down in our family, and when they did that book, Dad's family is mentioned several times. They came here in the late 1800s."

"From where?"

"England via Massachusetts."

Roxie smiled. "My mother's side came from Norway

and my father's from Ireland. He always said the Irish are part Norwegian, thanks to the Vikings."

Rich got a faraway look. "Now there were some real wood carvers and furniture makers. Dad and Mom went to Norway, and while she wanted to see the country, he wanted to spend all his time with the craftsmen. He even helped to restore a boat they were working on. Thrill of his life."

"What about you, Nate?" Roxie asked. "You have the desire to build and craft things too?"

He nodded. "I think we all inherited it. I minored in design at college, majored in business. Would have been more fun to do the other way around, but I figured I have a lifetime to do both."

Rich looked around at them. "Anybody getting hungry?"

"I am."

"Son, you are always hungry. I'll fire up the grill and get the steaks on. I can put on chicken too if anyone would rather?"

"He's been marinating the steaks since yesterday." Nate reached for another chip and a scoop of guacamole. "Don't know how I can be hungry after all these."

Rich pushed back his chair and stood to turn on the grill built into a brickwork wall, with a mini refrigerator, sink, and cabinet also built in. A fire pit surrounded by built-in seating took up the next level of the deck.

"Did he do the brickwork too?" Roxie asked Nate.

"No, he designed the plans but hired a real bricklayer to do the work. There's even a brick oven, which makes mighty good pizza. Takes quite a while to get it hot enough, though; you build the wood fire right inside it. Makes marvelous crunchy bread too."

"How does he have time for all this?"

"I personally think he has a touch of ADHD."

Roxie chuckled. "I've wished for that at times. So many things I want to do, and I have to take time out to sleep."

"She's pretty high energy too," Loren added. "Always has been."

"And you would rather hide out with a book. I know." Roxie said to Nate, "Loren's had her nose in a book since before she learned to read. She'd bring me the book to read, then tell me the story by the pictures."

"Both Mom and Dad read to us. I don't know how they did it all. But there are advantages to having your own business. Well, disadvantages too. You want some help, Dad?"

"Someone can set the table to start." Rich spread an assortment of sliced veggies out on the grill.

"I can do the table." Roxie pushed back her chair.

"Everything is laid out on the counter." Nate led them into the kitchen, where the marble countertop held all the dishware, some already on a tray. Loren picked up the tray and Roxie the basket with silver and napkins, already in bamboo rings.

How could such a dream kitchen also be so friendly and inviting, kind of like the whole place? Stepping back outside, Roxie caught her breath. Such a view. What must it be like to have early-morning coffee out here in the summer, with the breeze off the lake, birds singing, trees whispering. Of course, she had all of that at home but without the lake view—and enjoyed it immensely.

"How do you like your steaks?"

"Mine medium rare and Loren's medium." How long had it been since they'd had steaks on a grill? Probably last summer out at Ginny and Fred's. The thought stabbed her. They wouldn't be enjoying Fred's banter and whatever meat on the grill, not ever again.

"What is it, Mom?"

She sniffed. "I just thought of barbeques at Ginny's." This time she left off the Fred. And blinked a bunch. If it hit her this hard, what must it be doing to Ginny? Thank God Amalia was able to stay with her. She sucked in a deep breath and set the silver around. Loren had already laid out the placemats, also of bamboo.

"You want me to put the salads out?" Nate called.

"Yes," Rich called back. "I'm turning the steaks over. Vegetables look all done. So, please all, be seated. I like to serve hot food hot."

"And cold food cold." Nate grinned at Loren. "We have everything, please be seated. Dad, is there bread?"

"In the oven. Basket is on the table."

Nate returned with the breadbasket as Rich set the platter with grilled zucchini, eggplant, red onion, and Portobello mushrooms on the table. He returned again with the steak platter, each person's wearing a little flag, and sat down. "Shall we say grace?" He held out his hands. "Thank you, Lord God, for the food, the company, and the glorious day. In Jesus' name, we pray, amen. Now, help yourselves. The red bowl is potato salad, yellow is cucumber salad with the recipe from an old lady at our church, and green is for green salad." While he spoke, he lifted the covers off the bowls.

"This is too pretty to eat." Roxie motioned to the full table.

"Well, start with the steaks. Your initial is on the flag." He passed the platter to Roxie. "If it is too rare, we can flip it back on for a minute or so."

Roxie cut into her steak. She hardly needed the steak knife. "Ah, perfect, pink with a bit of red." As she chewed, she closed her eyes, the better to savor the flavor. She opened her eyes above a face-stretching smile. "You really know how to do steaks."

Along with everything else. Roxie looked at Loren and figured their faces must have about matched.

"I have it down to a science. The potato salad is from my German grandmother's recipe file. I like to collect recipes but, surprisingly enough, very few from on the Internet. Food is more personal this way."

"I think you outdid yourself this time, Dad."

"Thank you, but I think it's a combination of a lot of good things today. The weather, the company, the steaks are from that feedlot with the store and restaurant on the property south of here, so aged to perfection. That has a lot to do with it." His smile included them all. "You ever shop at the meat market on Fillibuster?"

"I used to once in a while. They make really good sausage."

"And they smoke their own hams. I think smoked pork chops are a special order."

The conversations seemed easy, as if they had all known each other for years instead of days and hours. After they'd worked together on the cleanup, Roxie joined Rich on a walk around the property, starting with the boathouse on the lake. Like the dock, it could be rolled up farther on the shore during the winter.

"I think my son is besotted with your daughter—told me he had a major crush on her in high school, and seeing her again brought it all back, but not puppy love this time."

"I had this feeling from him right away. When he sold us the perfect rug and when he delivered the rug, it was even more obvious. He is a fine young man; you must be very proud of him."

"I always have been proud of my kids. I told them early on that if they wanted to do something else, other than work in our family business, that was straight on up to them."

"But all of them chose to stay with the furniture business."

"They did." He nodded with a half smile. "Roxie, I am so blessed, I can never be grateful enough."

"Hard for any of us to be grateful enough." She looked toward the house. "Oh look, the sun is about to go down."

"Good, come on." He took her hand and half pulled her around the house. "We need to see that from the gazebo. Where did Nate and Loren go? We should have a spectacular display tonight, just enough clouds."

Roxie felt a jolt when he took her hand, which made her eyes grow wide. She'd not felt something like that since—since she had no idea when. What in the world was happening?

Chapter Fifteen

A ddy and Ginny are bringing cookies tonight," Amalia
announced. "They've been baking up a storm."

"Good. I know she mentioned she would rather join
the daytime group by wintertime." MJ pawed through
her bag to make sure she had everything.

"The fact she is coming at all is due to Addy. We attended the morning group, and Ginny held it together until someone came up at the restaurant and said how sorry
they were and that did her in. I know she got teary-eyed at
the UFO group but...after the restaurant she swore she
wasn't going out again until, well, she didn't know when."

MJ sat back in the easy chair. "So why is she coming
tonight?"

"Addy wanted to come, and you know, she'll do anything she can for those grandkids." Amalia leaned back
in her recliner, the one that fit her body so perfectly,
probably because of all the years she had sat in it. She
had a magnifying light on a swivel beside it for close-up
handiwork, a quilted coaster to protect the old end table
and hold her tea, and her quilted bag with other handwork beside the chair.

"So, are you coming?"

Amalia shrugged. "Still up for a vote. Feels good to be home."

"Will you be going back out there?" MJ asked.

"Possibly, if she wants me to. Perhaps Addy is going to stay with her, not sure yet. But I'm here for tonight for sure." She sipped from her glass with one hand and held the phone with the other.

"I'll gladly come get you."

"I know. Ginny volunteered too." Amalia looked around her apartment. It seemed small again after having been back in a big house for those days. But still her place felt like home. At least here, she knew where everything was, well mostly. But working out in that glorious yard and garden, in addition to the house, had been such a privilege. "I'll call you."

MJ nodded. "This UFO thing is providing benefits I wouldn't have guessed. See you later." They clicked off and Amalia sat a moment in quiet aloneness.

Her stomach informed her that it was suppertime. Taking a burrito out of her freezer, she popped that in the microwave.

To go or not to go, that was the question. *Face it, old woman, you're afraid you might miss out on something.* She spooned a dollop of sour cream on her plate, one of salsa, and careful to use a pot holder with the burrito, unwrapped it and took her plate out to her two-person round table on the lanai. The laughter of children playing on the playground across the street, birds singing in the tulip tree between her and the street, and a dog barking, all the sounds of her home. She loved it.

She almost ignored the chime of her cell phone but, when she saw it was Ginny, picked it up.

"Addy and I are down in the parking lot, waiting for you."

"Really."

"You don't want to go?"

"Come on, Miss Amalia," Addy piped in. "I baked your favorite cookies."

How could she resist that girl voice? "I would like to finish my burrito first."

"We'll wait."

So much for that. She cleaned the sour cream up with the last bite of burrito and heaved a sigh. "Sorry, Mr. Grump, I need to go." She slid the screen door shut behind them, locked it, and set her plate in the sink. Grabbing the bag that held the sweater she'd nearly finished, she ordered the cat to behave and was out the door again. "I'll be back in a while," she answered the plaintive cry.

"I'm glad to see you decided to go," she told Ginny as she slid into the front sidekick seat.

"I begged and pleaded. After all, what would we do with all the cookies we baked today?" Sometimes Addy could become rather dramatic.

"There is such a thing as a freezer." Ginny checked both ways and pulled out on the street.

"There are already a lot of cookies in your freezer and at Addy's house too," Amalia reminded her. "You could wrap up small plates and give them to those who live in my building. Some of them haven't had homemade cookies for who knows how long."

"That's a good idea."

"Uh-oh. Guess we're parking in the back." Ginny drove around the block and into the alley behind the store. Gathering up all the containers of cookies and their projects to work on, the three entered through the back door of the store, the hubbub already well under way.

"Saved your places." MJ met them at the coffee table. "We have more new people too."

Addy tucked the lids under the proper containers and followed Ginny to the table. "How about I sit on the floor, like last time?"

"You sure?"

"That way you can look down and make sure I am doing it right."

MJ stood and raised both her hands and her voice. Addy stuck two fingers in her mouth and blasted away. "Thanks, Addy."

"Welcome to you new people, glad you could join us. I hope you all picked up a name tag at the door. So, raise your hand if you found yourself working on your project during the week when before you would not have?"

A lot of hands went up, and a rush of chuckles swept around the room.

"Did anyone finish the project you brought last week?"

Three hands went up.

"I hope you brought them so that you can have your picture taken for the bulletin board and all the rest of us can be jealous. Please stand and hold yours up and tell us if you can remember when you started that particular piece." She pointed to the woman closest to her. She stood and held up the quilted table runner. "I started it at least two Novembers ago and then it got misplaced and I..." She rolled her lips together and nodded. "Busted, eh? But it is done and I am going to wrap and label it so I can give it away for an early Christmas gift. I would like a whole shelf of wrapped packages like that." She bobbed her head at the applause that commended her.

"Now, *that* is both a fine idea and a grand challenge for some of the rest of us."

The next said, "A bridal shower gift, a week of embroidered dish towels, she's only been married a year." More chuckles, whispers, and applause.

"And you, sir?"

He held up a carved bowl. "Not sure when I started it, but it was done except for the finish. Kind of the story of my life." He sat down to applause, giggles, and a snort or two.

"Please join my husband, Daryl, the guy with the camera, back by the bulletin board. He'll print the pictures and have them posted by next week. Anyone have a Polaroid camera by any chance? No? Oh, and the weekly newspaper wants a picture of the finished things each week to go with a column. Guess this concept is intriguing a lot of people."

"When is the morning group meeting?"

"Second and fourth Thursdays at nine thirty, at the senior center in one of the classrooms. Any other questions? All right, the coffee and cookies are ready, thank Addy Clarkson—raise your hand, Addy. She's sitting here on the floor." Addy turned around and waved.

Someone else raised her hand.

"Yes?" MJ asked, acknowledging the woman.

"Does she take orders for cookies?"

"I don't know. Addy?" Addy shrugged and looked to her grandma.

"They'll get back to you. And now, let the work resume."

The buzz of conversation rose immediately. There was not a lot of room to go get coffee and cookies but somehow they managed.

MJ dug out her crewel. "I'm glad I sorted through and straightened the yarns for my flowers. They were pretty globbed together."

"When did you have time to work that far?" Roxie looked over her shoulder.

"Been at this almost every evening. Daryl's been working in his shop and I decided to sit in the rocker on the front porch. Got to visit with a couple of neighbors, dual success. Once it got too dark out there, I moved in front of the TV and made Daryl turn on a movie."

Loren nudged her mother. "Look who's here."

Roxie looked up at the two men who had just walked in the door. "Well, I'll be."

"You know them?" MJ asked.

"I—we do. That's Rich and Nate Owens. I bought my rug from Nate at The Fond Furniture. Rich is his dad."

"You'd never guess by looking at them." Amalia said it sarcastically.

"They do look a lot alike, don't they?" Roxie went back to her work.

"You know, someone told me she saw Loren biking along the lake with a real good-looking guy." MJ stared at the top of Loren's head as she bent over her crocheting.

"Well, blast." Loren grumbled a bit more. "I hate ripping out."

"What did you do?" Amalia asked.

"Seems I can't even count right."

"Let me see." Amalia reached for her work as Roxie

and MJ stood to walk over to the newcomers. Amalia could clearly hear the exchange.

Rich smiled at them. "You need a bigger place to meet. I see you are fast at whatever that is you're doing."

Roxie smiled back. "Thank you, I try."

MJ waved an arm. "We do have more chairs; the guys seem to be congregating in that corner." But then two more newcomers entered, so MJ went off to greet them.

Rich was still smiling. "Okay, we'll go join them, but we plan on going out for coffee or ice cream or something afterward. We'd like you to come along," he said to Roxie.

"I'd like that. I'm sure Loren will too, especially if it's ice cream."

Roxie gave them name tags and took them to the men's group. "Please, all of you, introduce yourselves, and remember, there is coffee, tea, lemonade, and lots of cookies." She leaned closer. "Addy Clarkson baked most of them. She's the girl sitting between MJ and Ginny. She thrives on compliments."

One of the men snorted. "What woman doesn't?"

"On that note, I'll get back to my work." She returned to where MJ, Amalia, and Ginny were working.

"How do you know him?" MJ asked with a slight tone of accusation.

"He invited us out to his house for dinner."

Amalia studied Roxie very subtly. A mild blush rosied her cheeks. That tickled Amalia. Roxie was still too young to be a hermit.

"Did you have a good time?" MJ asked. Asked? Pried, as far as Amalia was concerned.

"We did, and we had wonderful food. Perfect day for eating outdoors."

"And?"

Roxie shrugged. "We talked and ate and came home."

Amalia could see Roxie's unease, so she stepped in. "And that young man is who was seen biking with Loren." It wasn't a question.

Roxie nodded and sent her a pleading look with a glance at Loren.

Amalia nodded, slowly but with a stealthy wink.

Thank you, Roxie mouthed back to her.

Amalia watched Ginny, trying to gauge how she was doing. She didn't have much to say, but the baby afghan was growing in her lap. She kept leaning over to help Addy with the dishcloth she was learning to knit, but the wrinkles in her forehead gave her away. *Hang in there, Ginny. The more often you do things out in public like this, the easier it will get. Turning into a mole slows the healing down.* She well remembered; she'd tried both ways.

"But, Grandma, what did I do wrong?" The plaintive cry made Amalia smile.

Ginny pointed to the dropped stitch. "Now we can use a crochet hook to pull it up and put it back on the knitting needles."

Addy handed her the yarn and needles. "Remind me why I wanted to learn to do this."

"Because your grandma makes it look so easy. I got hooked the same way." Loren shook her head. "But for me it was crocheting. She said it was easier." She gave her mother a look with a slight headshake.

Addy grinned at her. "And now you are doing pretty good."

"Most of the time. Until I try something new. Like this." Loren held up her piece. "I can't seem to make it come out right when I'm going to turn."

"Here, Addy, I'll show you how to catch the dropped stitch." With no effort, Ginny snagged the stitch with the hook and slipped the knitting needle through the loop.

"Seems ripping out is easier."

"You caught it before you did too many more rows, but if you hadn't, that might be true."

Addy shook her head. "Baking cookies is lots easier."

"It wasn't when you first started, remember?" Ginny laid her knitting down in her lap. "The egg broke on the floor and I made you clean it up."

"And I had trouble with the measuring spoons. I remember, but I don't think I will ever be able to knit and talk at the same time like all of you do."

Amalia laid her work on the table and stood up. "Need to move around before I get all stiffened up. Can I bring you anything?"

"Ice cream?" Addy grinned at her.

"Sorry, kiddo." Amalia patted Addy on the head.

A familiar woman stopped her. "You know, Amalia, we should start a group like this at our building. Surely the downstairs rec room is big enough to open it to the public like this, but in the daytime. Too many don't want to leave their apartments at night."

Amalia nodded. "Good idea. Why don't you talk to the manager and board and clear it with them. Then we can spread the word." She nodded again. "That's a very good idea." *I should have thought of that, but coming from someone else will be a lot better.* She was already known as a boat rocker for some strange reason.

She loaded a plate with various cookies, poured herself a lemonade, and returned to her chair. She leaned closer to MJ and Roxie. "These people are having a marvelous time. Listen to the laughter and the conversations. And a woman from my building just suggested we start one there. This just might be contagious. I mean, after all, we have a morning group already." She looked around. "Who is that over there with the camera?"

Roxie laughed. "I'll be...that's Grover Thurmond from the paper. You know—Rover Grover, their roving photographer. I wonder who is writing the column. I'm not. I've mentioned the UFOs twice so far in my columns, so I'd better lay off it awhile. Let Grover spread the word this time. Look. He's taking a photo of Rich Owens. What is Rich working on there, some sort of carving?"

Amalia smiled and nodded. "In a big way, we seem to be building community. Just think, it used to be quilting bees, but now we have UFOs."

"There are already how many quilting groups in Fond du Lac?" Roxie asked.

"At least two that I know of, The Quilting Guild and the one at the Lutheran Church, but all theirs go overseas for world relief." MJ laid her work down and stretched her fingers, then rolled her shoulders. "Anne isn't here tonight. I hope it wasn't an emergency that kept her away."

Maureen, the owner of the Yarn Shop, stopped beside MJ. "Do you think we need to give a signal that it's half an hour till closing?"

"Is it that time already?"

"'Fraid so. Usually I wouldn't care but that eight thirty class in the morning kind of cramps my style. Don't think I'll do that again, not that early at least."

"Not that I want to be nosy but..." MJ began.

Amalia accidentally snorted out loud.

MJ nudged her with her foot and rolled her eyes. "But did the last meeting bring you more sales during the off weeks?"

"Both sales and class signups. Enough to make this well worth my time. A couple of new people did not know my shop was even here. I know one was from out of town."

"Good." MJ nodded. "I'm glad. Daryl said the same thing; he hoped this benefited you. The funny, or rather, surprising thing is that article you posted on the bulletin board about the men who knit got his attention."

"Really?" Maureen glowed. "I'm going to order the books written by two young Norwegian men who travel the world talking about and teaching the European way of knitting. They are so fast. Wouldn't that be fun if on their next tour we got them to come here?"

Amalia gasped. "Are you kidding?"

"I was, but maybe I'm not. After all, it doesn't cost anything to ask."

Amalia could see the wheels turning in her mind. "Go for it. I'd sure come to listen to them and I am sure that taking a class from them would be a wild experience. They do teach, right?"

"They were at the Hostfest in Minot, North Dakota, last year. Some people from here who went raved about them. I just hadn't thought about inviting them here."

"If they came in May, they could perhaps do the Settendemae festivals too."

"MJ, you are a gold mine of ideas tonight."

"She's always really fine in the idea department." Amalia glanced around at the others. "Actually..." She nodded. "You have so many creative people here that the walls are pulsing with the energy."

"You're right. But how do we tap that?"

MJ stood up. She started to talk, but when no one noticed, Addy did her whistle again. The hush fell immediately. "Sorry to say but we need to be putting things away for tonight. We'll see you back here in two weeks. Happy UFO-ing. I hope we can include more pictures of finished projects for the columnist."

Amalia leaned over to whisper to Ginny, "You have done really well tonight. A major accomplishment."

"Th-thank you." Ginny sniffed. "I feel wrung out."

"Not surprising but you are moving forward anyway. Many people wouldn't."

Roxie nodded in agreement. "I remember telling my pastor I felt I should wear a sign on my back that said, KICK ME!"

"Why ever?" MJ asked.

"Because every time people were nice to me, it brought on the tears."

Ginny closed her eyes, silently nodding. "You're right," she whispered. "You are so very right."

Chapter Sixteen

O kay, my radar senses something is going on." MJ
and Roxie with their two furry family members
were halfway through their morning walk at a pace that
left them both with less breath to talk with.

"Ouch! Doggone it, Looper, you were doing so well."
MJ rubbed her shoulder. Looper lay on his tummy on
the sidewalk. He curled around and licked places polite
dogs do not lick, then squirmed a bit, apparently making
himself comfortable.

Roxie shook her head. "I think we wore him out."

"Looper, you cannot play flat basset just because
you've not had sniffy time." The look he gave her was
pure basset soulfulness. "No, I do not feel sorry for you."

"Aw, come on, MJ, how can you not." Roxie motioned
to Sir Charles, who sat panting. "And his legs are lots
longer than Looper's."

MJ leaned over to stroke her dog's long ears and
hopefully cajole him into moving.

"At least he's not in the middle of the street like last
time."

"Right. Come on, Looper, puppy treats at Annie's."
His ears perking up, he raised his head and lurched to

his feet. Even his whimper sounded like a child crying. "Good boy, we're almost there."

He and Sir Charles shared the dogs' big bowl of water outside the café and lay down, panting, in the shade.

"Blame Roxie, she set the pace. She's trying to walk all our legs off." MJ turned to her friend. "What's with you today anyhow?"

"Think I'll have my latte iced this morning." Roxie pushed open the door and set off the tinkling bell above it. "Ah, cool air."

"Missed you last night," Roxie greeted Anne.

"I know. We had a catering gig, and for some crazy reason, business has to come first."

Roxie nodded and rolled her shoulders. "I know, pathetic, isn't it? But I'm glad you are getting known for your catering. You do an excellent job."

"Thank you. So what will you two lovely ladies have this morning?"

They gave her their orders and moved to their table under the painting. They could hear the buzz of conversation and laughter from the back room.

"The Business Women are meeting back there," Anne replied when they asked. "They've opted to have their monthly meeting here."

"Good."

"We set up a coffee table with rolls and whatever they ask for, in advance, of course."

"You are getting more and more business. I am thrilled for you." Roxie nodded. "Are you doing lunch groups too?"

"I will if a group wants to. Why?"

"Thinking of the Realtors meeting, but there might be too many."

Anne set their drinks and orange rolls in front of them and took the coffee carafe to another table.

"Hey, Roxie, how was your ice cream date last night?" a woman called from a couple of tables away.

"Fine, they have good ice cream." Roxie flinched inside. Here it came.

MJ tipped her head forward to look at her over her glasses. "So that's where you went last night."

"Nate wanted to take Loren out for ice cream so we went along. Before you ask, 'we' is his dad and me."

"Really? A date?"

"Hardly, we went for ice cream."

"And had dinner at his house on Sunday, after Loren and Nate went bicycling?"

Roxie leaned forward. "Nate is really interested in Loren. I think seriously interested."

"Really? You mean...?"

"Oh, I hope so. I want her to be in a good relationship so bad." She was bursting to tell MJ the whole story but not here, where others might overhear.

"Face it, Roxie, you just want her to be happy."

"I know, how well I know. Not that she isn't now but..." She heaved a sigh. "I know we all want the best for our kids and life is so short."

"Not to them it isn't."

"I know, didn't used to be to me either, but losing Fred so abruptly really brought home to me that we never know how much time we get here on earth. You'd have thought I figured it out when Greg passed away so young, so perhaps this just exacerbated the knowledge. I mean, what if something happens to me sooner rather than later? It can, you know. After all, look at Fred."

"My word, but isn't this a bit morbid for such a glorious Tuesday morning? Not like you, not at all." MJ paused to savor the orange roll.

"Well, you asked, so there you have it." Leaning back in her chair, Roxie continued to nod her head.

"I guess." MJ wiped her fingers on her napkin. "My, but those rolls are good. Think I'll take one home for Daryl. He's been grumpy lately. This will fix it."

"Grumpy? I can't picture Daryl grumpy."

"He hit a snag on some project, and his car needs new shocks, and his favorite TV show was canceled. You know, a pile of little things. And I haven't been a bucket of cheer myself."

"Your car needs shocks too?"

MJ smiled briefly. "Late spring is the busiest time where I used to work as we geared up for summer. Ten-hour days making the business sing when it's practically tone deaf. So many things ended, for Daryl and me both. But are our lives finished? Productively, I mean. I sometimes wonder if I'm just another UFO." She suddenly sat up straighter. "Enough of this. I'm being just as morbid as you were. You showing any houses today?"

"This afternoon. I think I found the perfect one for them. Now we'll see if they agree." She pushed back her chair. "Come on." *Well, got around that one.* Whatever made her not want to tell MJ about Rich? After all, she was her best friend. They told each other most everything. And a horrible thought struck her. Was she jealous? She thought about last night, when MJ bounced right over to greet Rich and Nate when they came in. She greeted everyone—why did this bother Roxie so much? Possibly it was because MJ so easily took command of a situation without even trying to. What if…? Oh, that was silly!

Out the door they gave the dogs their crunchy treats and headed back home, grateful for the shade trees lining the streets. "You going to work on your crewel project today?"

MJ nodded. "Hope so. You know that drive to finish something once you get in the mood? Well, I have a bad case of it, and it is all the fault of our UFO group. Whoever dreamed it would affect me this much? Daryl hasn't left his shop other than for meals, and I'm sure if I volunteered to bring his out there, he'd agree."

"See, all kinds of good things happening."

MJ agreed. "All because you heard about it and we started one. Goes to show we have no idea what works and what doesn't. And you?"

"Might be able to find time after the showing. Depends on whether they want to make an offer or not. See ya." Roxie let Sir Charles free in the backyard so he could drink from the faucet, his favorite waterer. Stopping for a moment on the deck, she looked over her backyard. It might be relatively small but now that the flowers were starting to bloom, it grew lovelier every day. The geranium pots on the deck, the planters attached to the deck railing, the cherry tree about to burst into a glory of pink blossoms. One thing for sure, when the snow finally melted and spring came to Wisconsin, everything grew so fast, you could almost measure it. Her thoughts flew to the stunning place they had visited on Sunday. Like out of a magazine. Juno the cat called her to stop mooning on the deck and let her out. The indignity of being left in the house when *the Dog* wasn't was difficult to ignore.

"Oh, give it a rest." Roxie scooped up the fluffy critter and cuddled her under her chin. "You know, you're getting heavy. Maybe we better put you on a diet." She let the cat down, slid the screen door closed, tried to ignore Sir Charles's whine, gave it up, let him in, and now closed and locked the door. Not so much as she was concerned about someone breaking in but because she did not want her animals outside when she was gone. To her amazement, one of them had learned to open the screen door.

The buyers' appointment that afternoon went smoothly. She took the couple through the house again, as they requested, answered more questions, pointed out some things she might have missed before, and waited patiently, a skill she had developed over the years. People do not like to be rushed. When they turned to her with wide smiles, she knew it was a go.

"So, you would like to make an offer."

"We would." The woman pulled a list from her shoulder bag and handed it to Roxie. "These we would like them to leave, these to fix, and whatever price we come to an agreement on, we will pay half down. As you know, we are already approved. Oh, and it all depends on the inspection."

"Of course." Roxie already knew the inspection was clear but the formalities had to be gone through for the bank's sake. She read the list and smiled. The washer and dryer were really recent additions since the owners had remodeled the house in the last three years. "So what is your offer?"

They named an amount twenty thousand under the asking price, but with half down, they might get away with it. "You realize we are in a sellers' market right now?"

They nodded. They were moving here from out of state and wanted to close ASAP.

Roxie asked, "Anything on here a deal breaker?"

The woman looked to her husband, who shrugged.

"All right then, I will get your offer to them and we should have a counteroffer by tomorrow."

"Unless they accept everything and..." The woman looked hopeful.

"True. Do you have any other questions?"

"Not that I can think of."

"She'll come up with more in the middle of the night." The husband gave a slight shake of his head.

"Well, write them down. Sorry, I don't take middle-of-the-night-question calls." Roxie grinned at both of them. "But I am up at six a.m." She caught the nudge he gave his wife and turned to escort them out of the house. "I'll get back to you as soon as I hear anything."

Back home, she filled out all the paperwork and e-mailed the proposal to the owners, who were visiting one of their kids in Ohio to see a new grandbaby and looking for a new home there. The response came back so quickly, she didn't have time to go pour herself some iced tea.

Their response:

Thank you. We have found a house here and put it on contingency so the sooner we can sign the papers, the better. We will leave for home in the morning and get to packing. So, yes, we accept the offer. I hope they will love that house like we have.

Roxie reread the response. Not only did this promise to be close to the fastest turnaround she had ever done, but she had just brokered a blessing to two families. And since she handled this for both the seller and the buyer, this promised to be a lucrative sale. This called for a celebration. A picture of Rich licking his cone of rocky road ice cream last night danced into her head. "What?"

Sir Charles rose and came to put his head on her thigh, feathery tail wagging. He stared up at her as if asking if she was all right.

She stroked his head and fluffed his ears. "It's okay, big boy. I'm just surprised, that's all. Why would I think of Rich at the same time as celebrating? It isn't like he's a deep friend or anything. Just a nice guy who happens to be the dad of the young man who is making Loren try new things and have a good time." She leaned her cheek against the top of his head. "You and I and Juno just might be getting ready to live here by ourselves. Now, that will take some adjusting."

Sir Charles reared up and put his front feet on her lap, staring at her all the while. She hugged him and got her cheek washed for her efforts.

"You are such a good dog, you know that?" She rubbed his chest and under his chin. "I bet you want to go outside."

He dropped to his feet and headed for the door.

Downstairs she slid open the screen door to let both animals outside, then put ice in a glass and filled it with raspberry-flavored lemonade. She stared into the refrigerator. "What are we going to have for supper?" Nothing looked appealing. Same with the freezer.

She called Loren as she took her glass out to the deck. "Hey, you have any preferences for supper?"

"Fried chicken. Want me to stop and get dinner?"

"Oh, bless you, yes. Remember a pint of coleslaw. I have great news when you get here."

"Mother, you know how I hate it when you do that. Oops, I gotta go. See you in an hour or so."

Roxie chuckled to herself. Even Loren's voice sounded more chipper lately. She moved over to the chaise lounge and sank into its comfort. This might be a good time to work on her project. She watched two male humming-birds duking it out over the feeder. "Come on, guys, get along. See how much energy you waste?" They flew off and a female came and perched to drink in comfort. "Good for you. Smart woman." She left the drink on the table between the two loungers and headed to get her bag. If MJ could get hooked on finishing, perhaps it could happen to her too. *Wait, you better go get that paperwork together. That's much more important right now.* Some-times she wanted to strangle that self-righteous, bossy voice in her head. She left her bag and climbed the stairs to her office. She was deep in the well of paperwork when her phone chimed again. She toyed with letting it go to voice mail, but when she glanced at the screen, Rich's name came up. A little wiggle of pleasure crept up her spine. He had a nice deep telephone voice.

After the greetings, he continued, "There's a movie in town I've been wanting to see, and no, it is not a shoot-'em-up action adventure."

"Good thing."

"Figured you'd think that." He gave her the title. "Have you heard of it?"

"Sorry, I don't watch a lot of TV so I don't see the trailers and advertising."

"It's getting good reviews. I thought to go on Friday—are you interested?"

She glanced at her desk calendar. "Seven o'clock showing?"

"Yep. I thought we could catch a bite to eat at the Fond du Flavor first."

"Okay, sounds good to me." She sucked in a deep breath to slow her heart back down. *This is a real date. I've not gone on a date for years.*

His chuckle made her smile back. "I'll pick you up at five fifteen or so. Good, now that that's out of the way, how's your day going?"

"I sold a house today."

"That's great! Good for you. So what are you going to do to celebrate?"

"I was just wondering the same thing, deep in all the paperwork right now. Since I listed the house too, that means a lot of it."

"Nate said you are one of the top Realtors in Fond du Lac."

"Well, I don't know about that, but I've been at this for a long time, so I know the ropes and am well known."

"I tried to talk Nate into buying a house, but he said he's not ready for that yet. This house is pretty big since he moved out."

"Are you in your car?"

"Yep, left a bit early tonight. I'm going to work on one of my UFOs. It's not one I can take to the meeting. I started to build a storage unit in the boathouse last summer, so I'll see how far I can get."

"You too? MJ is pushing like crazy to get hers done. I was going to work on mine but the guilts got me and I came up here to work."

"Well, you know the old saying, all work and no play…"

"I know but these folks are so anxious to get this settled. Well, actually, both seller and buyer are. One is moving out of the area and the other moving in."

"Good for you. Good talking with you, see you on Friday."

"Yes, I'm looking forward to it. Thank you." They clicked off and she stared at her cell phone. "I have a movie date." She heard Sir Charles bark at the door. "Coming." She slid open the screen door and Juno entered with tail straight in the air. "Oh, knock it off, your highness, you haven't been waiting that long. Good boy, Sir Charles, I know, I know, supper time." She poured water over his kibble and made him sit and wait until she told him it was okay. The cat sniffed her dish, glared at Roxie, and crouched down to eat her wet food. The kibble was always up on the dryer for her.

She should go back upstairs and finish that paperwork. Later. "Don't you know we are supposed to be celebrating? I sold a house so I can buy your food, be grateful." She poured herself another glass of iced tea and went out to sit on the deck again, this time with the newspaper to catch up on the news, as always starting with the comics. She used to do the crossword puzzle every day but that was in the morning and now she and MJ walked instead.

When she heard the garage door go up, she folded the paper and went in to set out serving spoons, plates, and napkins. They'd dish up their plates in here and eat out on the deck.

Loren held up the bags so Sir Charles couldn't sniff them. "Here, please take these. I've got more to get out of the car."

Roxie inhaled the yummy fragrance as she opened the containers and put in serving spoons.

"We put out a sale table today at the library so I picked up some for us. Here's some of Louise Penny, and a couple of new mystery writers I thought you might like. After all, at twenty-five cents a book, we can't exactly go wrong."

"Oh, good."

Loren crossed to the sink to wash her hands.

"So how was your day?"

"Fine, now what great news do you have?"

"I sold that house. The sellers didn't even blink at the offer. They were so pleased because they have found a house near their kids so they are hoping both places close quickly. And the buyers love the house and now they're going home to start packing too. Glad it's them and not me."

"That's great, Mom. Sort of like double dipping, isn't it?"

"Yup. Was trying to decide what we will do this time." They had a tradition that she used some of the money from each sale to do an extra project around the house or yard. The rug was the last splurge.

They dished up their plates and took them out to the table. Sir Charles lay down between their chairs, always in the hope they might drop something.

"Guess who called today?" Loren said.

"Nate."

"Uh-huh. Asked if we could meet for lunch tomorrow."

"So where are you going?"

Loren shrugged. "It has to be someplace fast."

"Annie's?"

"I thought of that. More chicken? I'll get it. Anything else?"

"Bring the coleslaw out here, please. I brought some of Addy's cookies home last night. When I paid her for them, she was surprised. I told her she needs to think about that, filling orders and charging a decent price. She learned that from Ginny. You know Ginny, she'd give away everything. She never lets me pay for the eggs."

Should she tell Loren about her movie date for Friday? Why wouldn't she? Why did her date, an actual movie date, feel so private, a secret to savor, not share? She thought about that little tingle of pleasure she felt when Rich walked in last night. And here she was acting like an eighth grader with her first crush. *Roxie, Roxie, whatever is the matter with you?*

Chapter Seventeen

I can sleep in here, really I can.

Ginny forced her hands to release from the doorframe, one finger at a time. Addy had gone downstairs to sleep like she always did. Ginny made the excuse that she just wasn't ready to go to bed yet. So she sat in the living room and forced herself to pick up her knitting. It always helped her relax. She said she could knit in her sleep, just like she could transplant seedlings in her sleep.

She turned the gentle classical music station on so she could just hear it, something that usually helped her drift off. After dropping two stitches, she laid the knitting down and rubbed her eyes. Head back against the headrest on her recliner, her scratchy eyes drifted closed. The music played on.

Who turned on the AC? Another shiver brought her awake enough to realize where she was. In the living room, the sliding door open partway, good thing the screen door was locked. No wonder she was chilled. The big question, pick up the afghan from the back of the sofa and go back to sleep here or...or go to the bathroom. That always took precedence.

Standing in front of the mirror, she glared at the sleepy-looking face. "You will now get undressed, go into your bedroom, and go to sleep in the bed!" Yes, she ordered herself to do that. *Lord, help me.* She whistled for Spook. He would be more than happy to sleep on the bed. He charged up the stairs and skidded to sit in front of her in the hallway. "Come on, boy, let's go to bed." With him by her side, she marched into the room, folded back the spread, and reminding herself to breathe, slipped under the sheet and summer blanket. "Come on, Spook." She patted the bed, and with a grand leap, he stretched out beside her, head on her chest. "I know this isn't normal, but tonight we start a new normal." Refusing to let herself look around the room, now lit by moonlight, she rolled over and laid her arm over the furry body. "Good boy." For that she got a chin lick.

In the midst of the storm, praise Him! She'd read that somewhere. The words clogged in her throat. She swallowed. Whispering, she forced them out. "Thank you, Lord, for Spook, for getting in this bed. Thank you for Addy downstairs." The tears welled and seeped into her pillow.

Spook whimpered.

"Thank you for You, Jesus. Lord God, I praise Your mighty name. You promised to be here when I call, Lord Jesus, hold me close. You said You hold me in Your hand and keep me safe. Jesus. Jesus. Jesus. You said Your name is all powerful"—a song she had learned years earlier trickled through her mind—"there's just something about that name."

Spook snuffled and snored. *Please help me sleep, stop crying, get through.* Like a sweet balm, a voice whispered in her heart and mind. "I am here, I will never leave you, you are my beloved daughter. My love never leaves and never ends. Rest, sleep in my arms where you are safe."

Birds singing in the tree outside her window slowly woke her up. She lay there, Spook now at her feet, and breathed in the peace of the morning. *What is that fragrance?* she wondered, still not opening her eyes. She felt like she was floating in warm water, like the time they had gone to Florida. The rooster crowed. *What time is it? I don't want to know. I want to float longer.*

Spook whimpered and pawed at her leg.

"I know, you need to go out. Shame we never put in a doggy door for you." But then Fred never minded getting up early to let the dog out, not even in the winter. He loved greeting the morning.

For a change, thoughts of him did not make her cry. She sat up and swung her legs over the edge of the bed, feeling for her slippers. "Come on, boy. Out the kitchen door." Standing in the doorway, she watched a pair of robins fight in midair, flapping at each other. One fled, leaving a brightly rust-breasted male the victor. He returned to a perch in the crabapple tree. The tree was showing color on the buds. She needed to make crabapple pickles again this year when they were out. Fred loved pickled crabapples.

"Will this be the rest of my life, thinking of Fred and what he likes—liked?"

Spook barreled past her to his dish, then stared at her with a sharp bark. "I know, your food is not in your dish. Sorry, sir. I'm falling down on the job." She snagged a tissue off the box on the counter, blew her nose, wiped her eyes, and heaved a sigh. The cat had padded upstairs from sleeping with Addy at the sound of the refrigerator door opening. Cat food, dog food, fill the water bowl, make the coffee. Build a new morning routine. So far, Amalia had taken over the morning chores. *Today I am going to learn how to set the coffeemaker the night before so I can wake up to the smell of coffee.*

She grabbed her robe off the hook in the bathroom, slid her feet into her boots, and dog at her side, headed for the chicken house. She'd heard of a solar-powered gizmo to open the chicken house door at whatever time she set it. Might just be worth looking into.

Good thing she could open the door from the outside. She'd still not been able to force herself to go into the chicken house. Today was not going to be the day. Addy would gladly feed the chickens and collect the eggs. She left the gate to the chicken yard open so they would have free range like they usually did. Surely today she would see the hens drinking out of the low bird bath. One time she'd gotten a picture of them gathered around the concrete bath. The wild birds were not enthusiastic about sharing their bath with the big domestic birds.

In the barn, she dug grain out of the bin, dumped some in the manger for the pony and the donkey, and after throwing a couple flakes of hay in the steer feeder, poured a can of grain on top of that. "There you go, boys. Sorry to be late." Last stop was Boss Lady, the Hereford cow, and her heifer calf, Bets. Fred had named her, after they had bet on the sex of the calf before it was born. This was Boss Lady's first year to have a heifer, and they had planned to keep her. She was now

two months old and still not real sure about those crit-
ters that walked on two legs.

Ginny had asked Addy to come down and brush
Magic and Smoky. The kids used to ride them but had
pretty much outgrown them. They had talked about
buying a couple of horses so they could go riding, Addy
loved to ride and so did Andy. Ginny did too. Perhaps
if they—she—did, it would help loosen up her hips.
Something more to think about.

The bottom of her robe was wet from the dew on the
grass, but instead of going to change, she poured herself
a cup of coffee and took it out on the deck, where the
lounge beckoned her. Spook flopped down beside her
and started licking the wet off his feet. With a plaintive
mee-ow, the cat jumped up on her legs and walked up
to curl in her sort of lap.

A perfect morning like this, she and Fred would have
done this same thing. But while he was doing chores,
she would fix them some breakfast and they'd eat out
here at the table with the umbrella up. It was bungeed
closed. Amalia sat out here and must have closed up the
umbrella. Fred had brought it out from the storage in
the garage and inserted it in the hole. Usually she would
have washed it first. Whatever good that usually did.

She could hear her cell phone ringing in the bedroom. *Get up? No. Ignore for now.* She could always call
back. It quieted. But after a brief pause, long enough to
leave a message, it rang again and repeated the process.
"All right, all right, I'm coming."

"Grandma!" Addy came barreling up the stairs.
"Grandma!"

"I am right here. What's the matter?"

"Dad called me. He said he called and called and you didn't answer. I have to call him back if you're all right."

"Yes, I'm fine. My phone is in the bedroom and I was out on the deck and too lazy to get up to answer."

Addy punched a number and held the phone to her ear. "Easy, Dad, she's fine, she's right here." She inhaled deeply to catch her breath again, and handed the phone to her grandmother. "You talk to him."

"Sam, Sam, I'm all right. I was out on the deck and left my phone in the bedroom. I just figured I'd call back."

"For crying out loud, Mom, after all we've been through, how could I not hit the panic button? You promised to keep your phone with you all the time. *And* you are supposed to call when you get up."

"Did I agree to that?" Ginny tried to think when she would have said she'd call.

"Amalia has been doing so, but since she's not there, I guess I assumed you would do the same. And Addy..."

"Was still sound asleep." She glanced at the clock as Addy went back inside, disappearing downstairs. "After all, it's barely eight o'clock. Give us a break." She heard him suck in a deep breath. "If she hadn't answered when she did, I was heading for the truck. If you had one of the alarm buttons you wear around your neck, I'd have known if you were in trouble."

She started to tell him all she'd already done but none of it sounded significant enough. After all, the chores were part of the ordinary. Well, not anymore. Fred did all those things before...Would her life always be defined that way? BFD. Before Fred died. And AFD.

"I do not want one of those alarms."

"Yeah, well, Dad refused to have one too. He and I talked about it, or rather I talked about it and he shook his head." The silence screamed at her.

"Look, can we talk about this later? I would like to go get dressed and—"

"If Addy just got up…I'll be right over to do the chores. Or put her back on; she can go do the chores."

"I already did them. Well, most of them. I can't make myself go in the chicken house." She whispered the last words and sniffed back the immediate barrage of tears. "S-sorry. I'll call you back later." She pushed the Off button and laid the phone on the counter so she could blow her nose. *You have to stop crying before Addy comes back up. A few tears are one thing; a deluge could be scary.* It was all she could do to stagger into the bedroom and shut the door before throwing herself across the bed. Spook had gone from whimper to all-out bark before it registered.

"Grandma, are you all right?" Addy pounded on the door and rattled the knob. "Grandma!"

"Sorry, I'm coming." *No, I'm not. I knew having her here was not a good idea. Don't be stupid. She's a big girl now. Let her know what is happening. She can handle it.* She wanted to scream, "Shut up!" but sucked in a deep breath instead. "It's okay, Addy, I just had a crying jag. Do not call your dad, this just happens sometimes."

"You sure?"

Ginny could tell that her darling granddaughter was crying now. *Go to her.* Ginny blew her nose again as she crossed the room to the door. "It's okay, baby. I'm okay." How she had managed to push the lock button when she shut the door was beyond her, but then, right now, too many things were beyond her. She opened the door and pulled her granddaughter into her arms. "I'm sorry, I'm so sorry. But sometimes the grief just overwhelms me. Not quite so much anymore but I should have warned you. Pastor Mike said this is normal. Amalia said the same thing. I guess until you go through it yourself, you don't know."

"But, Grandma, I miss him too, so much that sometimes I want to scream at God. This is so not fair. I need my grandpa."

"I've already been yelling at Him, but you know, it is not God's fault."

"He's the only one who could have stopped it."

"Come on, let's go to the recliner." She sat first and Addy snuggled in beside her like they had done for so many years.

"We don't fit so good anymore." She sniffed and reached for a tissue. "Grandma, how come nobody wants to talk about Grandpa?"

"Ah, sweetie, it's because it hurts too bad, and they don't want to cry anymore. I don't either, but saying that doesn't do any good. I just cry—and cry. But I guess that is the way of...of grieving for someone you love so."

Addy's nodding head rubbed against her shoulder. "I remember when our baby died. I didn't think Mom would ever quit crying."

"You were pretty little then."

"I know, but I'll never forget."

"We don't forget, but after a while, it doesn't hurt so much." Ginny sucked in a breath. "I keep telling myself, this will be that way too, but right now..."

"Right now it seems to go on forever."

"Ah, Addy, you are so young to know that."

Addy shrugged and wiped a leftover tear from her grandma's cheek. "I love you, Grandma. I love you so much."

"I love you, baby, so very much, and so does your grandpa." Ginny reached for the tissue box and plopped it between them.

Spook barked his high-pitched *I want to help you* bark and planted both front feet on Ginny's thigh. He leaned forward to kiss Addy's tears away and then Ginny's. Both of them laughed, while Addy reached out and hugged the dog.

"Sorry, boy, didn't mean to ignore you. And you can't get up here because I am in your place."

Instead, he launched himself and landed right on Ginny. "Oof. Get down, you big lug."

But instead he leaned forward and tried to wash the rest of her face. She pushed him away. "Okay, this is it. We all get up before I am totally squished beneath a seventy-pound dog and an almost teenage girl."

Addy laughed and ordered the dog off too as she pushed herself upright. "That recliner just isn't big enough anymore. Come on, Spook, puppy treats?"

He beat her to the kitchen.

Ginny sucked in a breath and pushed it out. At least the tears had dried up. She stood and made her way to the bathroom for a cold wet cloth.

"Grandma, did you let the chickens out?"

"I did but I didn't feed them."

"I'll do that while you get dressed and then we can make breakfast, okay?"

Ginny smiled. "Fine, what would you like?"

"Can we have French toast?"

"We can, and sausage?"

"Yay!" She flew out the door, calling for Spook to come too.

Drained was the only word Ginny could think of. Like someone had pulled the plug and all her energy had gurgled down the drain. She held the cloth up to her face, wet it again, and did the same. Sinking down on the closed toilet seat, she leaned against the tank and let the coolness trickle down her neck. Her phone, now in her robe pocket, sang to her. She checked the screen, not daring a repeat from earlier.

"Hi, Amalia."

"Are you all right?"

"Getting there, why?"

"Your voice, and Sam called."

"Oh. I scared him by not answering my phone." Roxie felt bad about that now.

"Uh-huh. He about hit 911."

"He didn't."

"No, but he came close. The fact that he told me, that was the surprising part. You know his idea of the call button is not a bad one."

"Oh, for... Now that is playing dirty, enlisting my friends."

"I've thought about it. I would have gotten one had I stayed out on the farm."

Ginny's head shook without her volition.

"Where are you?" Amalia asked.

"Sitting on the john with a cold cloth that is now warm."

"Bad bout?"

"Yes, but I did manage to spend at least part of the night in our—my—bed. Spook kept me company."

"Bless that dog."

"I know. Thanks to him, I woke up to birds singing and got up and then went down to do the chores. After I fed him and the cat, of course."

"Did you go in the chicken house?" Amalia asked.

"Ah, no. But I opened their door and fed the rest of the animals. Addy is down feeding the chickens now."

"She's okay?"

"Yes, we had a good talk after I fell apart—again. Amalia, I tried so hard not to."

"And that only makes it worse."

"I know. I *am* learning, albeit slowly."

Amalia's voice soothed. "Ginny, life is not a contest to see how quickly we learn, which is an incredible gift from our God, who wants to help us grow. He never says, 'Hurry up.'"

Ginny blew out a breath. "Well, this seat is getting rather hard. I'll talk with you later. Got to get dressed and Addy wants French toast."

"Good for you both. Later." Amalia clicked off.

"Thank you, Lord, for my wonderful friends and family." She sniffed. "I take too much for granted. Way too much. Sorry, Father."

She was in the kitchen getting out the griddle when Addy and Spook burst through the door, the girl laughing, the dog yipping and bouncing.

"I won!" she announced.

"Won what?"

"I challenged Spook to a race up here and I won."

He sat at her feet, tongue lolling in a doggy grin.

"He thinks he won." Ginny nodded at him. "You better get him a puppy treat after accusing him like that." She pinched a large piece off the sausage for each patty. "You can start the egg and milk to dip the bread in. I use a pie pan."

This time she let the tears drip. French toast and sausage was one of Fred's favorite breakfasts. Today they would have it in celebration of him. "Make sure you pour orange juice too."

"Okay. Grandma, you're crying again."

"Nope, just drippy eyes." She sniffed and smiled through her tears. "Please hand me a tissue."

"Your hands are all greasy. You want me to wipe your nose for you?" Concern wrinkled her forehead.

"You think you can?"

"Grandma, I babysat the neighbor's baby, and he doesn't like to have his nose wiped. I'm sure you'll hold still."

Ginny snorted, then burst out laughing. "I can't believe this." She held still so Addy could finish her self-assigned job. "Thank you. Shoot, and I can't even hug you."

"Sure you can, just don't wipe your greasy hands on my shirt." They reached for each other, amid more laughter and tears.

Am I crying because I am sad or because this is so very crazy? Surely the latter.

Chapter Eighteen

Y ou know, this is the first time I've been on a date in, oh, ten years or more."

"Really?" Roxie leaned her head back on the car seat. "Let's see. My husband died sixteen years ago, and the last years when he was fighting cancer for his life, we did not do any dating. So that means, if you don't count husband-wife date nights, not that we called them that back then, I've not been on a date for...ah, let's talk about something else."

Rich burst out laughing. "Ha! You don't want to tell me how old you are. I am fifty-nine years old and proud of it."

"All right, smarty, I am fifty-four and proud of it. Turning fifty was the best birthday of my life."

He chuckled. "Well, how about us two old fogies going to the drive-in for milk shakes?"

"We could never afford milk shakes; we drank Cherry Cokes."

"You suppose they still make those?"

She shrugged. "I guess. Did you ever drink a Green River?"

"Now, that's a name I've not heard for a whole bunch of years."

"That was my favorite, Cherry Coke second."

He started the SUV. "Here we go down memory lane." When they arrived at the drive-in and gave their order for two Green Rivers, the mike went silent.

"Ah, did I hear you right? Green Rivers?"

"Yes." He grinned at Roxie, who was having a hard time keeping quiet.

"Ah, could you give me a bit more information? This is a fountain drink?"

"Yes."

Roxie thumped him on the upper arm and mouthed, *You are teasing him.* He nodded back.

"You could Google it probably for the recipe. I'm not sure what it is made from, other than fizzy water."

"I see. Give me a moment, please." The mike clicked off.

Rich nudged her and whispered, "You started this."

"I did not. I said a Cherry Coke."

"They most likely have that."

"And French fries," she added. "You have to have French fries with a Cherry Coke."

"Whatever."

"Come on, where's your party spirit?"

"Under the seat. It went into hiding when the kid didn't know what a Green River is."

The speaker clicked back on. "I—I'm sorry sir, but we do not have the proper ingredients for...for..."

"A Green River." His tone oozed helpfulness.

"Yes. Can I get you something else?" Hope reddened his request.

"Well, I'm really disappointed you do not have the ingredients for our Green Rivers but I know you have at least part of a Cherry Coke."

"Yes, sir, we do have that. What size?" Relief sounded a lot like pleading.

"I'd like two large Cherry Cokes and an order of fries."

Roxie held up two fingers and pointed to herself. He nodded.

"Two orders of fries."

"Ketchup?"

"Please."

When the speaker clicked off again, he turned to Roxie. "I didn't think to ask if you were hungry. I mean, we could order hamburgers or something."

"Fries and a Cherry Coke are plenty." She half turned and leaned against the door, one knee up on the seat. "So, how was your day?"

"Great, but then I have decided that every day I wake up breathing well, I have a roof over my head, a job to go to, friends and family, everything is all right with my world and I rejoice." His voice deepened. "Roxie, I am so grateful, I can't begin to verbalize it all and even more so now."

"What do you mean?"

"Oh, good, our order is here." He rolled his window down and dug his wallet out of his pocket. "Thank you, this looks great. That's how much?" He handed the server a bill and waved. "No change needed, thanks."

"Thank you, sir. Let us know if we can get you anything else." His smile lit up his face.

He must have given him a big tip, Roxie thought, to get a smile like that. One more mark in his favor. Whatever was she doing, keeping score? She took her sleeve of French fries and nestled her drink in the drink holder on the console. "Thanks but no ketchup," she answered in response to his questioning look.

"Good, then more for me." He handed her a napkin and straw. "A Cherry Coke. Do you think I'll like it as much as I used to?"

"Don't know. Last one I tried was pretty sweet." She stabbed her straw in the slash in the lid and watched as he took a swallow. He blinked and made a face.

"You're right! Sweet it is." This time he sipped. "But drinkable."

"The fries must have just come out of the fryer. They are good."

"I like mine hot too. You realize how many things we have in common?" He dangled a ketchup-laden fry over his open mouth and sighed in delight. "I never order fries anymore. That's one thing about getting older. My eating habits have had to change a bit."

"So, on a scale of one to ten, ten being high, what did you think of the movie?" She savored another fry.

"Hmm. Ten high. I'd say, oh, a seven point five, no, make that an eight. I'm glad I saw it; there's something about the big screen rather than on the TV at home, no matter what size the screen is. And you?"

She nodded while chewing on another fry. "I'm not sure how many movies I've given a ten to, but not a lot, so usually my high is nine. That would put this one about seven. Really good but not 'fantastic, superb, I want to see it again and tell all my friends.'"

"Now that's a really good definition. Can you repeat that, please? I should write it down."

"A cold drink and hot fries. What more can one ask for?" and she wasn't being completely facetious.

"In life in general?"

"No, for a trip to the drive-in." She didn't finish verbalizing her thought. *With a good-looking guy who has a good sense of humor and is a pleasure to be around.*

He set his drink back in the holder. "What are you doing this weekend?"

"On Saturday, Loren and I are going garage sale-ing, then I have a date with a prospective buyer to tour possible houses."

"I see. And Sunday?"

"Church first, then I'm not sure. I was thinking of going out to see Ginny."

"How is she doing?"

Roxie shrugged. "About as well as can be expected, I guess. Trying to adjust. Amalia spent much of the last couple of weeks out there with her, since her kids other than Sam went back home. Come to think of it, almost a month has passed since Fred died." Just saying the words caused a grab in her throat.

"There are a lot of people in this area who miss him. Nate and I were talking. I think Fred touched more lives than anyone realized. I've never seen that big a funeral here before."

"How did you know him?"

"Through a friend of mine. I commented on his garden one time and he said Fred and Ginny gave them many plant starts, he had the best tomatoes around, said Fred kept his own seeds from his grandpa's gardens. I guess they call tomatoes like that heritage, no, that's not right."

"Heirloom? Do you plant a garden?"

"Not a very big one anymore. Gloria, my ex, still makes my strawberry and peach freezer jams, blueberry syrup, and hamburger pickles. I provide the produce. Oh, and she makes great salsa."

"Really?"

"I know, it is really strange, but we are the best of friends; we just couldn't live together. I thought after she married again, that some of these things would change, but Norm is a grand guy, so we're all friends."

Roxie nodded. "You know how amazing that is?"

"I think I do." He nodded and half shrugged. "Another thing to be grateful for. When the children were still at home, they spent time at both of our houses, easy since our houses are so close together. I don't tell a lot of people because they'd think I am making it up." He flashed his lights for them to pick up the tray.

"Would you like to go sailing Sunday afternoon, if there is a breeze and no rain? I never have enjoyed boating in wet weather. A good wind is another thing."

Roxie nodded without needing time to think. "Thanks, I would love that."

"Have you ever crewed before?"

"Nope."

"I'll ask Nate to come and he'll ask Loren and... make sure you bring a windbreaker and wear nonslip shoes."

At the end of the date, he walked her to her door and smiled down at her. "Thank you for a really great evening. See you Sunday." He bobbed his head once and headed for his SUV. Halfway there, he turned around and blew her a kiss. "Night."

Roxie let herself in the quiet house and leaned against the door after closing it. And here she'd been wondering what it would be like to kiss him. She needn't have been concerned after all, not that she'd spent a lot of time thinking about it. "Hey, Sir Charles, where's Loren?" She peeked in the family room but the TV was dark. Surely she hadn't gone to bed already. Checking the kitchen counter where they left messages as to where they were, she found a note that said:

> Remember we are going to hit the garage sales. Leave here at 6:45. Breakfast at Annie's, post garage sales.

A bit cryptic but typically Loren.

The cat greeted her with a chirp and winding around her legs. Still smiling, Roxie scooped up Juno and headed for the stairs. Sure enough, Loren was sound asleep. How strange. She wasn't sick, was she? Roxie almost let her mother instincts take over but instead went on to her room and got ready for bed. Garage sales started at seven, as in a.m. That's why Loren went to bed early. Juno jumped up on the bed and Sir Charles flopped on the rug beside it. He knew that only by invitation was he allowed on the beds. And those invitations usually came from Loren.

❖   ❖   ❖

Morning came quickly, and Roxie had not dreamt of Rich at all. Of course not. He was very nice, but no dreamboat.

"You have the map and the list?" Roxie called to Loren as she finished putting on her makeup.

"Yes and the coffee jugs."

"Did you feed the animals?"

"Yes, come on, Mom, you're making us late."

Roxie added earrings and grabbed her leather bag on her way to the car, now out in the driveway. "You want to drive?"

"Fine with me, you navigate." Loren swung into the driver's seat.

Roxie looked at the map. "You already have our route laid out, good girl."

"So, did you have fun last night?" Loren twisted to back out.

"I did. He's a good guy. He asked if I'd like to go sailing on Sunday."

"You better have said yes." They got out onto the street and headed west.

"Loren, you sound like a mom." She glanced at the map. "Turn right here." There were already cars parked and people getting out. She recognized several as antique dealers who were almost always the first at the sales. "Are you looking for anything special?"

"Not really but you never know what we might find." They got out of the car and made their way among the tables. Roxie picked up a bag of yarn, Loren two books, and they headed for the car.

"Like you need more yarn?"

"Got it for Almira at church. She is always crocheting lap robes for the nursing homes." She tossed the bag in the back of her mini SUV. "The next one is two blocks over. A three-family sale. Might be good."

After hitting seven sales, they had, besides the yarn, a hanging basket of petunias, a pot decorated with zigzag rings to set a plain pot into, a new throw rug for by the door to the deck, three packs of sheets for the boxes made up at church for those less fortunate, several more books, and a catnip toy for Juno. They were almost to Annie's when Loren's cell woofed for her. She had recorded Sir Charles's welcome-home barks and made it her ring tone. Roxie had no idea how her daughter knew the things she did, but this one always made her smile.

While Loren talked to Nate, Roxie thought about her plans for the afternoon. She hoped she'd be able to take Sir Charles for a walk when they got home before she had to get ready to show houses.

"I'd like that, okay, see you then." Loren finished her call and stared at her phone a moment. "So we're going sailing tomorrow afternoon."

"Good. Hope it's not so rough I get seasick." Roxie parallel-parked on the opposite side of the street from Annie's. "Looks like they are busy. You hungry?"

Loren nodded. "Is today a cinnamon roll day?"

"Sometimes." She inhaled just before opening the door. "Smells like it." And she led the way inside.

"What'll you have, ladies?" Anne asked with a wide smile and sooner than they'd thought possible. "You hit the garage sales?"

"How did you know?"

"You have the cat-with-a-canary look. Any good buys?"

Loren shrugged. "Not really. You ever get to go anymore?"

"Not since we opened this. Lattes hot or iced?"

"One of each, make mine iced and mocha." Loren looked for a table.

"There's one over there." Anne nodded to the left. "Breakfast? Need menus?"

"Yes and yes." Roxie took the menus Anne handed her. "Recommendations?"

"Got fresh basil for the omelets, another batch of cinnamon rolls about out of the oven, and Gary is trying a new recipe for the corned beef hash."

"Cinnamon rolls for sure; can we get them without frosting?"

"Sure can." She handed them their drinks. "I'll be over to get your order when you're ready."

On the way to their table, they passed two ladies knitting away while they talked.

"Hey, trying to get your UFOs done early?" Roxie asked with a wide smile.

Paula, the woman with a bluish streak in her graying hair, raised her project out of her lap. "Wherever I go, this goes. I used to do this but got out of the habit. Actually I finished the one I started the first night."

"I bagged some of mine and numbered them," the other woman, Edith, said. "Getting this group going sure has been a good incentive. Thanks."

"What are you making?" Roxie asked.

"A poncho for my daughter. We bought the yarn a year ago and I got busy. She is really excited." She laid it on her lap and smoothed it out. "Pretty, isn't it? She has good taste when it comes to clothes. By the way, can I bring a friend to the next meeting? She's visiting from Iowa and is thinking of starting one there."

"Of course. How about that? Someone also called because of the column that has started in the paper. See you at the meeting." Roxie joined Loren at the table. "Did you order?"

"Not yet."

After they'd turned in their orders, Roxie propped her elbows on the table and sipped from her rapidly cooling latte. "What are you doing this afternoon?"

"Going over to the rescue place to help bathe dogs for their event tomorrow. I was going to help with that but instead I'm going sailing. Should I feel guilty?"

"Guilt is highly overrated. A quote I heard somewhere. Had you promised for Sunday?"

"No, nor for this afternoon, but I know they need help."

Roxie patted her daughter's hand. "Thinking of picking up pizza and taking it out to Ginny's. Want to go?"

"Sure, beats cooking."

Roxie picked up her phone and clicked on Ginny's number. "Hey, you want company who will bring pizza for supper tonight? Oh good. Any favorite kind? Addy too. I'll get a super-size with everything but anchovies. Good, they don't appeal to me either. Loren might come. Okay, see you sixish? You need anything else from town? Welcome." She clicked off, nodding. "She sounds more like herself again."

"Addy is how old now?" Loren asked.

"Going on twelve, I think."

"About the same age I was when Daddy died. Addy and Andy were really close to their grandpa, weren't they?"

"Yes," Roxie replied. "MJ said Andy still hasn't been over to the farm."

"Poor kids."

"Do you remember when their little brother died?"

"Sort of."

"They spent most of a couple of years with Ginny

and Fred." Roxie looked up when their food arrived. "Thanks, Sean. You working Saturdays here now?"

The boy nodded. "I can deliver food, clean off tables, and scrub pots and pans."

Loren grinned. "Having money you earned feels pretty good, doesn't it?"

"I don't know, I'll tell you after I get paid. Can I get you anything else?" His braces glinted when he smiled.

Roxie watched him walk off to pick up a pitcher of water and start around the tables.

"That's Anne's nephew, isn't it?" Loren asked.

"Looks like they're keeping the jobs in the family." She cut into her omelet. "Excellent. Reminds me, I didn't buy any basil at the nursery. That would look good in that new pot. I wonder if Ginny has started any herbs." Roxie dug her calendar out of her purse. "You have any things to add to the grocery list?" She flipped to the notes page, where she had started the list. "I'll try to stop after the house tour. If you get home before I do, please call the pizza order in to pick up at five forty-five."

"Sure. Do you have kibbles for Juno on your list? Almost gone."

Roxie smiled to herself. Getting low on cat food? Oh, my Juno, that would never do. She wondered, did Rich shop for his grocery needs, or did Nate do it for him? Considering his skill with cooking, she imagined he did his own shopping. Good cook, good sailor, good landscape designer...there was so much more to that complex man than Roxie would have guessed.

Chapter Nineteen

"R oxie and Loren are coming with pizza for supper,"
Ginny announced.

Addy looked up from the recipe file on the kitchen
counter. "What's their favorite kind of cookie?"

Ginny shrugged and shook her head at the same time.
"I have no idea." She closed her eyes, hoping to recall a
rather unusual fact like that, then nodded slowly. "Roxie
loves lemon bars but we don't have lemons."

"There's a bottle of lemon juice in the pantry."

"Really? Hm. Been there awhile then. Hope it hasn't
been opened."

"If it was, you would have put it in the refrigerator—
you always do."

Ginny stared at her granddaughter. "How do you
know so much?" She leaned her posterior against the
kitchen counter and crossed her arms. "You know what?
You amaze me."

Addy's forehead wrinkled. "Grandma, you're the one
who kept saying, 'Now pay attention.' Don't you
remember?"

"Since when do people do what I ask?" She got the
Oh, Grandma look that went along with a slight shake of

the head. "Okay, okay, sorry. You just caught me by surprise." At the singing of her phone, she fumbled in her pocket and hit the button. "Hi, Sam."

"Just checking up on you two. How are things going?"

"Addy is deciding what cookies to bake next. Roxie and Loren are bringing pizza out for supper."

"Good. You have any tomato plants left?"

"You planted all those you got the other day?" She watched Addy bringing the baking ingredients out to the counter.

"Just say you haven't tossed any in the compost yet. I'll be over in an hour or so." He clicked off.

"Your dad is coming over. We better get a plate of cookies ready to send home with him so he doesn't kidnap you."

"He's glad I'm here, says he doesn't worry about you this way." Addy checked the refrigerator. "Better put butter on the list, along with walnuts, oh, and powdered sugar. These bars will take the last of it."

Ginny turned and picked up the notepad she kept on the counter for just this purpose. "Oh, look." She pointed out the kitchen window. "Three hummingbirds on the feeder at once." The two watched, with identical grins lighting their faces.

"Remember the one we found that time we thought was dead?"

"I do and he was torpid. I'd never known about that before." Ginny looked off to the left to the birdbath. "Look, the hens are up here." Two of the lighter ones were up on the low birdbath, drinking.

"Do chickens like to bathe like other birds?"

"Nope, they take dust baths. You've seen their wallows inside their fenced area."

"I know but I thought maybe they did both."

Spook whined at their sides.

"Outside?"

He leaped and yelped. "Okay, okay." Ginny let him out the back door.

The lemon bars were cooling on the rack on the counter when Sam arrived. "Kid, do you never quit?" he asked after petting Spook and hugging his mother, in that order.

"Making up for not getting to bake while school is going on." She pushed a plate of chocolate chip cookies toward him. "Walnuts just for you."

"What else you two been doing?" He reached for a second one.

"Didn't your mother teach you not to talk with your mouthful?" Ginny asked, wearing an innocent look.

"That kid might take 'em away before I get enough."

"Right, you want coffee?"

"You have to make it?"

"You know that Keurig you bought me for Christmas last year? It works." She handed him a mug and pointed at the black machine on the counter by the stove.

"Yeah, we gave you the single one and yet you still mostly use the old one."

"Because it makes a potful. It has a timer to set for the morning so I wake up to the smell of coffee and it would probably poach eggs if I asked it to."

"Sure, coffee-flavored eggs. Ugh." He reached for another cookie. "What about the lemon bars?"

"Not ready to cut yet, sorry. Besides, they don't really taste good warm, oh hey..." She picked up the cookie plate and put it in the microwave just long enough to warm them. When she pulled out the plate, she sniffed the cookies. "Roxie taught me to do this. She says the fragrance of hot cookies or baking bread will sell a house almost every time."

Sam sniffed the cookies he'd snatched. "Good job, kiddo. Come on, Mom, show me what to take." He headed for the door, Ginny following. Out by the greenhouse, where she'd set pots to harden the plants off, he looked over what had become a meager collection. "You going to put any more in the garden here?"

"Doubtful. If they produced like last year, I'd never be able to keep ahead of them." Her voice broke. How would she do all the canning, freezing, drying without Fred to pick and peel and carry half the load? Tears welled up and over, too much to sniff back.

Sam turned from loading pots. "What is it?"

Ginny motioned to the plants and toward the garden. "I—I can't do it all without him." She dug in her pocket, only to find one badly used tissue. Sam wrapped his arms around her and held her close so her tears soaked his shirt.

"It's okay, Mom, we'll help. We all will. And you don't have to can and freeze like you and Dad did. I swear you fed half the city."

"I—I need a tissue." She raised her head. "S-sorry, that caught me by surprise."

"Does it happen often?"

"I don't know how to define 'often.' At least I am not crying all the time anymore, and I can sleep sometimes without waking to a wet pillow. Actually, I'm sleeping more like I used to lately." She looked toward the barn.

"I still can't make myself go in the chicken house. Addy takes care of the chickens, and feeds the other animals too. Magic whinnies now when she comes."

"And he used to nicker when Dad came. What about Smoky?"

Ginny sucked in a deep breath and let it all out. "Perhaps it's time to find new homes for them."

"Magic needs young children to teach about horse handling. Addy and Andy have really outgrown him."

"I know. More to think about."

Sam had all the remaining tomato pots loaded in his truck. "Looks like that pumpkin is too big to transplant. Why don't I dump some dirt around it right there and it can become a lawn decoration?"

"Why not. Go for it."

"Grandma," Addy called from the garage. "Telephone, you want to call her back?"

"Who is it? No, just tell her I'll call her back." She turned to Sam. "When you are done there, Addy will have a plate of cookies for you to take home."

"You get tired of having her around, you can send her home, you know." Sam shoveled a bucketful of compost for the pumpkin plant. "Where's your clippers?"

"In my apron pocket, where they belong."

"Yes, ma'am, I will put them back."

Ginny shook her head, heaved the stick for Spook, and made her way to the house. She could hear Addy on the phone in the family room, talking with a friend. It didn't seem fair that Addy should give up her summer to take care of her grieving grandma. She checked the light on the oven: sure enough, more cookies about ready to come out. Her sniffer never lied.

"You want me to take these out?"

"Yes, please, if they're brown enough. The last pan is ready to go in."

Ginny was moving the hot cookies to the wire rack for cooling when Sam and Spook came in the back door.

"Looks good. What kind are those?"

"Oatmeal with raisins and chocolate chips, I think. I know, your favorite so she baked them for you."

"Good thing, our cookie jar is sadly empty. Andy said she should come home, at least long enough to fill the cookie jars."

"How do we help him to be able to come over here again?"

Sam puffed out a sigh. "I don't know. Just give him time, I guess."

"Will he talk about his grandpa? Memories?" She watched Sam shake his head. "Can you talk about the memories?" She watched as the emotions raced across her son's face then his head began to move from side to side. "I see. Like father, like son."

"I can make myself come over here."

"I know, and Sam, I am so very grateful. Maybe— maybe..." She exhaled so her shoulders would come down from dancing with her earlobes. "I wonder if I should invite him out to lunch or if we should all go on a picnic where we could sit around a fire and talk about the good old days. That song by the Judds just blew through my mind. 'Grandpa, tell me 'bout the good old days.' You remember that one."

"I do, Dad loved it. Maybe that would help. Of course, we could build a fire in our fire pit. Let me talk to Erica—she has lots of common sense—but I agree with you, talking about the memories would help. Both him and me."

"Hey, Dad, you loaded?"

"I am. I was told you would have cookies for me to take home."

Addy took out a plastic container and filled it with the oatmeal cookies, which had cooled on the counter. "Grandma, would you please get that other container out of the pantry? The chocolate chip ones." She handed her father both containers. "Make sure you bring them back or you won't get any more."

"Whoa, tough taskmaster." He kissed his daughter's cheek and hugged his mother. "I'll get on that," he whispered in her ear. "Think on tomorrow night."

"Tuna salad sandwiches?" Ginny asked Addy.

"Sounds good. Think I'll go brush down Magic and Smoky after lunch."

"I think I will take a nap out in the hammock."

"Oh, good idea. Remember the time I was reading out there and Grandpa came and dumped me over? I started to get mad and then we both busted out laughing. I miss his laugh. It's like if I listen really, really hard, I will hear it again."

Ginny nodded. "I keep feeling he is right near me, and if I turn quickly enough, I'll see him." A sigh escaped her lips. She sniffed. "Just think, if I had baked bread this morning, ah, the sandwiches would be superb."

"Let's do that tomorrow. I want to learn to make bread."

"Okay. Let's eat on the deck. You pour the iced tea and bring it." Ginny grabbed the sack of chips and carried the two plates out to the umbrella table.

Later when she'd situated herself in the hammock, she fell asleep listening to the birds sing.

"Grandma, Grandma." Addy shook her gently.

"Wha-what time is it?" Ginny blinked and tried to smile up at her granddaughter. "I guess I really fell asleep."

"I thought you might want to be awake before they come." Addy settled cross-legged down on the grass.

Ginny looked at her watch. "Oh my goodness, I slept for nearly three hours. Why'd you let me sleep so long?" She carefully sat up and swung her legs over the side. "I had no idea a nap in the hammock could feel so good. You want it for a while?"

"I was thinking to do the chores early."

"Good idea. So what did you do all afternoon, after you groomed the animals, that is?"

"I cleaned up the kitchen, poured me some iced tea, and settled into the lounger with my book. Spook decided to share it with me so of course the cat got jealous and took over my lap. And they were sleeping so sound that it was contagious and I fell asleep."

"You think perhaps we should have one of those lemon bars to get us going again?"

"Hmmm, let me think on this." She laid the tip of her index finger against her lips. "Yep, definitely." She stood with one smooth motion and held out her hand to help her grandma. "Be careful or it will dump you."

Ginny stretched both arms above her head and leaned to the right and then the left. "Ah, what a lazy way to spend the afternoon."

"Isn't that what summers are for? And reading one book after another."

"You think we should make a salad?" Ginny asked.

"What? And ruin the pizza?"

Spook announced the arrival of a car that did not contain family. His barks were very different.

"We'll eat out on the deck." Ginny handed a basket with all the necessary table things to Addy and went to welcome the guests.

"Let's eat right away." Loren was carrying the biggest pizza box. "It smells so good, it was all I could do to not grab a piece."

Roxie gave Ginny a hug. "I had to threaten her to keep her fingers out of it. How are you, Addy? Grandma keeping you busy?"

Ginny snorted. "More like she is keeping me busy."

Loren set the box in the middle of the table and looked around. "This is so lovely. Look, Mom, a hammock. We need one in our yard." They all pulled out their chairs and sat, eyeing the box.

"Roxie, you want to say grace?" She did and they dug in.

Ginny wrapped a gooey string of cheese around her finger after taking a couple of bites. "Been a while since I had pizza. Thank you."

"Surely they deliver out here?"

Ginny shrugged. "I guess. We just never bothered to order here. We usually had pizza at Sam's. Addy and I make darn good pizza."

"Grandma used to let me and Andy spread all the toppings. Andy always managed to eat part of the cheese and the pepperoni and she'd swat his hand with the spatula."

"Did he learn?" Loren asked.

"To dodge the spatula, yes."

"So, how's your UFO coming along?" Roxie asked.

"Mine will be done fairly soon," Ginny answered and looked at Addy.

"I've ripped those stitches out so many times, I think the yarn is wearing out. I think I'll give up on it. Knitting just isn't for me." Addy reached for another piece of pizza and stared right back at Spook. "You know you do not eat pizza."

Loren chuckled. "Sez who? Look at those eyes."

"He has begging down to a science, not that it does him any good." Ginny reached for another piece. A bird singing made her pause. "A cardinal, what a nice serenade for supper."

"This is so peaceful. Amalia mentioned that more than once. She really enjoyed her time out here. I think she misses her farm far more than she lets on." Roxie propped her elbows on the table and nibbled at her slice. "You know, I was thinking the other day. I read an article about shared housing and then I had two sisters who were looking for a house to buy together."

"Shared housing, eh?"

"Yeah, there are books about it now and lots of articles. It might be something you could be interested in. I googled it and there's plenty of information out there." She licked some sauce off her fingertip. "Sorry."

"No problem. That's the way you're supposed to eat pizza." Ginny sipped her iced tea. Shared housing. Come to think of it, there were those women at the big Original Sewing and Quilting Show in Minneapolis one year. They were talking about the house they shared and how rewarding it was as everyone took a share of the work. Ginny was already feeling overwhelmed about keeping this place up. Might this be an answer to her prayers for the future?

Chapter Twenty

"You going to the morning group again?" Ginny's voice on the phone asked.

"Planning on it." Amalia laid her knitting down in her lap so she could hold the phone without her neck cramping from positioning it between shoulder and head. "Why?"

The breeze tickled bare skin, since she was only wearing a tank top and shorts and sitting out on her lanai with her feet up on the other chair. In all the pots surrounding her, plants were growing so fast she could almost measure them. The two tomatoes were nearing the height of the black iron railing. The fuchsia hanging from the ceiling fed several hummingbirds every day, and the pot of ruby penstemon was part of that feeding frenzy. She had affixed a trellis to the wall for the cucumbers to grow up. Most things she could buy at the farmer's market, but she could eat the lemon cucumbers like an apple with a ripe tomato for dessert.

"We're sort of counting noses to make sure we fit," Ginny explained. "The morning group is getting popular."

"Count two. A friend of mine from here at the home is planning on coming with me. By the way, did I tell you we started a UFO group here at the retirement apartments, meets every Tuesday morning? Talk about a refresher for some of these women. I heard one guy refer to this as the old age home. Could have castigated him but didn't want to get caught in his web of negativity." Sometimes Amalia threw in unusual words for the pure joy of it.

"I can't tell you how much it meant to me, your staying here all that time." Amalia could feel a smile as she listened to Ginny's thanks. "I miss you."

Amalia agreed with that. "I miss you. And the farm too. Anytime you want me back, let me know. I'm glad you and Addy have such a great time together. Ouch. Oh, cat's claws don't feel too good on bare legs."

Ginny snickered. "Cat's claws also pull runs in fabric. Your legs will heal; fabric doesn't."

Down inside, Amalia's heart sang. Ginny was beginning to sound like her old self again. "So true." She nodded, tucked her knitting in the bag beside her chair, and settled Jehoshaphat to be more comfortable, now that he would let her pick him up. "You should see my lanai. Thanks to you, I have tomatoes budding, cucumbers climbing up the trellis, and a basket of petunias starting to trail over the sides of the pot. Oh, and the basil smells so good. I made caprese salad last night, even though I had to buy the tomato to slice with the baby mozzarellas. The basil was grand. I could eat that salad every day."

She stroked the cat, hoping to set him to purring. A purring cat was about as relaxing as watching a fish tank.

She'd thought about getting one again, but decided to put it off until winter, if at all.

"What time is it now?" Ginny asked. Amalia knew she'd given up wearing a watch because something in her body chemistry stopped watches.

"Almost noon. I was trying to decide what I would have for lunch. Wanna go to Annie's?"

There was a pause on the line. Perhaps Ginny still felt nervous about going out in public. "Annie's it is."

Ha. Ginny was indeed coming back to life. "Okay, I'll meet you downstairs. See you in a bit." She clicked off her cell and stretched her arms over her head, only to feel sharp claws in her thigh. "Sorry, I wasn't going to dump you down." Inhaling through her nose, she held it then blew her breath out of her mouth. Immediately the warmth of relaxation bathed from head to toe. "Sorry, Cat, I need to go change clothes, wasn't planning on going out." She set the cat on the floor, got a dirty look, and headed for her bedroom. Slipping into capris and adding a white shirt to tie at the waist, she slid her feet into her walking sandals and made her necessary bathroom stop, one more indication of advancing years. Her knitting in a bag over her shoulder that also held her billfold, she moved the cat inside to close and lock the sliding screen door, just to be safe. Big as he was, he could probably reach the latch and open it.

Downstairs she greeted the woman behind the desk and sat down on the bench outside in the shade. The TV blared from the apartment right above her. The gentleman who lived there desperately needed hearing aids. Perhaps they should all take up an offering to assist him in purchasing some. Of course, that meant he would have to wear them. He fit the curmudgeon stereotype perfectly.

Ginny and Addy drove in, and Addy got out and climbed in the backseat. After the greetings, Addy leaned forward. "Grandma's dropping me off at the library for my volunteering time."

"And did you bring cookies?" Amalia smiled over her shoulder as she got in.

"Of course. Here's a box for you too. I thought maybe your UFO group would like some."

"Oh, I'm sure they will. How's your project coming?" She heard a dejected sigh.

"I don't think I'm supposed to be a knitter. The yarn is wearing out with all my pulling the stitches out again."

"Have you tried crocheting? I think it is lots easier for some people, especially those who pull the yarn too tight."

Addy said, "That's me, can hardly get the needles into the loops."

"I have an easy pattern for crocheted pot holders. Just chain and keep on single crocheting until the pot holder is finished."

"Is that the one where it looks like some sort of strange hat until you flip and smooth it out?"

Amalia smiled at the description. "That's the one. They last forever and you don't have to count stitches after the first single crochet. Rather monotonous."

"But is it easy?"

"As pie."

Ginny stopped in front of the library. "Have fun."

Addy bailed out and waved as she entered the glass and metal doors.

Amalia settled back. "She is such a good kid. Well, both of them are. Has Andy been back to the farm yet?"

Ginny shook her head. "No, but we're all getting together on Sunday for a bonfire picnic out at Monroe Park. I've been wanting hot dogs roasted on sticks over the fire. All the world of difference between a bonfire and a grill. Why don't you come too?"

"What can I bring?"

"I don't know, haven't thought that far yet. Think of something." She pulled into a parking place down the block and both got out, carrying a bag with a project in it. "I'm taking after you." She held up the bag. "Finished the afghan, so I pulled out a doily I started many moons ago. So very portable."

"So you'll get your picture up on the board?" Amalia reminded her.

"I will."

Sir Charles and Looper stood up as the friends approached, tails flailing. Ginny rubbed them both behind the ears. "Spook sends his greetings."

She pushed open the door to the café—and inhaled. "Must be cinnamon rolls day. I can still smell them."

"Probably don't have any left by now. Hi, Anne. Sure smells good in here." Ginny sniffed again. "Cinnamon rolls and bacon, and that makes me think I want a BLT."

"Hi back, the other two are in the meeting room. What can I get you to drink? I have mint iced tea today."

"Sounds great. That will be two BLTs with mint tea," Amalia answered.

"Fries, potato salad, or green salad, oh, and coleslaw."

"More decisions. I'll take potato salad. Ginny?"

"Make it easy, me too." They took their drinks and

headed to the room at the back, answering greetings as they went. Ginny managed to answer a how-you-doing question without it throwing her into tears.

"Whew," she said as she set her things down. "Made it."

"Good for you." MJ reached over and patted her hand. "Sit and be comfortable. Did you get the mint tea?"

"Hey, long time no see." Roxie grinned at her. "Amalia, how's life at the home?"

"My lanai is being taken over by plants and bird feeders. Any spare room left and Jehoshaphat uses that. At least the people down below have not complained. I hope they like birds. They don't know about the monster cat." She looked at Sean, who was their waiter today. "Thanks, good job."

"I just follow instructions."

"Ah, that's the mark of a good employee," MJ added.

He finished handing out the plates of food. "Now, can I get you anything else? Refills on the iced tea?" When they all nodded, he said, "I'll be right back."

Amalia commented, "This is his second summer working here. Addy told me one day she plans to work here, as soon as she is old enough."

MJ snorted. "She'll have such a big cookie business by that time, she'll be hiring some of us."

"MJ"—Ginny paused—"you really think so?"

"What's stopping her?"

Ginny shrugged. "You better talk with her. All I know right now is that she has two orders of three dozen cookies each to bring to the UFO group. Her oatmeal-plus are her most popular so far."

A woman dressed in pink capris, pink slip-ons, and a pink T-shirt stopped at their table to chat. After greetings, she smiled at Roxie. "Who is that handsome man you were with at the movies last week? He looks so familiar."

Roxie nodded. "His name is Rich Owens."

"The same family that owns the furniture chain?"

"Yes."

Amalia took a bite of her sandwich. Interesting. One couldn't get away with anything in this town. When the woman waved and left, Amalia wiggled her eyebrows at Roxie. "Do you have something you were just waiting to tell us?"

"Yeah," MJ chimed in. "Looks that way to me."

Roxie rolled her eyes. "It's no big deal. He's Nate's father, the young man who I told you has reconnected with Loren. They knew each other in high school. We had a barbeque at his house a couple of weeks ago and saw a movie last Friday, oh, and went sailing once."

"And?"

"And Nate and Loren are seeing more of each other and talking on the phone and..." She dropped her voice. "I think he is *really* interested in her, and he is a charming young man with a great deal of depth."

"And Loren?"

"She's beginning to talk about him and having a good time. They like a lot of the same things." She raised crossed fingers. "I think this could really be the one."

Amalia leaned back in her chair, nodding. "That is excellent news."

"I just want her to be happy. And he's not a typical guy of today; he's a real man with a good job, an education, and goals and dreams. Oh, and they both attend the same church."

"So he is a man of faith?" MJ asked.

"Yes, he is and not shy about it."

"Well, good." MJ finished her salad. "Anne sure has good food here." She grinned at Ginny and Amalia. "And now let's hear a bit more about his father." All three of them turned and stared at Roxie.

Two ladies, Paula and Edith, stopped by their table. "We just wanted to thank you all for starting the UFO club," Paula said. "You have no idea what a difference it made for us. Our husbands kept saying, 'Get rid of that stuff if you're not going to finish anything.'" They looked at each other. "We married brothers and they sympathize with each other. While I've not finished so much, it made me pull all the stuff out and sort it. Now it's organized and my laundry room doesn't need a closed door all the time."

"We did hers first and then mine," Edith went on. "I still have more craft stuff to go so I got a big idea. What if we have a swap meet at one of the meetings and people can bring stuff that they want to rehome?"

"Great idea!" MJ looked at Roxie, who nodded.

Edith dipped her head toward Paula. "We wanted to encourage you by telling you this."

MJ said, "You most certainly did encourage us, thank you. As of now, there is an evening group and a morning group, another group at the home, and several others are talking about starting a group at their church or in an organization. So, some of our evening members are moving to other groups."

"Well, I hope they let us know of their successes so

we can all celebrate." One of them patted MJ on the shoulder. "Thanks again."

The four stared at each other as the two left. "Can you believe that?" Roxie stared at MJ and then the others. "Do you all realize that all this started because MJ got fed up with her stuffed-full craft room and was ready to call in a bulldozer?"

MJ added, "But the UFO part was your idea. I sure hope other towns catch on like this. Or you think maybe we are just a fluke?"

"Doubtful, but all the encouragement is sure helpful." MJ pushed her plate back. "And people helping each other at the meetings. I heard one lady volunteer to take a person she did not know well to a doctor appointment because she lamented her car was in the shop. People just being helpful."

"Can I get you ladies anything else?" Sean asked.

"More iced tea?" MJ raised her glass. When he'd left, she muttered, "Not that I need more but it sure is good."

Ginny looked around for a clock. "I need to pick Addy up in half an hour."

"You should have told her to walk over here." Roxie cocked her head. "Call her and tell her."

"Can't. She turns her phone off when she's working in the library."

Knitting while their conversations continued, Amalia looked at Roxie. "So, when are you seeing him again? Rich, I mean."

"I figured who you meant. We're going to the concert at the Thelma on Saturday, after we go for supper somewhere. He said business casual."

"Oh, really? What does that mean?"

"Nice clothes but not fancy dress-up. Guess I'll wear a dress, not a cocktail dress, though."

Amalia grinned wickedly. "And what shoes will you be wearing to this affair?"

Roxie looked down at her feet. "Certainly not these shocking pink tennies."

"Interesting how seldom we dress up anymore. Life has gotten so much more casual." Ginny shook her head. "I don't even own a dress anymore. I have a couple of long skirts that hang there hoping." She looked at Amalia. "Uh-oh, I can see the wheels turning." She smiled up at their server. "Thanks for the refill."

Amalia nodded. "I just have this gut feeling that Roxie's life is about to change to include Rich and his son. And you all know how often my gut feelings are true. They happen."

"That's true, we've seen it." MJ looked to Roxie. "So, you ready for that?"

"Come on," Roxie insisted, "we're just friends."

"That's what they all say." MJ didn't sound convinced at all.

"Where does he live?" Ginny asked.

"North, up the lake farther. Incredibly beautiful place. He has three grown children, Nate is his youngest. He lives here in Fond du Lac."

"And manages the family-owned furniture store?"

"Yes. Nate has never married but Rich was divorced when his kids were still in grade school. Anything else you want to know?" She sounded a bit pushed.

"Does he make you laugh?" Amalia asked.

"Oh, yes."

"And feel special?"

Roxie nodded.

Amalia sat back smugly. "I rest my case."

"We'd better get going." Ginny pushed back her chair. "See you all later."

Amalia stood too. "Been a pleasure. See you Monday night, if not before."

Back in the car, Ginny turned to look at Amalia. "Not next Saturday but the one after, Addy and Andy will be going to Bible camp. At first I thought I could stay by myself and maybe by then I will be at that place, but right now it's looking doubtful."

"If you're asking me to come out again, I would love to. It is not a sacrifice, it's a pleasure, so let's leave it that way. If you truly think you'll be fine by yourself, that is fine with me too."

Ginny heaved a sigh and shifted into drive. "Thank you. I hate to impose."

"That's hogwash, how many years have we been friends? How often were you and Fred out helping me when I finally decided to sell?"

"That's what friends are for."

"Right. I rest my case."

They stopped at the curb, where Addy slung her backpack in the backseat and climbed in.

"You got more library books, I take it."

"How can you tell?"

"The weight of the backpack. No lighter than when you went in. What did you do today?"

"Shelved books. Several of them came home with me. Grandma, I'm starved."

Ginny smiled. "Figured you would be. Where do you want to stop?"

"Do you mind?"

"Not at all. We'll drop Amalia off first." She turned at the next stop sign. "You need anything at the store, Amalia?"

"Thanks but I'm fine. Just let me out at the street. You needn't drive in. Thanks for the ride." She waved them off and headed for the stairs. Much healthier than the elevator. A note on her door said:

Come on over for Mexican Train. There will be four of us. Seven.

It was signed with the initials of Lily, her friend two doors down who had been so ill. Wonderful! She opened her door to Jehoshaphat meowing as if she'd been gone for days instead of a few hours. Bending over, she scooped up her feline becoming friend and stroked his back before he squirmed to get down.

"Hey, you are settling in, I think there is hope for you yet." She slid open the screen door and stepped out on the lanai. A slight breeze cooled her on its way past into her apartment.

What if Roxie really did fall in love and get married? How would it change the group? Change. Good thing God didn't give them a laundry list of what was coming. Right now was enough to deal with. She went to stand in front of the freezer. What could she fix to take to the game night?

Chapter Twenty-One

Dear Roxie,

I am writing this to all of you but I have an address for you since you sold us a house many years ago. I have been a member of the UFO group from the beginning and so appreciate it. I began with a needlework picture I had started several years ago at least, for a friend of mine. She'd ask me about it once in a while because she was working on something too and we kind of challenged each other. I don't know if she finished hers but she has been fighting a recurrence of breast cancer that metastasized to her brain. I finished my picture, framed it, and took it to her two weeks ago. We had a marvelous visit and she showed me where she wanted it hung so she could see it when she woke in the morning.

My friend went home to Jesus two nights ago and her husband said she made him promise to call me and tell me, again, how grateful she was for our friendship and that I brought her the picture just when she needed it most.

So I am thanking all of you for the encouragement to finish something started. I never dreamed God would use my stitchery in such a way. And please share this with the others and the whole group if you want. I'll be back but not just yet. May our Lord God bless you all in that you do.

Blessings,
June Asbury

Roxie blew her nose and wiped her eyes. She picked up a box of tissue and took letter, tissue, and phone out on the deck, where the birds were singing, Sir Charles was snoring in the sun, and Juno greeted her with a chirp. She sat down at the table with umbrella shade, then Juno jumped up on the table and rubbed against her chin, purr already in full force. After another face mop, Roxie blew out a breath and hit MJ's name.

"You better be sitting down. I am going to read you something."

"Okay, give me a sec. You sound awfully serious." Roxie heard the chair squeal when MJ sat down. "Ready."

"Oh, do you have tissues at hand?"

"No, I'm outside on the patio."

"I'll wait."

When MJ sat back down, Roxie read the letter.

As soon as she could speak, MJ started, cleared her throat, and finally said, "Oh, my word. Roxie, this is beyond belief. All we wanted was to get some of the stuff done and out of the craft room."

"I know, but how often have we heard that God uses unusual things to get through to us. Even a donkey.

Little things, big things, but I am in shock. I mean we were joking about finishing baby blankets when the recipient is now in grade school and so many other things. We made a joke out of it and look what God did with our crazy efforts." She paused and blew her nose again. "MJ, I want to learn to listen better."

"Me too. *Me too.* We have to tell the others, read it to them. And I think we should read this at the next meeting. After all, June said that was okay. Which reminds me, better send her husband a card. Good thing we got addresses and phone numbers. You know, I thought it was the time together with people getting to know each other, but now I see it can be important in many different ways. Just never thought of God using this."

"I know, me either. I figured we'd have a fine time, feel good about finishing things, you know." Roxie blew out a breath. "I'm going to call Amalia and Ginny. Talk with you later."

"Thanks. Maybe it will be easier when you read it through again."

"Right."

Ginny broke down and said she'd call back later. And yes, Addy was with her. Amalia, the one who cried the least among them, sniffed and blew right along with Roxie. "MJ said she thought reading this again would be easier but not appreciably. She's going to have to be the one to read it to the group. I do not want to stand up there and blubber."

"You won't, but tears never hurt anyone. Someone I know told me about that."

"Hush, you know how I hate eating my own words. Have you read it to Ginny yet?"

"I did and she said she'd call me back. I hope this doesn't send her into a real crying jag again. She has said so often how tired she is of crying. I get that."

"Interesting that three of us in this group have lost a husband. You ever thought of that?"

"Nope. But true." Roxie glanced at the clock on her cell phone. "I gotta run and get changed. Meeting with a client in an hour. Thanks, my friend. Ah, could you call Ginny in a while, just to check on her?"

"Of course."

Roxie clicked off and stared at the phone while petting Juno. Sir Charles laid his muzzle on her leg and stared up at her as if pleading for her to be happy. "It's okay, fella." She stroked down his soft fur. "How about a cookie to help us both feel better." His tail thumped against the floor and he headed for the door.

Later that afternoon after meeting with one client to sign the final papers on their house and then explaining how the system worked to another who had called to learn about her services, she stopped by the grocery store on her way home. They needed something for supper and she had been so busy lately, the pantry was becoming depleted, along with the fridge and freezer.

With a car full of grocery sacks, she drove into the garage just before Loren.

"Yay, you're here to help haul this all in." She made a sweeping motion at the rear of the SUV with paper-to-paper bags.

"I hope you got something easy for supper."

"I did, deli salads and fried chicken." She leaned in and grabbed handles. "Those two bags are for the freezer if you want to start with that. Hurry, the ice cream is melting."

When they'd finished the groceries, they took their filled plates out on the deck and sank into the loungers. Juno joined Loren because she knew Loren was an easy touch and she smelled fried chicken. Sir Charles sat by Roxie wearing his terribly pitiful pleading look.

"It won't work," Roxie told him before she picked up the thigh and, after one bite, closed her eyes in delight. "I do love fried chicken. I think I could eat chicken every day of the week."

"We almost do." Loren gave Juno a bitty bite of the skin. "Now that is all, so forget it."

Roxie almost snorted. "You say that every time."

"I know, so why should I be surprised that she never believes me?" She tipped her head back. "So, how was your day?"

"Busy, but I got the most interesting letter that I'll read to you once I no longer have greasy fingers. I was planning on doing some cold calling but I had too many inquiring phone calls."

"That should tell you something. Ouch, Juno, not the claws."

"I need to keep in practice, though, if I ever need to again."

"Nate called and asked if I wanted to go biking later. He's going to ride over here and then we'll head for the park, sans car."

"Good for him. He is such a nice guy."

"I know." Loren studied her plate. "I think I kind of like him."

"Good. Me too. I know he likes you; you can see it every time he looks at you."

"Really?"

"Really, big time."

Loren sniffed. "He said he had a crush on me in high school. I hardly even knew him. I mean, he was one of the nerds."

"And you were pretty quiet yourself."

"Maybe you think that might be changing now?"

Roxie nearly dropped her chicken. This was her daughter, the one who hardly said a word in public. *Thank you, Lord.* "I think that is entirely possible. Good for you."

"I read an article that said change is difficult."

"That is so true, but not impossible and hopefully part of growing up." She handed Sir Charles the gristle off the ends of the thigh bones and reached for her iced tea. "Sometimes life forces us into change and other times we can make choices and work at it. But some people are paralyzed by fear and others refuse to do the hard work." She shrugged. "The way of life. You ready for ice cream?"

Loren shrugged. "I thought we could wait and have dessert when we get back."

"I think that is a fine idea. Shame we don't have some of Addy's cookies."

"Mom, we can bake our own. I'll stir up the batter, and if he gets here before they are baked, would you please finish?"

"I will and I'll wait to read the letter until later."

"What smells so good in here?" Nate asked when he arrived. He stared at the rack of cooling chocolate chip cookies on the counter.

Loren pulled out the last cookie sheet. "Help yourself and then let's go before the mosquitoes are out."

"I did bug spray. You?"

"I baked cookies." She handed the turner to Roxie. "See you in a while."

"The insect repellent is in the front bathroom." Roxie grinned at Nate. "Take some if you'd like but we have ice cream to go with them for later."

"Ah, bliss."

Roxie waved them off, poured herself more iced tea, snagged two still-warm cookies, and headed upstairs to her office. The never-ending to-do list called her name.

For some strange reason, she could not quit smiling. *Besotted* might be more fitting than *liked* in Nate's case.

She'd just sat down at her desk when her cell chimed. "Roxie here."

"Sure glad to hear that."

Rich. She'd recognize his voice anywhere. The tingle started somewhere about her knees and zipped to the top of her head. "Hey."

"I was just thinking about you and wishing I had time to see you tonight, but since I have a meeting in a few minutes, I thought I'd ask if you'd like to go out for breakfast in the morning."

"Yes, I would like to go out for breakfast. What time?"

"Pick you up at eight, or might seven thirty be better? You are a morning person, right?"

"I'm usually walking with MJ at seven thirty so I guess you can call me a lark."

"That sounds better than 'morning person.' I love the song of the larks out in the field in the morning."

Roxie chuckled. "Me too, though we don't hear them often around here. So, see you at seven thirty?"

"Good. Although if I had my druthers, we would be eating together out on my deck. Mornings, the lake is beyond beautiful."

"Rich." Even her fingers tingled. "I—I'll see you at seven thirty…here."

"Sorry if I offended you."

"Oh, believe me, you did not offend me."

"Uh-oh, gotta go, wouldn't you know he'd be early. Sleep well."

Roxie stared at her phone. Had they really had this conversation? To quote her Norwegian grandmother, "Don't that put the sizzle in the meat!"

The sun was nearing the horizon when Loren and Nate returned, both of them beaming. They came in the kitchen with her laughing at something he had said. Seeing Loren laugh out loud always made Roxie's heart sing.

"Oh, Mom, the lake was so beautiful, just enough white caps to sparkle. We need to bike over there more often."

Roxie watched the look on Nate's face. Yep, besotted. "I made lemon iced tea, figured you'd be thirsty."

Loren smiled at him over her shoulder as she opened the refrigerator door. "We have chilled bottle water if you'd rather."

"Lemon iced tea sounds good, thanks." At the same time he reached for a cookie, giving Roxie a questioning look. He grinned at her when she nodded and one bite equaled half a cookie.

Sir Charles greeted him with his usual exuberance and Juno paraded past with her nose in the air. Snubbed, typical cat style. At least she didn't run and hide.

"We have rocky road, vanilla bean, or mint chip ice cream, so what is your flavor and would you like chocolate syrup drizzled on top?"

"Choices even?"

Roxie nodded. "I'm having rocky road, Loren usually has vanilla bean, so what would you like?"

"Rocky road and vanilla bean."

"Hmm, that sounds good. Me too."

"Drizzle?" Loren asked.

"Why not? Splurge all the way. And just-baked cookies. Dessert fit for a king."

"You want to be king?"

"Not really but I feel like one." Nate grinned at her. "I've learned that living alone makes for a simpler life, like with cooking and, well, everything. Fast food is too easy to go for."

"Let's go outside," Loren said as she and Roxie finished the dishing up. Around the table with a plate of cookies in the center, they finished off the sundaes in short order.

"Pretty soon the days will start getting shorter again." Nate looked toward the west, where oranges, reds, and yellows ribboned the sky. The clouds right above them wore shades of pink into purple. "Spectacular." He reached for another cookie and eyed it. "These should be outlawed, they are so good."

"We'll send some home with you. Do you have a basket or a backpack?"

"Backpack, although I'm thinking since I'm using my bike to get to work and around town that a basket might be better. Or one on the rear."

"I saw one with a crate on the rear, full of grocery bags."

"It does keep me from buying a lot when I do go."

"Good for you, leaving your car parked so much of the time." Roxie gave in to another cookie. "Your mixing was delicious, Nate. Thanks for the idea. Are you coming to the UFO meeting again?"

"I'm not really working on a project, although Dad reminded me I could use his shop anytime. He's coming right along on refinishing that boat. I think he put it off only a year or two. He plans on giving it to my brother's kids but keeping it at his house, painting it really bright colors so it will be easy to pick out with binoculars."

"Smart man. Oh, that reminds me, Loren, we are supposed to celebrate tonight. Marcie is pregnant. Their announcement came in the mail today." She paused to explain to Nate who Marcie was.

"They didn't call with news like that?"

Roxie shrugged. "Guess they do things differently nowadays."

"Oh, yeah, reveal parties when they learn the baby's sex. There's parties for everything."

"Maybe because there is so much bad news these days, we need to celebrate the good more than ever."

"You could be right." Loren nodded slowly. The two of them exchanged a special kind of look.

Roxie kept her joy to herself. This was looking better all the time. And going faster than she ever dreamed possible. Not that she'd spent a lot of time dreaming of her daughter's future—or had she? A picture of Rich floated into her mind. Two men from the same family? This was absurd. Or was it?

Chapter Twenty-Two

"G randma, are you sure this is okay?"

"Yes, Addy, your leaving me is okay. I will see you later this evening." Ginny smiled at her granddaughter and hoped she was nodding with encouragement. "You go and have a good time. Now promise me you are not going to worry about me. And I'm sure the oven will manage to not be heated today, but I promise you that if I hear it crying, I will bake something."

Addy rolled her eyes. "Grandma." A car honked so, with a wave, she flew out the door. Spook followed her, hoping she would throw the stick for him, but instead she shut the door in his face, with a "you be a good boy and take care of Grandma." He went to the big window in the living room and watched the car leave then came back to flop at Ginny's feet.

"Sorry, boy, but she can't be here all the time." Ginny patted him and gave him a belly rub for good measure. "There now, better?"

Now was a good time for her devotions so she rose from her recliner, picked up her Bible, devotional book, and journal, and headed out to the table on the deck with a padded chair. She stared at the floral cushions

Fred had picked out, knowing her love of flowers. Heaving a sigh, she fetched a box of tissues and made sure she had her cell phone. Sure enough, her eyes blurred and the tears spilled over. *Lord, will I ever get over the tears? Such little things that evoke memories and make me cry. I miss him so much. How will I ever manage without him?* She let her Bible flop open and read one of the verses that she had underlined. "He will gather the lambs with his arm and carry them in his bosom." She wiped and blew and wiped her eyes again. "Lord God, why did You take him home so soon? You know how I need him, why?" The sobs took over until she whimpered inside, "Are You mad at me? Did I do something You are punishing me for? Lord, I know I get so angry! You are the only one who could have stopped it from happening." She slammed her fist on the arm of the chair. "Screaming does no good. Nothing does any good. Can You hear me? Are You really listening?" She leaned back in the chair and let the tears run.

Spook put both front feet on her thighs and licked the tears away, whimpering all the while.

"It's okay, boy. They say crying is good, but will this ever stop?" Arms around his neck, she whispered in his flopped-over ear, "It's okay. Thank you, I know you miss him too." Spook sank back on his haunches and nuzzled her hand.

"Fred, look what you left. Remember, you refused to see the doctor! You wouldn't go see him! How could you do this to us?" She yelled the last line and heard the chickens at the water basin flutter. Spook raised his muzzle and howled!

Ginny choked on her tears and coughed. Spook

howled again. Laughter choked her this time. She leaned over and wrapped her arms around her curly-haired, oh-so-loving dog. "Thanks, Spook. Good boy." Looking into his dark eyes, she smiled and nodded. "Good boy, you have more sense than I do. Or maybe you were telling God you're mad too."

Blowing her nose again, she read her devotion book for the day. More words about the Great Shepherd. She sure agreed with the author when she wrote that Jesus referring to us as sheep wasn't a compliment. Sheep stink and get full of bugs in their wool and are afraid of everything. Sheep truly can be scared to death. She underlined this sentence: *But thank you, Jesus, for loving us anyway, beyond what we can dream or imagine.*

She stared at her ringing cell phone, not going to answer it, until she saw it was Amalia and punched the button.

"Hi."

"Are you all right?"

"Why?"

"Something just told me to call and check on you. I am trying to obey those hunches."

"Hunches, right." Ginny used the last of the tissues to wipe her eyes and again blow her nose. "I'm getting okay again."

"You got snagged on a memory?"

"I did. The floral cushions on the outside chairs. Fred picked them out."

"And it made you furious."

"How do you know?"

"Remember, I've been there. I was so mad at Ernie for leaving me behind to take care of the farm and everything, I almost broke a tooth my jaws clenched so hard and for so long. But—the anger is just another stage to the grieving. Yell and scream and pound it out, whatever it takes."

"I sorta did."

"Good, and how do you feel?"

"Better. All this time he would not go to the doctor. Said he was in good shape for his age. Kept making excuses. I know he was busy, but—"

"Hate to add fuel to this, but how long since you've been to the doctor?"

Ginny shrugged, trying to think back. "Several months ago I had my yearly, and other than some common things 'for your age,' blood pressure was up some and he sent me for a chest x-ray because of the asthma. I don't go to the doctor any more than I have to."

"And you think grieving doesn't take a toll on your body, let alone your mind? I happen to know that grief scuttles all your resistance, not just to disease but to everything physiological." Ginny was silent until Amalia asked, "You there?"

The sigh could probably be heard without the phone. "I am, and right now I don't like you too much either."

Amalia snorted. "Ah, well, the cost of being a friend at times. Is Addy still there?"

"I told her to go to the swimming party her friends had set up. I don't want her giving up her summer for me. We're planning a party for their twelfth birthday next weekend here and I'm hoping that will make coming to the farm again easier for Andy."

"He's still not come?" Amalia asked.

"Nope, and the longer he puts it off, the harder it will be."

"You going to be okay there now, for today?"

"Yeah, hopefully did my crying for today. Addy will be back for bed. They are having a bonfire at the girl's house that has the pool. Erica has already volunteered to come over, but I think it's time I have at least a day here by myself."

"Okay, good for you, my friend. You're going to make it. Remember, one step forward, two back is normal."

"You mean two forward, one back?"

"Nope, said what I meant." She clicked off, leaving Ginny to ponder the last couple of hours. She turned to writing in her journal, another way she had found to deal with the day-to-day, pouring out her thoughts and feelings. When the sun came around to catch her chair, she got up for a glass of raspberry lemonade and moved to another chair to continue writing.

When the phone rang, she checked the number but, since she did not recognize it, ignored it. Too many tele-marketer calls lately. Since she and Fred had canceled the land line, they didn't get those kind of calls for a while. Another thing that aggravated her. She used to be able to ignore irritants like that more easily. Easily ir-ritable. Was that part of the grieving process too? She hoped so because that wasn't normally like her.

❖   ❖   ❖

There weren't very many dry eyes the night MJ read the letter to the UFO group.

She cleared her throat and sniffed before continuing. "We never even dreamed of such things when we started this. All I wanted to do was get some of the stacked-up stuff in my craft room finished, to sell, or give away, or put to use. Just out of that wonderful room my husband created for me, since he did all the cabinetry work. And yes, he finished that rather major project." She nodded to Daryl, who shrugged as usual. But he did grin when the applause broke out.

"So thank you all for coming tonight and can we have our finished project creators please stand."

Amalia stood with the child's sweater she had finished. "Now I need to find someone to fit it. The original recipient is about to enter high school." Two hands went up. She nodded. "Come talk to me."

MJ showed her crewelwork. "I thought I'd never get it done." She smiled at the applause. "Now maybe I'll make a real supper again rather than something quick."

"I hope so." Daryl grinned at those who clapped for him.

One of the men stood to show the lamp he had made out of an oak burl. The general consensus was awe. "My wife is really glad too. She'd about given up."

The fourth one was an afghan, crocheted for an aging mother. "She didn't have so much trouble staying warm when I started this, but finally threatened to finish it herself. She taught me all kinds of handwork, needlework, whatever you want to call it."

"Can I be your mother?" someone called.

"Good, good. Remember we need pictures, so as soon as the photographer gets here, oh, there he is."

"Sorry I'm late," Rich said, "but I did remember to bring the camera. Of course, that's why I am late, because I had to go back for it."

Others chuckled, MJ nodded with a smile. "Thanks for the effort. So, folks, anytime you can go back for your picture. And with that, I see some of you are working already, but now we all can be. Oh, any questions?"

"Not a question, but I think we need to start a scrapbook of things like that letter and other comments along with the pictures of the finishers," one woman said.

"Good idea. Anyone want to volunteer? Especially someone who won't let this become a UFO?" MJ looked around the room.

A woman named Judith raised her hand. "I just finished a scrapbooking project. I'll get this started."

"Thank you. Anything else? Good, have at it. Drinks are up here along with Addy's cookies. She said to tell you the orders she received at the last meeting are here and boxed. Raise your hand, Addy, so they can see you."

Addy stood up shyly.

"You taking more orders?" someone asked.

"Yes, just come talk to me." Addy sat back down.

MJ picked up her finished crewelwork. "Was hoping to get this framed before tonight, but Daryl is working on the frame."

"Another UFO?" Roxie asked with a grin.

"Nope, he promised for tomorrow. Had to go buy glass and some kind of tool first."

Roxie snorted. "Interesting how men always need one more tool to do something and they go and buy it, while women make do."

"They are smarter that way. Wish I would do the same sometimes, especially with new gadgets for the kitchen. Saw an ad on TV for a salad cutter that looks really good. I never did like to chop a lot of things. Seems simple things are coming out, not like a food processor and those fancy kinds of machines."

Loren looked up when Nate pulled over a chair beside her. "Hi. Thought perhaps you decided not to come."

"My closer had an urgent errand, so I'm running a bit late."

"What are you working on?" Roxie asked.

Nate laid his sketchbook on the table. "I started a series of pen-and-ink drawings years, er, some time ago and almost tossed them when I moved. But I kept the book and I'm still working on the beginning design sketches. I finished one pen-and-ink years ago, and Dad was so pleased with it, I figured to try again."

"How many?"

"Doing a triptych." He held out his hands to show the size. "Each needs to fit a frame. Or maybe my dad"— he gave Rich a teasing look—"would like to create the frames."

Rich grimaced. "Or perhaps he would teach you how to use the tools so you can make them."

"I need a frame for my stitchery. Hint hint," Roxie said with a grin. She held up a counted cross-stitch eight-by-ten of hummingbirds and fuchsias.

Nate groaned. "I can be bribed with ice cream after our meeting."

MJ laughed. "Who couldn't?"

Addy sighed heavily. "I don't think I'm cut out to be a knitter or crocheter." She held up the piece that was supposed to be a square and looked more like a trapezoid. "I started to knit a scarf but none of the edges ever matched. Then this silly potholder and it isn't working. And I tried to crochet that one you showed me, Grandma, and it's a mess too. I'd rather bake cookies any day."

"Did you bring the crocheted one?" Loren laid down her knitting. Addy shook her head. "I didn't think I'd ever be able to knit either but I finally got it." Loren held up a soft fluffy scarf of various blue tones that flowed into each other. "I love this and it is finally working."

"Here, I have a crochet hook and some extra yarn. Come and show me how you started that potholder. I love that design," a lady from across the table said.

Ginny nudged her granddaughter. "Go on, try it."

"I'm going for a plate of cookies first."

"Girl after my own heart," Rich muttered, staring at the bird he was carving in bas-relief on a block of wood.

"You have trouble too, Mr. Owens. I think cookies can cure about anything." Addy rose and headed for the refreshment table.

"That is one special girl. How old did you say she was, Ginny?"

"Almost twelve. She's pretty grown-up for her age. Both of the twins are but girls are always ahead of boys. They had a baby brother who was born with severe health problems that took him home to heaven at three. They were six and had lived with Fred and me for much of those earlier three years." Ginny choked on the last line. "Both Fred and I are so proud of them and love being with them. I have been to their home a couple times since Fred died, and Andy and I get along fine. But he still can't handle coming to the farm." She blinked rapidly.

"Losing someone we love like that is so hard on everyone." Rich smiled at Addy as she set the plate of cookies down. "What kinds are they?"

"Chocolate chip, oatmeal with raisins, snickerdoodles."

"Three of my favorite kinds."

Nate shook his head. "There is no kind of cookies not my dad's favorite kind."

"Well, what's your favorite kind?" Rich looked at each of them.

"Ginger cookies." Roxie didn't have to think. "Especially the ginger cookies at Annie's."

"I'm like Rich, I can't think of one kind I don't like. I even like those lemon or ginger ones in the box at the grocery store," Amalia said.

"Lemon bars," Loren said with a smile. "Mom makes the best lemon bars. I think Addy uses the same recipe. Yum."

Addy took her yarn and crochet hook around the table to sit with the other woman. "I can chain just fine now—ripping out gives me lots of practice with chaining."

"Done!" a woman announced. "I finally finished something."

"Stand and take a bow," MJ called, laughing and clapping with the others. "Hold it up. Counted cross-stitch no less. Good for you!"

"This baby picture will be appreciated by her mother even though the child is in kindergarten. My daughter had given up hope. She even bought the frame for it years ago." She inhaled and blew out the breath. "I really finished it. Thank you, all of you. The encouragement stuff is almost addictive. I can't wait to decide which to work on next."

Roxie felt Rich's knee touch hers. She looked up to catch his smile. Between the touch and the smile, the tingles shot to her middle and settled in. Her breath did a jig. She was beginning to wonder if she had reverted back to teenhood. This was crazy; after all, she was nearing her mid-fifties. She needed a man in her life like she needed, ah, needed...Nothing came to mind. Ouch, she stuck herself with the needle.

Chapter Twenty-Three

"Are you sure you want to do this, Mom?" Her daughter-in-law sounded doubtful on the phone.

Ginny smiled and nodded, even though Erica couldn't see her. "I do. We have always had the twins' birthday parties here. You know how tradition-minded Addy is. She wants it here and I don't want to break the tradition. Besides, we have to help Andy."

"Did Andy mention anything about birthdays when you were over here a couple days ago?"

Ginny replied, "No, but I did. I told him Addy wants it here, but it's his birthday too. So I asked him to try, and if it's just too much stress, we will move the whole birthday to their house, banner and all."

"And he said...?"

"Nothing, really. He just shrugged. Addy and I have had plenty of deep talks about Fred and what happened so I know she is handling it. Is Andy talking with you or Sam?"

"Not really." Erica sounded tired. "We need to force ourselves to talk about it. Dad's dying brings back all the old experiences of death, pets and people, and too often we still fall apart."

"So Andy is being left out."

"By his choice," Erica said. "He stones up when I try to talk with him and pretty much hides from me. When I asked him what he wanted for his birthday, he shrugged and said, 'Doesn't matter.' I know he is having nightmares but he won't talk about that either."

"Perhaps it's time to bring in a counselor," Ginny suggested. "Much as I hate to say it."

"I thought of that. He and Addy can usually talk about the deep stuff but—"

"But Addy is here and he refuses to come," Ginny finished the thought for her.

"Exactly. I can remember a line of yours, any excuse is a good excuse. Never did understand that but seems to apply here. He hides away with his guitar, and when I asked him what he was working on, he just shrugged. But I know he's working on a song."

"That's good. I'll see if I can get anything out of Addy. I know she's worried about him. So often they talked best when they were down at the barn with the donkey and pony."

"Thanks, Mom. We'll take care of the food for the birthday. Neither of the kids has asked to or planned on inviting their friends so it will be just us. So hard to believe I have almost teenagers."

And then an interesting thought struck Ginny. "Have they ever been out on a sailboat before?"

"I don't think so, why?"

"Just trying to think of something unusual to do with them. Perhaps Roxie's friend Rich would take them out on the lake. I'll look into it. I know he already thinks Addy is pretty special."

"From the UFO group?" Erica asked.

"Right."

"All right, see you later. Love you."

"Love you too." Ginny sat tapping her cell phone against her chin. Oops, she forgot to tell her. She quickly called back. "I forgot to tell you, I ordered their ice cream cake."

"Okay, one thing to cross off my list for tomorrow. Of course, two would not go to waste. When they turn thirteen, we'll get them each one."

That left Ginny with a smile as she put the phone back down.

"Hey, Grandma," Addy called from the far end of the central flower bed. "Come see." She beckoned with a "hurry" hand.

Ginny slipped on her garden shoes and headed for her granddaughter, who was beaming in delight. When Ginny was nearly there, Addy pointed at something in the thickest part of the little Japanese maple, a close tangle of leaves and branches that looked more like a bush.

Ginny leaned closer. A mama chickadee glared up at her, daring her to come closer. "Oh, how wonderful," she whispered and backed away. "How did you see her?"

"Her mister brought a dark blob to her and then flew off with an empty beak."

"Isn't that pure wonderful?"

Addy frowned. "She's low enough for a predator to get her. Wish we could put a screen all around her. I want her to hatch her eggs and teach her babies to fly." They looked up at a bird yammering. "That's him. He's not happy with us."

"Being yelled at by a bird, definitely not my first

time and probably will be many more." Ginny dutifully backed away. "I wish we could move her to one of the bird houses for safety but…" She locked arms with Addy. "We will do as he says."

"We could leave a tray with mealworms on it so he doesn't have to work so hard."

"We could surely do that. You go get some worms from the feed house and I'll figure what to serve them on." She rounded up an old pie pan and, with a piece of duct tape, fastened it to a wooden stool she kept in the garden shed for when she needed to sit down.

"I brought sunflower seeds too." Addy returned carrying two of the cheap plastic bowls Ginny kept for general use. They set the stool under an over-hanging branch, not far from the nest. "You think he'll find it?"

"All we can do is try. Birds are pretty smart." Ginny stretched her shoulders and heaved a sigh. She should go clean out the greenhouse, now that all the plants were out of there. A lot of "shoulds" hung around. This was Thursday and the party was Saturday.

Ginny should make a formal list; she kept randomly thinking of things. "We need to go buy special plates and napkins tomorrow at the party store."

"I think Mom already did. I have an idea, though, of something special." Addy pulled her phone out of her hip pocket and hit one number. "Mom, did you already buy party plates and that kind of stuff? Okay. Thanks." She clicked her phone and shoved it back into her pocket. "She did."

"That solves that. Now what was your special idea?"

"We could roll out chocolate cookies and bake them

real crisp. Soften some ice cream and form it in circles and put them together for ice cream sandwiches."

Ginny grinned. "Sound like fun. We could make the circles with strips from a cereal box."

Ideas popping, they strolled back up to the house, with Addy stopping every once in a while to throw the stick of choice for Spook. Today it was a small length of split wood. "Crazy dog, you get splinters in your mouth, don't come whining to us."

❁   ❁   ❁

Ginny noted that Addy was up earlier than usual on Saturday morning. "You're up early! Happy birthday, dear Addy."

"So that after chores, I could groom the pony and donkey," Addy explained while Ginny made breakfast. "Then I tied ribbons in their manes and brushed off that hat with the holes for the donkey's ears." She reached for Ginny's phone on the table. "Today is a perfect day to go riding."

"That it is. Omelets will be ready in a couple of minutes." Ginny pulled a pan of blueberry muffins out of the oven and turned them in the pan to cool.

"Wow, how come?"

"A birthday girl deserves a special breakfast too."

She grinned as she punched a number. "Andy, are you up yet? Good. I decided that I want to go riding on my birthday and I want you to go with me, so either ask Dad to bring you over or get on your bike and get over here. No, we are going to do this, hear me? This is your big sister talking." She snorted. "Tough. So only by one minute makes no difference but for right now." Her voice softened. "Please, Andy, for me, for us. And to top it off, Grandma baked blueberry muffins. I'm sure there are enough for you too." She paused and listened, nodding, a smile spreading over her face. "Thank you, Andy."

She sniffed and turned to Ginny. "He's coming. Can you make him an omelet too?"

"You can bet your sweet smile I will do that. We could keep this one warm and we'll eat together. How soon?"

"Five minutes. Dad's bringing him. He wouldn't come last week to go riding, but he will today." She leaned into her grandmother's warm hug. "He's coming. That's the best birthday present of all."

"It is." Ginny snagged a tissue, blew her nose, and pulled the ham out of the fridge. "You beat up four eggs while I chop, oh, and get out the half-and-half too." Between the two of them, they had the batter ready to pour into the pan when Spook did his family's coming bark.

"Our early warning system." Ginny pulled the omelet pan back on the hot burner and proceeded to put the omelet together.

"Wow, something sure smells good." Sam ruffled Spook's ears before the dog left him and leaped for joy around Andy, who knelt and hugged him close. When his face was thoroughly cleaned, even to his ears, he pushed the dog away and stood. When Ginny spread her arms, he went to her and nearly fell into her embrace. "I'm sorry, Grandma."

"Sorry? Dear, there's nothing to be sorry about. It's okay, my love. You were taking care of what Andy needs,

and I admire that. You're here now and that is all that
matters." She spoke softly into his ear, followed by a kiss.

"Thank you."

"Thank *you*. You have no idea how happy I am to see
you. Oh, the omelet." She turned to see Addy and Sam
taking care of serving the breakfast.

"Have you eaten, Sam?"

"I have but you can count on my eating at least one
muffin. After all, we don't want them to go to waste."

The four of them carried the breakfast out to the deck
table and took chairs. Spook glued himself to Andy's leg.

"Sam, will you please say grace?"

"Lord, bless this special day for these two birthday
kids of mine. Thank you for the food, the sun, the
breeze, and for Your love that never goes away. Amen."

Ginny passed the muffin basket and then the butter
dish. "If anyone wants jam, it's in the fridge."

"With blueberry muffins? Sacrilege." Sam took his
first bite and sighed. "Mom. Addy bakes the best cookies, but you excel in muffins, along with lots of other
things too many to name with my mouth full."

Addy giggled and rolled her eyes. "D-a-a-a-d." She
told them about the bird's nest and added, "He's been
bringing the worms to her. We watched him with the
binoculars. He was doing his best to keep her fed."

"Wait until they're feeding the open beak brigade. If
he thinks he's tired now, there is more to come." Sam
grinned at his mother. He glanced at his watch. "I better
get going. Erica has a list two feet long. So we'll be over
here about three then?"

"Perfect."

After Sam left, she watched the two kids head for

the barn to saddle up. Addy would just as soon ride bareback but the rule was saddles when off the farm. The kids rode away out across the pasture toward the back gate and hiking trail. Their feet nearly touched the ground. They were getting too big for the pony and donkey. Perhaps Ginny should look into buying horses for them.

But this farm was so hard to take care of already. Why would she get two more animals? Horses took time to tend, every day.

They had promised to be back in two hours so Ginny dug out the wrapping paper and finished the packages. They never went overboard in the gift-giving department, but she'd been collecting some little things for the last couple of months. Fred had bought Andy a handmade knife in a leather sheath so she wrapped that with tears leaking down her face.

When Spook announced their return, she had just finished stacking the boxes in the living room. She watched them unsaddle at the barn and put Magic and Smoky in the stalls to cool down, then put the saddles and bridles away. Fred had taught them well on how to care for their mounts and the tack. So many things he had taught them, would that they would remember them as the years passed. She swallowed and sniffed.

"Oh, Fred, I miss you all the time, but today will be so hard. You taught Sam well on grilling, but you were the best." She mopped with tissue before the kids came up. Andy seemed to be doing well, but Grandma tears might rock his boat.

She had hung the HAPPY BIRTHDAY banner from the drapery rod in the living room, the same place it had hung for perhaps the last ten years. It was starting to look a bit worse for the wear but Addy had insisted. She was definitely tradition minded, not like so many kids of the day.

Ginny fixed a pitcher of lemonade and smashed some strawberries to mix with it. "You two ready for a cold drink?" she asked when she heard them come into the house.

"Out on the deck?"

"Of course. Pick it up and take it out."

"Any cookies?" Andy's voice crackled from low to higher and back.

His voice is already changing. Ginny poured the now-pink lemonade in the glasses with ice. *Lord, these two are growing up so fast. Please keep them from pulling away. We all have tried hard to help them become independent and responsible adults. But please, no hurry.*

She set the plate of several kinds of cookies in the middle of the table. "So what did you see?"

"There were four deer out in the meadow at the east end. We just sat and watched them graze. They didn't mind us being there at all."

"The Harrises' dog barked at us and spooked Smoky." Andy always rode Smoky.

"Ah, he was just looking for something to startle him. Any excuse to jump." Addy sipped her drink. "This sure is good. Hope you made a lot of it."

"Easy to make more."

"I'll go down and brush Magic and Smoky, turn 'em out." Addy pushed her chair back. She shook her head at Andy. "I can do it. You visit with Grandma. She's missed you."

"Addy!"

Addy shrugged and gave her a sort of apologetic look, along with a wink.

"Glad you came over early." *Actually I'm just so glad you came, I could fly.*

"Thank you, I tried before but..." He studied his fingernails, then looked at her. "Grandma, I couldn't."

"I know, honey, I know. There have been lots of things I've put off because I just couldn't do them yet."

"Like what?"

"Like sort all his clothes and give them to people who could use them. I open his closet door and then just close it again."

"Oh."

"And the hardest of all..."

He waited for her answer before finally asking, "What?"

To tell him or not. She inhaled and sniffed. "I can't...I can't go to the chicken house. At all."

"Because that's where you found him."

"Yes." *Please, Lord, keep me from crying.* She watched as a tear leaked over his lower lid and meandered down his face. The face that reminded her so much of Fred when he was younger, actually when they first met. "You look so much like him."

Andy stared at nothing far away. "I think he was my best friend."

"Mine too."

Andy looked at her. "How come God took him to heaven?"

"I ask the same question, but there is no answer."

"Do you think he and Grandpa Bill are together?"

"Yes, I do. The Bible says there will be a great crowd of people to welcome him home. I know your mom's father is one of them."

"I want him to come back but I know that won't happen. But sometimes I dream he did come back but then he leaves again and won't take me with him."

"Nightmares?"

"Uh-huh. I feel like I'm screaming. Dad said sometimes I do scream in my sleep."

"People tell me all these things will go away with time, just part of the grieving. And I can tell they're right. But one thing I know he wants me to tell you is how much he loved and still loves you and always will. Andy, he was so proud of you. He loved to spend time with you and teach you how to take care of the animals and the land, use the tools. You learn so fast and try so hard. I'm so glad you can see that you weren't just related, you are friends too." She refused to use the past tense.

"I miss his cheering at my ball games. Remember how he'd yell at the umpire sometimes? At first it embarrassed me a little but all the guys on my team thought he was the greatest."

"Such good memories we have."

He was silent awhile but she could see he was struggling with something he wanted or perhaps did not want to say. His voice dropped to a whisper. "Grandma, I got mad at God and Grandpa too."

"Boy, do I understand that!"

"Really?"

"Oh yes. Andy, such feelings are part of this whole thing. But they will go away, and the more we talk about him and remember the good times, the sooner we will be better. Pastor Mike has told me that several times. He stops by now and then." She smiled. "He says it's for the cookies. So I guess I finally believe it. I am so glad you are talking with me. I needed this and I think you did too."

He nodded and reached for a tissue. "Yeah."

Spook announced family again.

"They're here." He sat up straighter.

"So let the party begin." She stood and reached for him. "I'm afraid that one of these days you won't let me hug you anymore, so I'll get them while I still can. I love you, Andy boy. I love you enough for both of us. And I know Grandpa is smiling down on us right now. He's not here in human form, but I believe he is watching over us and cheering us on."

Andy kissed her cheek, something he'd not done for the last couple of years. "I love you, Grandma." He hugged her again and headed for the car to help unload.

Ginny watched him go. *Thank you, Lord God, oh, thank you!*

Chapter Twenty-Four

Roxie stared into her closet. The red or the ever-faithful little black dress, of which she had three.

"What's up?" Loren sat down on her mother's bed, her lap immediately occupied by Juno, who gave Sir Charles a superior look.

"Rich said to wear something dressier."

"Where are you going?" She rested her cheek on Juno's fluffy head.

"I have no idea. Red or black?"

"You already wore one black out with him, right?"

"Yeah, the plainest one." She pulled out one with a band of black beading around the scooped neck and a short jacket with matching beading down the front. "This one?"

"They all look good on you. I think we need to go shopping."

Roxie stared at her. "Are you feeling all right?"

"Mommm." Loren heaved a sigh. "I think I need a little black dress and dress shoes too."

"Considering you have, what—two skirts, one short, one long?"

"Yes, and the long one is black so perhaps I could just look for a dressier top."

"Along with a dress, shoes, and perhaps even a bag."

"I can use one of your bags."

"True. How about tomorrow? There's a good sale going on at the mall."

Loren pouted. "I should have kept my mouth shut."

"But you want to look extra good for Nate?"

"Well..." Another sigh. "There is that." She stroked the cat. "I guess my style is casual, huh?"

"Ultra-casual. But you always look nice. Casual is good but even better is a willingness to dress up when you need to." Roxie laid the chosen outfit on the bed. "Do not let Juno touch that."

She was dressed and sorting through jewelry when her cell chimed. Rich. "Hi, I'm about ready."

"Good, but I'm running about fifteen minutes late. So you needn't rush. See you soon." He clicked off.

She returned to her jewelry and the decision of what to wear. Rich was so considerate. Amazing how they had become good friends so quickly. As soon as she was ready, she sat in her office chair to return several phone calls, something she had to remind herself to be grateful for. Returning phone calls as soon as possible was part of her reputation as a top Realtor to work with.

One was a possible new listing; she said she'd call on them early tomorrow. She and Loren would go shopping in the afternoon. The other two were asking for more information about certain listings. When she clicked off, she readied a packet to send to an out-of-state address. Someone needing to move here for a job who planned to buy immediately. The other she marked in her calendar for a Monday meeting. Life was far different now that people could go house hunting on the Internet.

She was just on her way down the stairs when she heard Rich in the driveway. "See you later, sweetie. Remember, there are leftovers in the refrigerator."

"Thanks, Mom. Nate might be coming by later so we can go for a bike ride."

"Oh, good." That made her smile as did the doorbell. She opened the door to feel her heart kick up at the sight of Rich. "Just had time to return phone calls, so perfect timing."

"Thank you, I try. You look lovely."

"Thank you, kind sir." She felt like curtsying, like laughing. When he extended his bent arm, she slid hers through and together they walked to the car, a silver Lexus, not his usual truck. He opened the door and assisted her to get seated. "How come this car is sporting the new car smell?"

"The air freshener. I like it and I think she does too." He patted the roof as he closed the door. After he settled his seat belt, his smile lit up the car. "You look good enough to eat."

"Hardly. I'd be tough and stringy." She shook her head. "You must be crazy."

"I think I am, crazy in love with you."

Her mouth dropped open. "Ah, Rich, we've only known each other for, say, six weeks. You can't—"

"Oh, yes I can. I've known since I first saw you walk around my house to the deck. I almost said so at that very moment but I didn't want to scare you. Besides, I was in shock. Sorry, I was planning on this conversation at the restaurant."

"Really?" Her voice squeaked. She stared straight ahead as he backed out of the drive and headed north. "W-where are we going?"

"Country club, François is head chef tonight and I asked him to make us something special. No idea what it will be, but he outdoes himself when given a chance."

"I see." But her head was still reeling.

"Have you eaten there before?"

"Perhaps, a long time ago." She could feel his glances because her body heated up with each one. How could she tell him that she'd never planned on something like this happening, that she was very comfortable with her life as it was. Simple, busy, and so rewarding.

He laid his hand on her thigh. "Don't stew about this, okay? We'll take it one step at a time."

"Right." How could she not think about it? He tips her world upside down and sends it spinning off its axis, and her heart is screaming "woohoo" while her mind is just reeling. *Okay, think about something else. Now, Roxanne Jean Gilburn!* "Ah—how was your day?"

"My day was splendid. The latest sale is giving us a solid boost, drawing in many new customers, my daughter announced last night that she's pregnant, and Nate is happy with Loren." He grinned at her. "And yours?"

"I have a new out-of-state client who wants a house *now* because he would like to have some things in place before he starts work here in two weeks. He and his wife will arrive Monday and he asked if I can give them all the time they need to make good decisions. I think I have the perfect house for them from what he described. In fact, I have several to show them. My son is planning to come here for a visit now that school is out, so you'll be able to meet him and his family."

Rich's head bobbed. "Good, that's one of the things I was thinking about. It is time to meet each other's family, beyond Nate and Loren. Thinking of hosting a barbeque at my house not this weekend but next. Are you available?"

"I think so, let me check." She dug out her cell and called up her calendar. "Yes. What can I bring?"

"Yourself and Loren. I was hoping you'd come right after church and help me get ready."

"Really?"

"If you don't mind."

The glow that warmed her insides seemed to be spreading. "No, I don't mind. I'd love to. What else can I bring?"

"Let me think on that." He turned off the highway at the sign and followed a paved road that curved around with lovely trees and flowering shrubs to the parking area. Of course the restaurant overlooked the lake.

"Do you golf?" she asked.

"Yes, but not as often as I'd like, just too busy, and I'd rather sail. I use both golf and sailing to entertain clients sometimes. We have the contract for furniture and furnishings for the new hotel in Green Bay." He parked and turned to look at her. "There is so much I want to tell you about my life and learn about yours. Do you ever handle business properties?"

"I have, but I specialize in private homes."

He came around the car and held out his hand to assist her. How long had it been since a man helped her in and out of a car?

Their table overlooked the lake with bright-sailed boats tacking back and forth across the water.

"Ah, perfect, thank you, Mark." The man seated Roxie and laid her white napkin in her lap. "I have your order all under control, Mr. Owens. Your server tonight is Julian, and in the meantime, may I get you anything else?"

"Not that I can think of, thank you." Rich turned his attention to the lake. "Perfect wind, see how the sails billow? If the wind is like this tomorrow, I'll be taking my boat out. You want to come?"

"I have a meeting with a client in the morning, but after that I could." She stared out over the amazing calm of the lake. How peaceful. "*Swee'Pea!*"

"What?"

"Jeff has his little peapod out on the lake. It's finished and in the water! Look!" She pointed.

He watched the tiny craft a few moments. "Well, I'll be. So he did finish it. It's a cute little boat, just right for one person. Spritsail and rudder. Must be fun to sail." Rich studied her with what looked like admiration. "All right, so you make people's lives better by finding them the perfect home. But your good works go in all sorts of directions. Like that one. I'm proud to know you."

What could she say? She sat kind of thunderstruck. She managed a "Thank you."

Thank heaven he changed the subject. "Our dinner is all ordered, but would you like a glass of wine now or a mixed drink?"

"Wine would be nice."

"Good, he'll be bringing that. I ordered a Riesling, since that is what you drank before. So much I have to learn about you."

"Well, uh, what is your favorite color? Mine is turquoise."

"The blue of the lake in the sun."

"Why am I not surprised?" She smiled back at him as his fingers reached across the table and clasped hers.

"Okay, what is your favorite sport?"

So they were playing a game of sorts. And she loved it. "Personal or professional?"

"Both."

"I guess walking and biking and I have no great love for anything professional. Although Loren and I love to watch horse shows and rodeos."

"Really?"

"Yes, we do."

"Do you like to attend horse shows and rodeos?"

"Sometimes. I do love to watch Little League and softball games, especially when I know the kids who are participating. Like I usually go to Andy and Addy's games. Those are Ginny's grandchildren, twins who just turned twelve."

"I see. What about your grandchildren?"

"Too far away and too small yet for team sports. At least that's what their mother thinks. They are five and three. We did go to Regina's dance recital last year. She wanted Grammy to come so we did."

"My children seem to be late bloomers, although this pregnancy is Mara's second. Jason is nearing four. They live in Green Bay so it is not that far away. Jason loves anything to do with water."

"Your boat?"

"Oh, yes, and I keep a rowboat for fishing and

puddling around in. He loves to fish and usually snags more than his dad."

By the time they'd finished their out-of-this-world dinner, as Roxie described it, they settled in to sip Irish coffees and to listen to the music. The string quartet added an ambiance that few other places offered.

When they played "Bring Him Home," Roxie's eyes watered. "I love that song."

"I know, me too. Do you ever go to Chicago or Milwaukee for stage and concerts?"

She shook her head. "No, only local productions and sometimes to Madison."

"Would you like to go to Chicago when something really good comes?"

She half shrugged. "I guess, just didn't think much about it. Would you?"

"Yes, and I am a Chicago Cubs fan, so while I usually watch them on TV, Nate and I have gone down for some games. And we have season tickets to the Green Bay Packers."

"Really? Football, eh?"

"Yes, but usually home games, not when they travel." His thumbs massaging the palms of her hands made it hard for her to concentrate on what he was saying. They finished their coffee and prepared to leave.

"Thank you for this." She gestured around.

"You're welcome."

Back in the car, they paused to see the moon rising on the other side of the lake. So instead of leaving, he pulled to the edge of the parking lot that faced the water. "You know these modern bucket seats sure make cuddling difficult." So he took her hand instead. "One of these days you'll get to see this from my deck or the great room windows that overlook the lake for scenes just like this." They sat quietly for a moment, just taking in the view, enjoying each other's company.

"You know," Rich said softly, "I didn't believe in love at first sight before meeting you. Sure made a believer out of me. I truly believe God brought us together and plans for us to share the remainder of our lives."

"Truly?"

"Truly." He reached across the console and, with one hand on each side of her face, kissed her, gently but long enough to leave her shaking. "I sure hope that shaking is from joy and not fear."

"Oh, I think you are so right." She touched her tingling lips with her fingertips. "Oh, my."

He rested his forehead against hers. "I knew when I kissed you, it would rock my world. I think I better take you home."

She nodded. "I think so." How long would it be before her heart settled down again? There was surely no doubt that they had chemistry, volatile chemistry. But was this love or merely attraction? Not that "merely" had anything to do with it. There was also no doubt that she had kissed him back. None of that fainting damsel stuff.

At her door, he wrapped his arms around her and this time kissed her with depth and fervor, as if searching for her answer. "I hope this clarifies your confusion; it sure erased any hesitancy I might have felt as to the rightness."

Please don't pressure me, Roxie's mind cried while her body sang for more.

"I'll see you Sunday if not tomorrow." He tipped up her chin and kissed her again, lightly this time but filled with promise. "Night."

"Night." She realized later that she'd floated into the house and had almost forgotten to shut the door. She could hear the TV on in the family room so Loren was home. She wandered into the room to see that Nate was still here too. Sir Charles leaped up and came to greet her rather apologetically, head down. "That's okay, Sir Charles, I snuck up on you." She petted him and smiled at the two on the sofa.

"Did you have a fun ride?"

"We did. And stopped for pizza on our way back." Nate released Loren's hand and stretched his arms over his head. "I think I better head home."

"Don't leave on my account. Stay and watch the rest of that if you want. Either way, night." She headed for the stairs, Sir Charles at her side.

She undressed and removed her makeup in a daze. Had that really happened? She'd not been dreaming of such a thing so it wasn't that. She touched her finger-tips to her mouth again. Crawling into bed, she reached for her Bible and her journal and didn't bother to open either one, instead sat propped against her pillows and let her mind wander back over the evening. She was still sitting like that when Loren poked her head in the doorway.

"All right, Mom, what is going on? You floated in the house and up the stairs."

"I'll tell you about it when I have a better handle on this evening."

"Really? What does that mean?"

"I think it means I have no idea. But when I figure it out, I'll tell you." Roxie smiled. "Night. Remember we are shopping tomorrow afternoon."

"I know. Night." Her look was as puzzled as Roxie felt. Perhaps her reaction was because it was so many years since she'd been kissed by a man. What she did understand was she had some major decisions to make. And she might need to make them sooner rather than later.

Chapter Twenty-Five

"Miss Amalia, this is Addy and I have a favor to ask."

"Oh, and what might that be?" Amalia swung her feet up on the lounge on her lanai.

"Well, Andy and I leave for Bible Camp on Saturday and I hate to leave my grandma alone for a whole week. I mean, she says she will be fine and I shouldn't worry but..."

"She's right, you know."

"Maybe, but I don't want her to get so sad again."

"You're a good kid, Addy; your grandma is very blessed to have you." Amalia thought a moment. "Tell you what. I'll call her and ask if I can come out on Tuesday. That will give her a couple of nights alone. Tell her that if she really needs me, I can come earlier, but she could pick me up Tuesday morning or even Monday night after the UFO meeting. How does that sound?"

"The strawberries are ripe. I was going to help her make regular jam and freezer jam, but maybe you can."

"Good. That's an even better reason. My mouth is watering for strawberry freezer jam."

"Thank you. I'll bake you a batch of cookies."

"I'd love that. Bye, Addy, and you have a good time at camp and don't worry about her."

"I won't with you here."

Amalia stared at her phone. What a kid. When she and Ginny talked after the birthday party, she was so grateful Andy had talked with her, enjoyed the party, and come back to help around the farm the next day after church.

She dug her calendar out of her bag and checked to see what she would have to change. Not a lot. After tapping in Ginny's phone number, she leaned back on the lounger and watched the birds flitting about in the maple tree. She was sure there was a robin's nest in the higher branches. She'd seen both parents bringing nest materials.

"I heard the strawberries are ripening. Would you like the company of your I-don't-want-to-wear-out-my-welcome house guest as of after UFO on Monday night?"

"Now that was a mouthful. Addy called you, didn't she?"

"I'll never tell."

"They are," Ginny said. "Already, I think, there are enough for jam. You want to come help and take some home with you?"

"Hm." Amalia thought a very brief moment. "Ginny, come get me and let's pick strawberries. Are you up for it?"

"I would love that. I'll be there in a sec."

It was more than one sec, of course, but Ginny showed up promptly. Amalia slid into the passenger seat. "Thank you, my friend. How big is the job? Any estimate?"

She sniffed, and tears appeared. Again. "Fred always picked. I don't know."

"Well, we're about to find out."

Spook greeted them as they pulled into the farm. Ginny brought buckets as Amalia walked down to the strawberry patch.

"What do you see?" Ginny asked as she stepped in beside Amalia.

"I see enough to make a batch of preserves already. Looks like you're going to have a bumper crop this year."

They began at the east end of the patch. As they parted leaves, ever more ripe strawberries appeared.

Amalia asked around a mouthful of strawberry, "So we're on that I come stay with you after UFO on Monday?"

"That would leave me with Saturday and Sunday nights to get through and I am determined to do just that. I must admit that being on my own the whole week was beginning to concern me."

"At least you're being honest and keeping track of your feelings. I am proud of you, my friend."

"Taking one day or even one minute at a time has various levels of difficulty. You know how Fred loved his strawberries. I even thought of not picking them, but that would be a waste and..."

Amalia gave her time to fight off the deluge. She even offered a tissue. "We'll take care of it. And the raspberries and the blueberries and anything else. You know, Sam and Erica..."

"Yes, but they have their garden and berry patch too. Summer is always a busy time." Ginny suddenly stood up and left.

Should Amalia get up and follow her or keep picking strawberries? Ginny returned with two more shallow buckets. "I had no idea there were so many ripe ones."

Rocking back on her heels and wiping her forehead with the bandanna she kept in her pocket, Ginny asked, "Amalia? Do you like your little apartment?"

"Very much."

"So you're happy where you are."

Amalia thought about that. "Yes, I am. Mostly. I like being able to bike nearly everywhere, but I sometimes miss not driving. And I miss this right here: being close to the earth, planting and harvesting. I have the pots on my deck, of course, but I miss the open space a farm provides."

"Would you consider moving out here, to my farm with me?"

Amalia whipped her head around so fast, she got dizzy. "Here?"

Ginny tossed another handful of strawberries into her pail. "I don't know. Maybe it wouldn't work. But we could remodel the basement into an apartment, so you and I could each have alone time." She smiled. "You know, get away from each other now and then. And together, I think we could do what has to be done to keep the farm going. I know I can't do it all alone."

Amalia quit picking and sat back, thinking and nodding at the same time. "Interesting idea." She continued to nod. "I'll consider this. Yes. A lot to think about. I take it you've already given it a lot of thought."

"Yes—and prayer. The idea came to me when I was praying the other morning. I figure God had a hand in that."

❀   ❀   ❀

"Okay, Roxie, what's up? You are not yourself today?" MJ stopped them in mid-stride.

"What do you mean?"

"Well, for starters, you're not talking."

"Sorry. I have a lot on my mind, several new clients, things like that." *And what do I do about Rich?* That was the biggie, as she well knew, but she was not ready to talk about it yet. Mostly because did she, could she, love him like he apparently loved her?

"See, there you went again, off in some world of your own."

"Okay, I have some decisions to make, and until I am sure of my answers, I'd prefer not talking about them. Nothing personal, mind you. You know what it's like when you're trying to figure out what God wants you to do."

"I do, but I usually gain help and perspective by talking it over with Daryl or my friends."

"Well, I don't have a Daryl in my life to talk things over with." And since that might be remedied sometime in the near future, oh, my land... "The answer will come, I know it, in God's good time. After all, He promised."

"Sometimes His promises take a long time to come through." MJ got a good yank on her arm by the basset taut at the end of the leash, nose to the concrete.

"We need to hustle if we're going to stop at Annie's. I have a ten o'clock meeting with a buyer who wants to see the two houses I showed him before and make a decision." Lucky man, has only two choices, or so he thinks.

She and Sir Charles caught up with MJ, who was being pulled along by a strong-willed hound.

"Looper, no, we are not going that way." She planted her feet. "This way, Annie's, puppy treats." Looper liked the biscuits at Annie's. They tied the dogs to the dog hooks and went inside the café.

"Hey, Roxie, someone this morning said she saw you at the country club with a good-looking man." Anne grinned at her while making the lattes. "She was going to say something to you, but she said you were mighty cozy and she didn't want to interrupt."

Between the two of them, they were both too well known around here to even dream of privacy. "He's just a friend of mine." *Liar.*

"Right." Anne gave her a knowing look. "I'll bring your cinnamon rolls as soon as they are warmed up."

They sat down in their usual place, as if it were kept vacant just for them.

"And? The puzzle pieces are falling into place. You must be speaking of Rich Owens, father of Nate Owens, who is dating Loren. And from what I hear, real often. Perhaps all these ice cream dates after UFO?" MJ's eyebrows arched.

"All right, Mrs. Inquisitive. Good grief, one can't keep anything private in this town. Yes, we went out to a very nice dinner at the club house, where I haven't been for a very long time. And yes, we are doing things together. He is a fine man and we enjoy our time together. Now that is all I am going to say right now, so—" She looked up. "Thanks, Anne, oh, this smells so good."

Speculative looks were becoming more frequent on MJ's face. "He's in love with you, isn't he?" She nodded, her sleuthing look visible in her grin.

"No comment. Now, can we please drop it?" Roxie

glanced at her watch. "I have to leave here in fifteen minutes. You know how I feel about being late for a client."

MJ raised both hands in the air. "All right, all right, but you better promise me you will bring me up to date when you come to a decision. Now, how are Loren and Nate doing?"

"This afternoon Loren and I are going shopping for a little black dress for her, along with accessories."

MJ clapped her hand over her heart. "Well, I never... How wonderful."

"Now don't go getting them married yet, all right? I am sure he's in love with her..." *Like father, like son.* "But I don't think she's aware of it yet, thinks they are just friends." Roxie stared hard at her best friend. "I better not hear from anyone that you passed on this tidbit, got it?"

"Yes, ma'am. Besides, Roxie, you know I don't gossip."

"Not to Amalia or Ginny even?"

"That's not gossip, that's good friends sharing." She rolled her eyes toward the tin ceiling. "All right, I will not mention anything to anyone." She did the motions as she said, "Cross my heart and hope to die..."

"Don't get carried away. We're meeting Ginny and Amalia for lunch here on Friday, right?"

"Yes, I have it on my calendar for noon. Looking forward to it."

"Me too." Roxie ate the last bite and drained her cup. "I'm out of here. Coming?"

"Two minutes, er, one minute." She chugged her latte and took the last bite of roll. "Yum."

After a fast walk home, Roxie met with her clients and recorded their offer on their favorite of the two homes they had seen before. "This is a good solid offer, but you know there will probably be negotiations. Are you willing?"

"To a degree," the man said while he and his wife looked at each other and both nodded. "And all depends on the inspection. How soon will that be able to happen?"

"The owner has to accept your offer before we schedule an inspection. But I feel strongly that will go through easily. I'll submit to their Realtor this afternoon and we'll see. Be prepared."

"We are." They grinned at each other. "Looking forward to hearing from you."

Roxie drove into her driveway half an hour later than she had hoped. She hurried inside to use the bathroom. "You ready?"

"Yes, be right down."

Within minutes they were on their way to the mall. "Did you have lunch?"

Loren shook her head. "I got involved in planning my next display and the time disappeared. Let's shop first."

"You sure? You might need sustenance."

"If the shock is too great, we'll take a break."

"Okay."

It took two stores before they found a possible dress. "What do you think?" Loren modeled the dress in front of a mirror.

"I think it looks very nice, simple but decent-quality fabric and construction." She had checked that out before Loren put it on. The others she'd tried were too frothy. "You can dress it up or down by the accessories. That print jacket on the rack would make it more casual, and the black one with the scroll trim would look dressier, not that you'd want a jacket so much in the summer anyway. And before you ask, it is very slimming. Now let's get you a black bra, and panties, and then we hit the shoe department."

Loren groaned. "All in one day?"

"Might as well while we're here. By the way, why the change of heart?"

"Nate wants me to meet his mother so he's taking us both to supper tomorrow at her favorite restaurant."

"Which is?"

"The Royal Crown." She flipped the dress over the fitting stall door.

"Okay, this will be fine. You can use my turquoise jewelry, will look great on that, and my black shawl if it gets chilly. Knowing that restaurant, you better take the shawl."

Loren stepped out of the fitting room, shaking her head. "Jeans or khaki pants are much easier." She glanced in the mirror and pulled her T-shirt down. "Let's get this over with."

"You are not sentenced to the guillotine."

"Almost. And besides, what if she doesn't like me?"

Roxie put her arm around her daughter's shoulders. "She can't help but love you. I've heard all good things about her."

"If she's so wonderful, why did they divorce?"

"Couldn't get along in the same house but reverted to being the friends they were before the marriage. Rich said, 'She gave me great children.'"

They finished their shopping, got Loren through the shock of spending that much money on fancy clothes, and stopped at Loren's favorite restaurant, where the hamburgers were superb. They had celebrated many life events there through the years. "Let's get that dress hung up and we'll steam it. You'll look smashing tomorrow for supper." Roxie pulled into their driveway. "You might want to wear your hair up, look even more sophisticated that way." She grinned at her daughter. "Want a bowl of ice cream?"

"Need you ask?"

A message from Rich was waiting on her house phone. She returned his call. "You called?"

"I did. Since Nate is taking Loren and his mother out for dinner, you want to come out here since you'll be all alone?"

"You think I can't handle being alone?"

"And here I was trying to be nice. So much for nice. Will you please come out here? We'll have chicken on the grill, veggies, garlic bread, and some kind of potatoes, I suppose. Then we can watch the sunset over the water and the moon come up. What do you think?"

"I think it sounds heavenly."

"Whew, you scared me there for a moment. Oh, I get it, you were teasing me."

"You got it. See you about . . ."

"Three, no four. I have some things I need to get done."

"So do I, so I will see you then." She set the receiver back in the stand and went to check on Loren, finding her in front of the bathroom mirror. "How are you doing?"

"About done. It didn't wrinkle much. I'll be wearing brand-new shoes, with heels no less."

"Your espadrilles have heels so don't worry about it. Relax, sweetheart, you'll have a good time, Nate will see to that."

"Thanks, Mom." She tucked the steamer back in its place under the sink. "You going out to Rich's?"

"At four so I will help you get ready if you need me."

"I'd rather go there."

"Now, now. Let's go have ice cream. I'm having rocky road."

"Me too." Sir Charles padded down the stairs in front of them, and Juno met them in the kitchen, reminding them it was time to feed their furry-faced kids.

❀   ❀   ❀

"Just think, when we're married, we can have evenings like this all the time." While the breeze had driven them inside, Rich and Roxie were seated on the love seat looking out over the lake.

She sat straight up to turn and stare at him. "Pretty sure of yourself, aren't you?"

"It's all a matter of time. When God gives you a gift, He'll also say when to open it."

"That is not a Bible verse."

"Bet I can find one or many to support it." He pulled her back with his arm around her shoulders. "I see our whole relationship as a series of mini miracles, starting with how we met, or rather, how you met my son. At just the right time. You realize Nate is in love with Loren?"

"I got that feeling. His eyes light up when she walks into the room."

"And now he is making sure she meets his mother. First woman he has ever done that with. I tell you, it is only a matter of time."

"Oh, look, the rim of the moon. How lovely."

"Yes."

She glanced at him. "You're not looking at the rising moon."

"I know, you look at the moon, I'll look at you." When the moon had cleared the trees on the far side of the lake, he tipped her chin with one finger and kissed her, lingering to savor the moment. "There, I've been waiting for that."

Sometime later, she pulled away. "I need to get home; I have to submit a proposal and I have an early morning appointment."

"I know. Me too. Two busy people." He brushed her lips with his. "Just to remind you that I'm not kidding. I love you." Hand in hand, he walked her to her car. "Call me when you get home."

"I will."

Glancing in the rearview mirror, she saw him still waving. She punched the horn twice and reminded herself to pay attention on the roads. His comment about evenings like this all the time when they were married: That idea was seeming more appealing all the time. *Crazy woman*, she scolded herself. The main question? *Are you certain you love him?*

❖   ❖   ❖

"We're celebrating," Roxie announced the next day when the four friends were gathered around a back-room table. "I sold another house, a very nice one." They all clapped. "Loren met Nate's mother, she even bought a little black dress and accessories, and Nate looked stunned. She was indeed beautiful. Oh, and his mother thinks she's perfect for her son. Now, who's next?"

"I lost five pounds and have not yo-yoed this time." MJ spoke firmly, as if warning the weight away. "I will get rid of the next five and keep them off." More applause.

"I finally got Mr. Grump to turn down his TV by bringing him those earphones that I saw advertised. They work and the rest of us at the home are rejoicing in the relative quiet."

"Brilliant." They applauded.

"And Addy and Loren are both at the library. I think Addy is going to help Loren with her display because she wants to learn how. So much to be thankful for." Ginny blinked. "Sorry, most anything makes me tear up, even happinesses like these." She raised her glass of lemonade and iced tea. They all touched glasses and nodded.

"Okay, now Roxie, isn't there something you've been meaning to tell us?" Ginny's smile looked innocent.

Roxie glared at MJ, who raised arms and eyebrows. "I did not say anything."

"If you are referring to Rich Owens..." All three nodded. "Yes, we have been seeing each other often and talk most days on the phone."

"And?" The three leaned forward in unison.

"And..." Roxie sucked in a deep breath and dropped her voice to a whisper. "He asked me to marry him." At their gasps, she held up a hand. "But..." Heaving a sigh, she frowned. "But I'm not sure I love him enough to change my life all around. I love to be with him, he's a wonderful man, and he says God has given us this gift of each other and I am beginning to think so too but..." Her head moved side to side slowly, as if of its own accord. "I like my life just the way it is."

"Don't turn your back on more happiness and God's gifts, please?" Ginny implored. "We all need to use and appreciate every gift He has given us. Please pay attention. Too often, good gifts go away before we're aware how good they are."

MJ stared at Ginny. "You're right, we overlook too much."

"Preach it, sister." Amalia leaned forward and patted Roxie's hand. "You'll know for sure. When the time is right."

When their orders arrived, MJ offered the grace and they fell to, as always starting with the homemade rolls that came in the basket with butter.

Anne stopped by their table. "Everything okay?"

"Come on, Anne. Always better than okay or we wouldn't come here all the time." Roxie pointed to what was left of her roll. "You or Gary?"

"This time it was me. He was doing cookies. At least we have the super-duper mixer now with a dough hook that really works. With the other one, I'd finish the kneading but now we are using more dough so I broke down and invested in a new one."

"Good for you. You know, the only complaint I've heard about your café is that the portions are so big." MJ pointed to her salad. "See, it's huge."

"I know, but I don't want anyone to go away hungry. Take after my mom, I guess."

"She didn't run a restaurant."

"How about more Arnold Palmers?" At their nods, she motioned to her young waiter, who brought the pitcher over. As she left, she stopped by Roxie. "Anytime you can dispel the rumors, which by the way, are all excited for you."

"Anne!"

"Just sayin'." Her grin made them all chuckle.

Roxie rolled her eyes. She raised her refilled glass. "Happy Friday to all of us."

As they left the café a bit later, Amalia turned to Roxie. "I just have one question."

"What?"

"What are you waiting for?"

Roxie stared at her friend. "Good question."

"Ginny was so right. Grab your moments, every moment you can, and be thankful. You never know what tomorrow will bring." Amalia nodded with a smile that spoke of love and experience and sound advice.

Roxie hugged her. "Thank you. I will."

"That's what friends are for. I mean, after all, we are all UFOs when you think of it. God said He would do the finishing."

Roxie stared at her wise friend. She nodded slowly and sucked in a breath. "I will. Tonight." Inside, she felt like fireworks going off. She headed for her SUV. What she wanted to do was drive out to Rich's office and ask him out for coffee. Or did she want to call him and set up a date for this evening? Or take the time to plan a celebration? Or... She stared out the windshield.

Was something memorable important? No matter what she did, telling him was the important part. But where? How?

Her cell blipped with a text from Loren: *Going with Nate for hamburgers and movie. Later.*

She texted back: *Thanks for letting me know. Have fun.*

Then one for Rich: *Want to watch the moon come up again? I'll bring dessert.*

He replied: *Sounds good. I have a meeting that should be over by about 7:30. See you at 8 at my house?*

She responded. *Perfect.*

She spent part of the afternoon following up with several clients, getting some papers out, and then she baked brownies, with walnuts, just the way he liked them, powdered sugar dusted on top, no frosting. She stopped for a bottle of good champagne, grimaced at the cost, and set it in the cooler with the ice cream wrapped in plenty of ice.

Driving up his driveway was always such a pleasure. The big gray heron patrolled the banks of the pond while ducks paddled out in the middle. Green lawn made the beds of columbines and tuberous begonias sparkle. How he found time to take care of all this was amazing. But then, he was an amazing man. And he loved her. The smile started in her middle and tickled the edges of her mouth. Yes, his truck was parked in its assigned place.

He and Sophie got to her door before she could gather her purse and push down the handle, Sophie barking excitedly. "What a fine way to end this day."

Her heart kicked up. "It is." She reached for the cooler on the backseat.

"Let me get that."

She greeted Sophie, ruffing her ears and murmuring doggy greetings.

"Okay, back off, girl, she's here to see me." Sophie sat, her fluffy tail sweeping the concrete.

Rick took Roxie's hand and with the other swung the cooler. "Did you see the general at the pond?"

"If you're referring to the heron, yes." She gripped the container with brownies.

"Did you eat supper?"

"Yep." Not that she'd had much but it was enough.

Instead of walking around the house, he opened the front door and gestured her in. "I take it there is ice cream in the cooler?"

"How'd you guess?"

"What else would need a cooler?"

"Let me put this in the freezer, and since it's breezy out here, how about lighting the fire pit?"

"Okay, I'll do that." He gave her a questioning look that she made sure she answered with an innocent smile.

She put both the champagne and the ice cream in the freezer and the brownies on the counter, then followed him outside, where Sophie greeted her again. Roxie stared out over the dancing lake. Bright sails were still billowing in the wind, with many of them on their way to the docks. Seagulls dipped and squawked, some settling on the ridge of his boathouse. Her hair fluffed in the wind and she wrapped her arms across her middle.

"Are you cold?" Standing behind her, he put both arms around her and nuzzled her neck.

"Just chilly. This view is so peaceful and lovely."

"It is. I come out here to unwind after the crazy days and putz with the pots and planters. Always reminds me to breathe and let it all go."

She let her head fall back against his chest and did as he suggested—took a deep breath and let it all out. Turning in his arms, she clasped her hands behind his neck. "I am a woman on a mission."

"Oh, really?" He kissed her nose.

"Stop that or I can't think clearly."

"Okay. I take it thinking clearly is important."

"It is. Number one." She stared into his eyes. "I love you, Rich Owens, as much as I am able and plan on loving you more day by day. Number two, I think you mentioned marriage."

"Yes, I distinctly remember that."

"Would you like to ask me again?"

He nodded, his smile spreading. "Roxanne Jean Gilburn, will you do me the honor of becoming my wife?"

"Yes, Richard Donald Owens..." She started to say something more but talking and kissing did not work together.

"You have just made me the happiest man alive."

"Good. I'm glad to hear that. Oh, Rich, is this really happening?"

"I think so. You better pinch me to make sure I'm not dreaming."

"You're not. Two people cannot share the same dream at the same time." This time she initiated the kiss. "Now, let's get the champagne out of the freezer; it should be chilled enough by now. And while you pour that, I will dish up the ice cream to go with the brownies

I baked a couple of hours ago." She leaned her forehead against his chin. "I love you. I really and truly love you, and I am still in the shock of realizing that."

"Good. Stay that way because our next order of business is to set a date. I do not want to wait. In fact, we could elope tomorrow."

She shook her head. "I want a very small wedding with just our families and very closest friends. I want it in my church because Pastor Mike has seen me through many life events and—"

He laid a finger against her lips. "Whatever you want to do is fine with me. But let's make it soon." He popped the cork and poured the champagne. "To us, with God's blessing." He touched her glass with his. His grin kicked her heart into even higher gear. They took their glasses and dessert back out to sit by the fire pit, snuggled where they could see both the moon rise and the fire crackle.

"You make the best brownies, just the way I like them. How did you know?"

"Nate mentioned one time when we were talking about the brownies Loren had made."

"I'm curious, what happened today that made you sure?"

"Amalia reminded me to not waste a moment of God's gift to us. And then she said something really interesting. She said we are all unfinished objects and that God promised to finish us in His good time. I really like that idea, so down to earth, just like her."

"Hmm, I'd think at our age, we must be half finished, don't you think?"

She thought a moment. "I don't think age has anything to do with it."

He paused. "Roxie, are you familiar with Robert Browning?"

"The poet?"

"Yes. This is from 'Rabbi Ben Ezra': *Grow old along with me! / The best is yet to be, / The last of life, for which the first was made: / Our times are in His hand / Who saith "A whole I planned, / Youth shows but half; trust God: see all, nor be afraid!"*

He paused and swallowed, along with a sniff. "I want lots of years ahead with you right here beside me." The glory of his smile made her eyes fill. "Unfinished objects, eh?"

They stared across the lake as the moon floated free of the horizon and rose on its journey. Their journey together was just starting. Who could dream what great things God would do with the remainder of their journey?

Epilogue

MJ stood behind the podium looking out over the faces gathered to celebrate the one-year anniversary of the UFO group. Around tables that sat eight, the laughter and conversations made her nod and smile especially when she looked right in front at their table. Roxie and Rich, inseparable since before their marriage eight months earlier; her daughter, Loren, and his son Nate, who finally had announced their wedding date; Amalia, wearing a new hat in honor of the occasion; Ginny, also wearing a hat thanks to Amalia's influence; and MJ's husband, Daryl, who gave her a thumbs-up sign. She tapped the mike but that did nothing to attract attention.

She looked to Addy, seated with her family at the next table. Addy and Andy both nodded and the double whistle blasted around the room. Instead of quieting, the crowd first laughed, then waved to MJ, and then quieted, in spite of a few more giggles and chuckles.

"I can tell we are all celebrating and so busy chatting and sharing that I could just sit down, but since we are here tonight to honor those who completed UFOs and catch up on all our news, we shall begin." She puffed out a breath and straightened. "First of all, we now have five UFO groups in Fond du Lac and who knows how many elsewhere." She held up her spread fingers. "When I call the group you belong to, please stand. And yes, I know, some of you go to more than one. So if you do, please stand for each one. Now, the beginning group that still meets at Maureen's Yarn Shop. Roxie, please count for us and while you do that..." She started the applause.

"Twenty-three." Roxie stayed standing as the group waved to others.

"Thank you. This group has altogether finished sixty-one projects. By the way, I hope you look through all those finished projects displayed on the table around the room. Jeff's peapod greeted you at the entrance. That little boat has already seen many hours on the lake."

Jeff waved and did a half bow. "Just remember, I had lots of help. Helping each other is at the heart of these groups. The canoe we worked on didn't quite make it here tonight but not for lack of our trying."

"Group two, the first spinoff meets in the morning at the senior center, please stand. Roxie, please count again. This group has finished twenty-eight projects." The applause brought on plenty more smiles.

"Seventeen," Roxie called out louder, to be heard over the murmurings. "They have more members who couldn't be here tonight."

Amalia and Ginny gave each other a high five. Ever since Amalia had moved out to the farm in the fall, their shared housing story had encouraged several other people to do the same. And they had managed to finish even more unfinished objects, especially from Ginny's collection.

"That young lady with them is the proud owner of Addy's Cookies, and her project is a tasty success. Many of you have ordered cookies from her, and she says she has started a fund for her dream to go to cooking school."

"Not that she needs more training in great cookies," someone called out.

"Thank you. The third group started at the senior housing complex, and while it is a small group, they have not only completed twelve UFOs, they pooled their resources and donated four baby quilts to the pregnancy center."

Amalia stood for the third time.

"So, what does Amalia do? Count her same UFOs with every group?" That question came from another table.

"Hardly." Amalia rolled her eyes and raised her voice. "Now that sounds like a good idea. Why didn't I think of that? Sorry, but I work on something different in each group. Fabric, crochet or knit, and other."

"Sometimes she helps someone else finish something too. Like many of you, she always has something to work on in her pocket or bag." MJ nodded to Amalia, who held her ball of yarn and the beginnings of a crocheted lap robe in the air. "Any more questions?"

"By the way, before I forget, don't you all forget to forage in that bin of yarn we have back there and take home what you can use. We wouldn't want you to run out. Our next group meets at the Lutheran Church and it too is open to the public. They meet in the afternoon after a potluck lunch, so we have mornings, afternoons, and evenings and all on different days of the week." She motioned to Roxie, who came to stand beside her.

"I have a letter here that I thought you all might enjoy." Roxie took a card from an envelope and held it up for all to see. "This is from Hawaii. 'Dear Roxie and all our friends in the Fond du Lac UFO groups. Ours is the story of another kind of unfinished objects. We had both been single for a few years and then met at the first UFO group. We found ourselves enjoying the visiting at the meeting. One night I mentioned I was frustrated with the latch on my front door. George volunteered to come see about it. He ended up putting in a new handle and latch so I offered to cook supper in return since he refused payment. The rest is history. We were married ten days ago and are on an extended honeymoon spending time on each of the islands. We will be sure to attend the first meeting when we get home, unless we choose to take a round-the-world cruise that leaves not long after we get back. We both dreamed of having a travel companion but marriage was not in our plans. That is, before UFO.

"'All this goes to show, you just never know what might happen. Again, thanks and see you one of these days.

"'Blessings,

"'George and Alice Nelson.'"

The applause burst out, along with a few hoots and whistles. Roxie held up her mike again. "As we have said, you never know what might happen when people get together to finish UFOs. We know there are groups in other places because they have read about us and asked for suggestions. We thank you all for coming and I hope you'll take time to admire all the displays we have, including the scrapbook maintained by Judith, the pictures of all those who finished, and the yarn bin, of course. Our Supplies Swap was a huge success also, but all it did for me was add another project that I couldn't resist. I have a feeling I was not alone. Anne, will you and Gary stand up?" She waved to them with both hands. "Our supper tonight was catered by Annie's Fountain City Cafe. Didn't they do a superb job?"

This time people stood to applaud.

Anne and Gary bowed and waved. Anne raised her voice. "MJ, you forgot the UFO group that meets early Friday mornings at the cafe. We have anywhere from four to ten in attendance, and since we are fairly new, I'm not sure how many projects have been finished but we sure have fun together."

"Sorry." MJ flinched.

"That's okay." Anne grinned. "This was our biggest event to cater and are we ever grateful for good helpers so we could celebrate with all of you. Thank you."

"Thank you. MJ and I walk most mornings and stop at Annie's for lattes and sometimes breakfast. I see more people there who are eating and often they have a project along with them. See, Amalia, what you have started."

Amalia raised her hook and yarn again to more laughter.

"What an evening. Thank you all. And now Pastor Mike—his wife joined our group early on—would you please give the benediction?"

He stood at his table and smiled around the room. "What a gathering of unfinished objects. Good thing He has a plan to finish each one of us. As I look around, I see so many whose lives have changed dramatically this year, both for the good and the sad, but you people have stood by each other and offered whatever help you could give. So many unknown lives too have been touched by what you have been doing as God multiplies our efforts. Thank you." He nodded. "Amazing." He lifted his hands. "And now, may our good Lord bless and keep us. May His face shine upon us and above all, may He fill us with His peace. Amen. Congratulations, everyone. Keep it up."

❀   ❀   ❀

The next day, the four gathered at Annie's to do some Monday morning quarterbacking. MJ sighed and leaned back in her chair, staring at the remains of the orange roll on her plate. "Anne, m'dear, you have done it again. You did a fantastic job catering the celebration supper last night and now..." She swept her hand to indicate the entire table.

"And now we have rolls to die for." Roxie grinned back at the innocent-appearing Anne.

"Don't you ever sleep?" Ginny leaned forward. "I mean, I would still be in bed if it weren't for—"

"All your animals and chickens to feed," muttered Amalia.

"Well, that too, but..."

Anne shrugged. "All I can say is magic, and yes, I did sleep, just not terribly long. As I have said so many times, we have an amazing group of workers here. They took care of last night from beginning to end. You saw them."

"And who hired and trained them?" Roxie's eyebrows tickled her half bangs.

"Okay, thank you, but let me remind you all, you are the ones who dreamed up and created the first UFO group and—"

"And then hung on for the ride." Amalia looked up from the poncho she was knitting on big needles as a surprise for Addy. "Like Pastor Mike said, look at the lives that have been touched by such a simple thing. We had no idea this could happen..."

"All I wanted was to get some stuff out of my room." MJ used both hands, elbows resting on the table, to sip from her latte. "Think back. Look at our lives, let alone all those others. Roxie and Rich met and are married, Loren and Nate are engaged..."

"Which was my dream." Roxie's head wagged. "Whoever would have thought this?" She looked at Ginny. "Your life had the hardest change but you made it through. I know you can't say you are over the grief, but you have come so very far." She reached across the table and patted Ginny's hand, but when Ginny turned hers over, Roxie squeezed her friend's hand.

"And now Amalia is sharing my house, the twins are back in school, and Addy is building a cookie empire. Can you believe she was featured on that cooking show?"

"And from what I hear, more creative kinds of things are in the works. Her dad is flabber-dusted." Amalia chuckled. "He tickles my funny bone all right."

Anne braced herself on the table and stood. "Thanks, ladies, for doing so much to increase our business here. I better get back to work. Can I get you anything else?"

"You and I need to talk. I am pushing for you to cater the Realtors event," Roxie said.

"And Rich has scheduled a company celebration at his, er, your place. See what I mean?" Anne grinned at all of them. "By the way, breakfast is on me." She stared at each of them. "And don't bother to argue." She headed for the kitchen.

"Thank you," they chorused. Anne waved without looking back.

"Whoever would have thought that one woman's frustration when some tubs of her unfinished projects hit the floor, I know, and her head on the way down, along with a play on words, would turn into this...this vehicle for blessings for so many unknown others?" Amalia nodded as she spoke. "And you know what? I kind of appreciate knowing I'm an unfinished object, à la Pastor Mike. There is freedom in that."

Roxie blew out a breath. "What a year this has been. I used to wish I could see into the future but no longer. I'm grateful for right now, for all of us, and for all the UFOs ahead." She raised her iced latte so the others did too. "Onward!"

Acknowledgments

From the very beginning of my writing career, I realized that some books take a bigger team than others but all books are a team effort. And this is before the manuscript gets sent to the publishing house.

Some years ago I heard of the term *UFOs*, that is, *Unfinished Objects*, in reference to handicraft projects and items. Mostly those I knew of focused on crafts or needlework, quilting, painting, woodwork, and the list grew. A few of us from our church decided to form a group to assist each of us (and anyone else who wanted to join in) to finish something. I'd have loved to offer a prize to whoever could guess the number of those kinds of projects in my sewing/laundry room, but to do so would have meant digging them all out and counting them: totally intimidating. Many of us are great starters but then we often get distracted and start something else before we finish. So my thanks to the core group: Pat, Diane, Judy, and also to the others who floated in and out.

When I mentioned this book idea to Wendy, my agent and encourager, she got excited. We talked the idea over with Christina, one of my editors, and she got excited:

all of us because we have such UFOs stashed in various places in our homes and offices. I have talked with many people, always with the question: "Do you have UFOs?" (And then I add, "unfinished objects.") Only a few have been able to say no. So, my thanks to all of those who took part.

When I was doing a book tour for *The Second Half*, another novel set in Wisconsin, I visited a Facebook friend in Fond du Lac to see her glorious gardens. Kathy Sable showed me around her gardens and her town, and introduced me to her family, and the story became more than an idea. Fond du Lac is a lovely town with lots of interesting places, especially her daughter Ann's new Fountain City Café. Ann agreed that I could use her café as a location in the story. Actually, she got excited about it. So thanks to Kathy and Dick Sable, and Ann and Gary Culver.

Besides all these folks, my thanks go to my husband Wayne, who is a frequent sounding board, Sandy, my first reader, and all the folks at FaithWords, who are the teams that continue on after I've turned in the manuscript. One of my mind pictures is of God sprinkling ideas over the earth from a mighty saltshaker. Some ignore the ideas, some start them and never finish, and some take the ideas and carry them out to the end. Through the years I have been all those. This one I did finish. So, thank you Father, for all those projects in my possession completed or not, and may they be used to bless others. But mostly for the idea and the people who helped *Half Finished* come about.

About the Author

LAURAINE SNELLING has been writing since 1980, with over sixty-five books published, both fiction and non-fiction, historical and contemporary, for adults and young readers. She received a Career Achievement Award for inspirational fiction from *RT Book Reviews*, and her books consistently appear on CBA bestseller lists. A hallmark of her style is writing about real issues within a compelling story. Lauraine and her husband, Wayne, have two grown sons and live in the Tehachapi Mountains in California with a basset named Sir Winston.

Dear Reader,

Thank you for reading *Half Finished*. Of course I hope you enjoyed it and I hope you found a take-away from these characters in this story. I wrote the book out of a need of my own, to finish some of my UFOs. We started a group at our church and—thanks to getting together—we all finished our waiting projects, some very long-waiting. My dream is that you will find this helpful in finishing your own. I've learned the best way to get something done is to take a class or meet with some friends who agree to work on something, too.

Thus began our original small group, and after writing *Half Finished*, a new dream for me. What was good for us, and for my characters, might help other people, too. So, if you just happen to think you might like to belong to such a group, here are some very simple guidelines.

1. Invite creative people to meet with you.
2. Keep it simple: no board, officers or agendas.
3. Choose a day, time, and place.
4. Agree to bring a project to work on. Choose one and begin. Stay with that project until it is finished.
5. Refreshments are always enjoyed but not necessary. We do potluck lunch, our preference, since we meet in the morning.
6. Cheer each other on. Celebrate every finished project.
7. Choose the next one to do.

8. Have fun.
9. Be prepared for wonderful things to happen.

I would love to hear from any groups that start. You can contact me via my website: laurainesnelling.com, where I will be posting updates as we go—success stories, I hope!

Have fun turning UFOs into the item you had in mind when you started. Hmm, guess I'd better get back to the baby afghan I started to crochet when I went traveling and didn't bring it along. Oh and by the way, people who stash UFOs are really good at making excuses.

Blessings,
Lauraine